LI
GIRL
MISSING

BOOKS BY J.G. ROBERTS

As Julia Roberts
THE LIBERTY SANDS TRILOGY
Life's a Beach and Then…
If He Really Loved Me…
It's Never Too Late to Say…

Christmas at Carol's
Carol's Singing

Alice in Theatreland
Time for a Short Story

One Hundred Lengths of the Pool

LITTLE GIRL MISSING

J.G. ROBERTS

bookouture

Published by Bookouture in 2019

An imprint of StoryFire Ltd.

Carmelite House
50 Victoria Embankment
London EC4Y 0DZ

www.bookouture.com

ISBN: 978-1-78681-918-5
eBook ISBN: 978-1-78681-917-8

PROLOGUE

Day One – 7.26 a.m. – Friday

Naomi's head felt fuzzy and her eyelids heavy. The start of another new day without Charlie. After taking a herbal sleeping pill the previous night, she had climbed into bed waiting for, but not expecting, sleep to come. One minute she was wide awake, the next a little dizzy, and then oblivion. Although grateful for the much-needed rest, she knew it was going to be even more of a struggle to get going this morning.

Forcing her eyes open, Naomi was surprised to discover it was almost 7.30 a.m. *Have I really been asleep for over ten hours? I don't remember the last time I slept for more than three.* She snuggled deeper under her warm duvet, listening for sounds of movement from Cassie in the next room. Nothing. Despite feeling a pang of guilt, she was glad to have a few more minutes without needing to respond to the constant demands and questions of an inquisitive five-year-old. There was something safe and comforting about the touch of soft flannel against her cheek and the faint smell of lavender lingering from the drops she sprinkled every night. Each morning was more difficult than the last to summon the energy needed to get up and go through the motions of a normal day, but she knew she had to, for Cassie's sake.

Everyone, from her friends to the medical professionals she had reluctantly agreed to see, advised her that routine was the best way to get through each day, but it wasn't them who had to come to terms with life after Charlie. The silence dragged on, suggesting that her little girl had also slept well. *I'll have to wake her if we're going to make it to school on time*, Naomi thought, pushing back the duvet as though it contained lead weights rather than feathers. She slid her feet into sheepskin-lined slippers and crossed the short space to her bedroom door, tying the belt of her dressing gown as she went.

'Come on, sleepyhead,' she said, opening the door to Cassie's room, a smile plastered on her face. One look at the crumpled cover and she realised why there had been no sound coming from her room. Since her daddy had gone, Cassie had begun waking up in the middle of the night and going downstairs to the living room to curl up on the sofa with Pumpkin, the cat. Naomi had worried about it at first, but after her GP had explained that such behaviour could be brought on by anxiety, and that the best thing was not to make a big deal of it, she now treated it as perfectly normal to find the two of them snuggled up together. Usually, she was aware of Cassie's nocturnal movements as she lay sleepless in her bed, tears seeping from the corners of her eyes, but the herbal pill must have dulled her senses.

Naomi was only mildly surprised when Pumpkin met her at the bottom of the staircase, brushing against her legs and purring, before he headed upstairs and trotted into Cassie's room.

'She's not up there, silly, have you forgotten you've been cuddling? I thought it was only goldfish that had a three-second memory.' The words froze on Naomi's lips. Cassie wasn't on the sofa as expected. 'Cassie, where are you?' she said, pushing through the door to the kitchen, a mildly panicky sensation starting in her chest. The room was empty, but one of the kitchen chairs had been moved from its place at the table and was now beneath the row of hooks near the back door where all the keys were kept safely out of reach. *At least, I assumed they were out of reach*, Naomi thought, noticing the door to the garden was ajar and her daughter's pink-and-white spotted wellingtons were missing from the piece of newspaper on which she had stood them the previous night to stop any mud being trodden into the house. *Why would Cassie reach the keys down and open the back door when she knows she's not supposed to?* Naomi wondered, *unless she was trying to be helpful by fetching the spent sparklers in from her sandpit to create whiskers for the pumpkin cat we carved last night for Halloween?*

'You should have waited for Mummy…'

Her words hung in the frosty air. There was no sign of Cassie in the small enclosed space. Naomi was acutely aware of her heart thumping in her chest. No need to panic, she told herself, turning back into the house, there will be a perfectly simple explanation. *Perhaps she's in the bathroom. Yes, that must be it.* Taking the stairs two at a time, she prayed that she would find her daughter proudly lathering up soap on her hands to wash away the sand. Her heart sank.

'Cassie, where are you? Are you hiding? Come on now, it's not funny. You'll be late for school.'

Naomi grabbed at the wardrobe doorknob in her daughter's room, but it held only clothes and toys. She tossed the bedclothes onto the floor and then looked under the bed, her breath coming in increasingly short gasps. Back in her own room, she wrenched the wardrobe doors open, staring for a moment at the neat row of clothes on her side of the wardrobe and the empty space where Charlie's used to be. Tears were forming in her eyes, but she refused to let them fall. *Think logically – Cassie can't simply have vanished into thin air.*

'Cassie,' she called again, trying but failing to keep the panic from her voice as she stumbled back onto the landing. The peace and quiet she had been grateful for only minutes earlier was now a deafening silence. Then she noticed Pumpkin standing on his back legs, clawing at the front door. As with the back door minutes earlier, she noticed the key was in the lock. A cold fear gripped her heart.

'Oh my God, no,' Naomi muttered, running down the stairs as fast as she dared. She tried to turn the key to the right. It didn't move; it was already unlocked. She flung the door open. The pumpkin she had carved to resemble a cat's head was exactly where she had left it a few hours previously, only now it had sparklers stuck haphazardly around its triangular cut-out nose. Frantically, her eyes darted around the small front garden, searching for a flash of pink coat or wellington boots, but there was nothing. Then her gaze rested on the front gate, which was normally fastened shut. It was hanging loosely on its hinges, creaking slightly with each breath of wind. She began to shiver uncontrollably. *Why would Cassie open the front gate and wander out onto the street? Where was she going?* Naomi tried to take a step towards the gate and the road beyond, but her legs buckled beneath her.

'Help me,' she cried out, her voice shrill and desperate, tears she had been holding back now flowing freely. 'Please, somebody help me. My little girl is missing.'

CHAPTER ONE

The Night Before – 6.30 p.m. – Thursday

Knife in hand, Naomi looked dubiously at the large orange vegetable in front of her on the kitchen table and wondered where to start. Pumpkin-carving had always been Charlie's domain, but he wasn't here, and she was determined not to be defeated by an inanimate object.

'Can we make it look like Pumpkin, Mummy?'

Glancing across at Cassie, who was sitting on a battered old club chair stroking their family pet, Naomi was thankful for the comfort he had brought them both over the previous five weeks. He was quite simply the best cat ever. No amount of young Cassie pulling him around or holding him like a baby had ever caused the ginger tom to scratch or bite; it wasn't in his nature. It was as though the brush with death he had had as a kitten, using up the first of his nine lives, had made him eternally grateful to his saviours.

*

Naomi could clearly remember the snowy December evening, almost six years ago, when Charlie had pushed open the front door holding his woolly hat rather than wearing it. The tops of his ears were tinged pink with the cold and snowflakes had settled in his raven-dark hair.

'Why aren't you wearing your hat?' she had asked, gently patting Cassie's back to bring up her wind, to which Charlie had replied,

'Someone needs the warmth more than me.' He had pulled open the sides of his hat to reveal a pink nose and the perfect 'M' head markings of the tiniest ginger kitten Naomi had ever laid eyes on. It was love at first sight.

*

'I think you need to start, Mummy, or it won't be ready to take to school in the morning,' Cassie said, a note of anxiety creeping into her voice.

'You're right, sweetie, and I think I'll be able to use the shapes I cut out for the eyes as the cat's ears if I make them big enough, but first we need to scoop the insides out. Fetch me one of the big plastic bowls from the cupboard, will you?'

'Get down, Pumpkin,' Cassie said. 'I've got to help Mummy, now that Daddy's not here.'

Naomi swallowed hard and kept her head down, pretending to focus her attention on scooping out all the seeds. Cassie often came out with innocent statements such as this, totally oblivious to the impact they had on her mum.

Almost an hour later, urged on by Cassie's delighted squeals, Naomi had carved the pumpkin into a passing semblance of a large ginger cat's head, with the triangular ears held in place by cocktail sticks. The nose was also triangle-shaped with a narrow vertical slit leading to a wide grin, not dissimilar to the Cheshire Cat's in *Alice in Wonderland*.

'It's very good, Mummy, but our Pumpkin's got whiskers.'

'Hmmm, you're right. What could we use, I wonder?' Naomi said, casting her eye around the kitchen for inspiration. Her gaze rested on the two packets of sparklers she had bought that morning which were intended for Bonfire Night the following week. 'Go and put your coat and wellies on, Cassie, Mummy's had an idea.'

Pumpkin, who was once again curled up on Cassie's lap, jumped down and began to stretch, only to be swept up by Naomi and carried through to the lounge.

'You stay in there, boy,' she said, closing the door on him, 'you know you don't like fireworks.'

She and Charlie had been surprised by Pumpkin's terrified reaction to Cassie making giant circular shapes with her sparklers on Bonfire Night the previous year. He had been shut in the kitchen to keep him safely away from noisy bangers and whooshing rockets, but had jumped up on the window ledge to see what the family were up to without him. The moment Charlie had set the sparkler alight and placed it in Cassie's gloved hand there had been an almighty crash from the kitchen. In his rush to get away from the window, Pumpkin had sent the basil and mint plants hurtling to the floor in their ceramic pots, then he had buried his head deep into the old fleecy jacket that served as a blanket in his cat bed.

'Ready,' Cassie said, appearing in the kitchen in her bright pink Puffa jacket and pink-and-white spotted wellington boots.

'Put your gloves on, too, we're going to light some sparklers. Do you remember how Daddy told you to hold them?' Naomi asked, a rush of emotion almost overwhelming her. This time last year they had been the perfect little family. Brushing a tear away from her eyes, she reached for a packet of sparklers and the box of long matches, and then opened the back door, letting a cold rush of late October air into the warm kitchen.

Cassie carefully lined the toes of her wellington boots up with the edge of the paved patio area and held one outstretched arm over the grass, with the other hand in her pocket.

'Like this, Mummy,' she said, triumphantly.

'Perfect. I'll light the first one and we'll hold it together until you feel confident to hold it on your own, okay? When mine is lit, we can make shapes together, but you have to keep your arm stretched out as far as you can and your other hand stays in your pocket.'

Charlie had come up with the pocket idea. If Cassie kept her free hand in her pocket, she wouldn't accidentally touch the searingly hot end of the sparkler.

'When it finishes sparkling, wait for me to take it off you.'

'Yes, Mummy, I know. I don't want to get my fingers burnt cos it will hurt.'

Out of the mouths of babes, Naomi thought, holding out the first spitting sparkler for her daughter and encasing her small, gloved hand in her own.

The tension and despair of the past five weeks eased as the two of them moved the sparklers around in big circles, the bright white light illuminating not only the small fenced-in back garden but also Cassie's smiling face, coloured pink by the cold evening air. As each pair of sparklers was spent, Naomi walked across the stepping stones in the lawn to Cassie's sandpit in the corner and placed them burnt side down to cool off safely.

'They will make purrfect whiskers for the pumpkin cat, Mummy. Did you hear I made a joke?' she laughed. 'Pumpkin purrs, doesn't he?'

'Very clever, missy,' Naomi said, hugging her daughter tightly after placing the final pair of sparklers hot end down in the sand. 'Now, let's get you in the bath, it's already way past your bedtime.'

It was Naomi's favourite time of the day. Cassie would sit among sweet-scented bubbles, chattering excitedly about her day and what was to come tomorrow, with Pumpkin sitting on the closed toilet seat, not wanting to miss out on anything. He had come into their lives five weeks after Cassie was born, and Naomi had always harboured the belief that the two of them shared the same date of birth. They had always been inseparable, and he even appeared to enjoy listening to Cassie's nightly bedtime story, curled up contentedly on the end of her bed, occasionally twitching an ear. Tonight's story was quite short as the little girl's eyelids were drooping after the unexpected excitement of playing in the garden with the sparklers.

Just before she fell asleep, Cassie said, 'Remember to put the pumpkin near the front door, Mummy, so we don't forget to take it to school tomorrow.'

'Will do,' Naomi said, kissing her daughter's forehead and feeling suitably reprimanded. Since Charlie had gone, she had occasionally forgotten things that her daughter was supposed to take in, most recently her contribution for the Harvest Festival. She had realised her oversight on arriving home from walking Cassie to school. The gingham-covered cardboard box that was to be distributed to the elderly people in the area, filled with tins of vegetables and jars of honey and jam, sat reproachfully in the middle of the kitchen table.

'And Mummy?'

'Yes, sweetheart?'

'You did a very good job with the pumpkin, nearly as good as Daddy. I wish he could have seen it.'

'Me too,' was all Naomi could manage without her voice breaking to match her shattered heart.

CHAPTER TWO

8.40 p.m. – Thursday

Charlie was about to leave the safety of his hiding place behind some bushes across the road from his former home, when the front door opened. Naomi came into view, holding a pumpkin. He shrank back into the shadows and watched as his wife bent down to place it on the top step, a candle illuminating it from within. *Is it really Halloween already? What happened to the last five weeks of my life?* It all felt like a horrible nightmare, one he was desperate to wake up from. *If only I could turn the clock back to the night of the argument, I would do things so differently.*

For days after Naomi had thrown him out, he had taken refuge in his old bedroom at his mum's house, refusing to eat and struggling to sleep. Three weeks ago, after the initial shock had worn off, and following a lot of encouragement from his mum, he had returned to work, although he was pretty sure he wasn't currently the most productive member of staff. Only today he had been called into his manager's office and asked if he needed a sabbatical. Charlie knew it was less out of concern for his well-being and more of a coded warning: get your act together or we'll have to let you go. Losing his job would be a disaster. Going through the motions of a normal day at work was the only thing that was keeping him sane, and it also gave him the opportunity to make his nightly detour on the way back to his mum's, hoping for a glimpse of his little girl.

It was a familiar routine. At around 7 p.m., the light would go on in the bathroom, followed about fifteen minutes later by the light in Cassie's bedroom. Sometimes, when he was still part of his family's life, she would jump up on her bed to draw her own curtains but, since he had been watching, it had always been Naomi shutting out the world.

Everything had been much later than usual this evening and, shivering in the sub-zero temperatures, Charlie had to keep telling himself to wait just a few minutes more, tonight might be the night. When he had heard shrieks of laughter coming from the back garden shortly before the bathroom light went on, it had almost broken him. It sounded like Naomi and Cassie were doing just fine without him. *She's even carved the pumpkin*, Charlie thought, watching his wife lean back against the door frame to admire her handiwork. *That's always been my job.* He buried his face in his hands for a moment, wondering how it had all gone so catastrophically wrong, and when he raised his head, he could have sworn Naomi was looking straight at him. It was so tempting to walk out of the shadows, up the front path and beg forgiveness from the only woman he had ever truly loved. But even as this thought formed, Naomi retreated to the warmth of the house, closing the door behind her and extinguishing all light but the flicker of the candle from the depths of the pumpkin. *That's all I have to cling onto, a tiny glimmer of hope that one day she'll listen to my side of the story.*

Although he knew he should be heading back to his mum's, certain she would be worried sick about him, Charlie wasn't sure that it was safe to leave the candle burning. *What if it gets blown over and somehow sets the house on fire? I'd never forgive myself if I could have done something to prevent a terrible tragedy.* He decided to give it a few minutes, and then make his way silently up the path to blow the candle out.

Before he had a chance to move, the hall light was turned off. Naomi must have decided on an early night, he thought, picturing her heading upstairs to the bed they used to share. He closed his eyes and imagined himself holding her against his chest before she raised her face to his and their lips met. He could almost taste the minty freshness of her breath and smell her perfume, The One, by Dolce & Gabbana. He had bought it for her on their first Christmas together as husband and wife, in part because he liked the smell but mostly because she was 'the one' for him. *And now I've ruined everything*, he thought, creeping stealthily up the path. He glanced down and realised that he should have credited Naomi with more sense. It wasn't a real candle, after all.

CHAPTER THREE

9.05 p.m. – Thursday

There was no way Naomi was going to forget about the pumpkin, but to be on the safe side, she put it on the step outside the front door where she and Cassie would more or less fall over it the following morning. She turned on the artificial tea light candle to illuminate it from the inside and leaned back to admire her handiwork. Understandably, the school wouldn't allow real candles, but the artificial ones flickered in almost the same way.

Naomi shivered. *It's probably just the cold,* she thought, peering into the inky darkness beyond the reach of the street light, *but it does sometimes feel as though someone's watching me.* She closed and locked the door, then headed through to the kitchen to double-check that the back door was secure too before she hung the keys on a metal holder shaped like a black cat. Despite his promises to paint it orange to more closely resemble Pumpkin, Charlie hadn't got around to it. *He was probably too busy seeing Jessica behind my back,* Naomi thought, an image of the curvy blonde kissing her husband filling her mind. She reached for the work surface to steady herself. Simply thinking about her husband and what they had lost was overwhelming. Although she had tried her hardest to banish all thoughts of him, there were times, like earlier in the evening, as she had been carving the pumpkin, when it was impossible. It was hard to deny his existence when there were so many daily reminders to the contrary, not least of which was looking at their beautiful daughter, who was the image of her dad. Naomi had felt guilty at times for preventing Charlie from seeing Cassie, but it was a form of self-preservation. Explaining to a five-year-old the reasons why her mummy and daddy were no longer living together was something she couldn't face at the moment. It was easier for him not to be in their lives. Eventually she might be strong enough to allow him to visit, but not yet; it was too raw, too painful to even contemplate.

'Right, Pumpkin. What do you fancy for your dinner tonight, rabbit or turkey?' she asked the ginger tom in an effort to blot out her thoughts of Charlie with routine. Pumpkin had purred rhythmically and brushed past her legs repeatedly in response.

'Rabbit it is,' Naomi said, spooning the food into his bowl and placing it on the plastic mat covered in miniature paw prints. 'At least you love me,' she added, tickling him behind his ears, 'even if it is only because I feed you.'

She flicked off the kitchen light, leaving the door to the lounge ajar to give Pumpkin the choice between the comfort of the sofa or his fleece-lined basket.

Although it was only a little after 9 p.m., Naomi was barely able to raise one foot in front of the other as she had dragged herself up the stairs and undressed for bed before heading to the bathroom.

The harsh overhead light was less than flattering as Naomi examined her face in the mirrored bathroom cabinet while she was brushing her teeth, observing that even the soft lighting used on a film set would have a job disguising her dark circles and bloodshot eyes. Despite her exhaustion, she suspected sleep would elude her the moment her head hit the pillow as it had done since that fateful night. Stretching out ahead of her were hours of lying in the dark, torturing herself with the same thoughts. *If only we hadn't argued. If only Charlie hadn't slammed out of the house in a temper. It was too late now; nothing could ever be the same again.*

She opened the cabinet to put the toothpaste away and her eyes rested on several unused pregnancy testing kits. It was almost as though they were taunting her. How many times over the past three years had she held her breath after peeing on the test sticks, waiting for the word 'pregnant' to appear? *How many times have I cried myself to sleep when the word didn't appear? Charlie always said he wanted a brother or sister for Cassie as much as I do, but it's not him that feels an utter and complete failure every time the test is negative. Well, I won't be needing them now.* She grabbed the boxes and threw them with force into the metal bin. *But maybe I should give these a try?*

Naomi looked at the picture on the side of the packet that her best friend Kate had handed her in the school playground that afternoon while they were waiting for their children to finish for the day. It was of a person lying down with 'z's in various sizes surrounding their head. Kate had suggested she try the pills several times over the past few weeks, but Naomi always resisted, reminding her friend that she hated taking any kind of medication.

When the subject of lack of sleep had come up again, Kate had reached into her bag and produced the box that Naomi was currently holding in her hand. 'They're herbal,' Kate had assured her, 'so not really medication. They're aimed at relaxing you sufficiently to fall asleep naturally, not filling you full of chemicals. They're the ones I take when I'm a bit stressed out, so I'm afraid there are only a couple left in the pack. Look, I wouldn't dream of saying this if you weren't my best friend, but it all seems to be getting a bit much for you on your own. I'm worried that your lack of sleep will eventually affect your ability to look after Cassie. Just give them a try tonight, and if they don't work for you, or you don't like the way they make you feel, you never have to take them again.'

After further gentle persuasion, Naomi had agreed to try them. Kate had made her promise that she would by saying 'Brownie's honour'. A faint smile momentarily found the corners of Naomi's mouth as she remembered the two of them making their first solemn oath together when they were only eight years old. They had been playing in the park when Naomi had said she was hungry. While she distracted the owner, Kate had stolen two bags of crisps from the shelves of the corner shop opposite.

'It's our secret,' she had said once they were safely back in the park, munching on the salt-and-vinegar potato snacks. 'You have to promise not to tell anyone.'

'Brownie's honour,' Naomi had replied. From that moment, whenever either of the friends promised using those words, they had to stick to it.

*

'Is everything okay, Mummy? I thought I heard a noise.'

Naomi spun round to see a sleepy Cassie in the doorway.

'What are you doing out of bed?' she snapped.

'I came to see if you were all right.'

'Well, you can see I am, so go back to bed,' she said, immediately regretting the sharpness of her tone of voice. 'I'm just tired,' she explained to Cassie's retreating back. *Unbelievably tired,* she thought, turning back to her reflection in the mirror. *I can't go on like this. It's not fair to take things out on Cassie. Kate's right; she has to be my priority. I have to get a decent night's sleep, or I'll crack up completely.* Reaching for the packet of tablets and her glass of water, Naomi pulled the cord to extinguish the bathroom light and headed towards her bedroom and another solitary night.

CHAPTER FOUR

9.15 p.m. – Thursday

'Is that you, Charlie?' Hazel called out. 'You're late tonight, love.'

'Sorry, Mum. I'm still catching up on stuff at work. I hope you didn't wait for me for dinner.'

'Of course I did, I don't like you eating alone. Get your coat off and wash your hands and I'll dish up. I've done a nice warming sausage casserole, it's bitter out there tonight. That's the trouble with bright sunny days in the autumn – it translates to cold frosty nights. Mind you, I bet the weather will turn for the fireworks display on Saturday, it always seems to rain and spoil things.'

Charlie was grateful to his mum for letting him stay with her after Naomi had thrown him out, but he did find that her constant chatter grated on his nerves, as did her repeatedly asking him if he was okay. He wanted to say, *no, I'm not okay, my heart is breaking*, but instead he always smiled and said, 'Getting by, Mum'. He knew the whole situation was difficult for her, too. Naomi had always welcomed her mother-in-law into their home, but since the break-up she had said she thought it would be less distressing for Cassie if Hazel stayed away. Having her grandma around would only remind the little girl that her daddy was not, and Naomi insisted that she didn't think that was fair on Cassie. Charlie suspected this wasn't entirely the truth, but under the circumstances he could hardly argue against her decision. It was as though she wanted to wipe him from her memory by pretending he didn't exist, and who could blame her? Nevertheless, it was really upsetting for his mum. She worshipped her only grandchild and, living on the next street, was used to seeing her on an almost daily basis. *What a cock-up*, he thought, instantly cringing at his choice of words.

'It's on the table.'

'Coming, Mum,' Charlie called back, trying to ignore the haunted look in his eyes reflected in the mirror above the basin. He plastered a smile on his face as he walked into the kitchen.

'Mmm, that smells good.'

At least he's eating now, Hazel thought, clearing the dishes away and filling the sink with warm soapy water to tackle the washing-up. Charlie had offered to help but she assured him she could manage, urging him instead to get an early night after reminding him that she needed the garage door opening. He hadn't argued, kissing her on the top of her head on his way to retrieve the garage key from the hook near the back door.

It was a huge improvement since the first few days after Naomi barred him from their home. Initially he had shut himself away in his old bedroom, refusing even the cups of hot sweet tea Hazel offered him. After a fortnight off work, he managed to rally a little, and toast and coffee fuelled him sufficiently to leave the house each morning. Gradually things were improving, but he still refused to talk to her about exactly what had happened.

Hazel had her suspicions, but found it hard to believe her darling Charlie would treat a woman in the same way that his feckless father had treated her. She knew all about bringing up a child single-handed and it wasn't something she would recommend, although the closeness she shared with her son was some compensation.

In Hazel's opinion, Charlie and Naomi were made for each other, unlike her doomed relationship with Frank, Charlie's dad.

We never stood a chance, really, she thought, carefully washing each dish in the soapy suds before rinsing it under the cold tap and placing it in the draining rack. *With Charlie already on the way when we got married, we had barely got used to living as a couple before there were three of us. Charlie and Naomi were married for five years before Cassie arrived on the scene, but maybe that wasn't entirely planned,* she reflected, knowing Naomi's recent history of miscarriages and difficulty in falling pregnant. *It doesn't seem fair somehow. I became pregnant so easily, almost forcing Frank into 'doing the right thing', and those two can't conceive a much longed for brother or sister for Cassie. Life can be so cruel. Maybe that's what has finally come between them. The pressure to have another baby is taking all the fun out of their sex life.*

Whatever the reason, Hazel had initially felt confident that the two of them would sort things out, but the weeks were dragging on and there was still no indication that Naomi would ever speak to Charlie again, let alone reconcile with him. Not wanting to be accused of interfering, she had to stand by and watch from the sidelines, feeling completely helpless, as the three people she cared most about in the world slowly drifted apart. It was bad enough not seeing Naomi. She really liked her warm, caring daughter-in-law, but it was being refused access to Cassie that was truly heartbreaking. The little girl, with her happy, smiling face and cornflower-blue eyes, the exact same shade as Charlie's and Frank's, had brought so much pleasure to Hazel from the day she was born. The thought of not being allowed to resume the close relationship she had always enjoyed with her only grandchild caused a lump in her chest that made it difficult for her to breathe at times. She brushed a tear away from the corner of her eye with the back of her yellow rubber washing-up glove, leaving a residue of foam in her greying hair. *I just can't let that happen. I can't live the rest of my life without Cassie in it, and neither can Charlie. I know she's hurting and needs the reassurance of her daughter's unconditional love, but if she doesn't come round to seeing things from other people's points of view, I'll have to make Charlie go back and see the lawyer chap to get some kind of access agreed.*

Absent-mindedly, Hazel cut up the half-sausage left on Charlie's plate and scraped it into Alfie's bowl. The golden retriever wagged his tail in anticipation.

'Not yet, boy. You'll have to wait until after your walk, and then you can have it with your biscuits for supper.'

As if the dog had understood every word, he went over to where his lead was hanging on the wall next to the back door and lay down with his chin resting on his front legs, whining softly.

'All right, boy. Let me finish this washing-up and then we'll pop out. Only a short walk tonight though,' she warned. 'I've got an early start in the morning if I'm going to beat the traffic.'

CHAPTER FIVE

Day One – 8.02 a.m. – Friday

Rachel closed her eyes and stepped forward under the sharp needles of water, allowing them to stream down her face and wash away the saltiness, a mixture of tears and perspiration. Her panic attacks had lessened in frequency, but were no less severe than when she had first experienced them nearly thirty years ago. *At least when I get to menopause, I'll already know what it feels like to wake up drenched in my own sweat.* She reached for the shampoo bottle and squeezed out a large dollop before lathering it vigorously into her scalp. The aroma of apples filled her nostrils, catching her by surprise. She had run out of the brand that she bought on her quarterly trip to the hairdressers so had grabbed a bottle, along with a shepherd's pie ready meal for one, from the shop at the garage when she had filled up with petrol on her way home from work the previous evening. She opened her eyes, risking getting foam in them and making them sting and glared at the bottle. Sure enough, the label read 'crisp apple fragrance'. *That's going straight in the bin. The last thing I need is a reminder of the first time I met him.* She shivered, turning the heat up on the water in an effort to cleanse her mind of unwelcome memories, even at the risk of scalding her body. She rinsed the foam from her hair and applied a generous amount of her usual conditioner, leaving it on while she washed herself, in the hope that it would mask the smell of apples.

As she stepped out of the shower and reached for a towel to wrap around her head and a larger one to cover her body, she could hear her mobile phone ringing out from the kitchen where she had left it on charge overnight. By the time she got downstairs it had stopped ringing, but she could see on the screen that there were two missed calls. Both were from Graham. *It must be important if he's ringing me this early.* She pressed the screen to return the call.

'Morning, Guv. I was just about to try you again.'

'Talk to me.'

'We've received a call about a five-year-old girl going missing from her bed overnight. I thought you would want to know as soon as possible.'

Rachel's throat constricted.

'Guv, are you still there?'

'Yes.'

'Do you want me to head up the investigation, or do you want to take the lead?'

Rachel hesitated. Her DI was perfectly capable of leading the investigation but, due to the nature of the case, he had rung her first.

'I'll take it. Has anyone gone to the child's home?'

'I'm leaving now, but it's your side of town. I wanted to let you know so you can go straight there rather than coming into the station first in rush-hour traffic.'

'What's the address?' Rachel said, unravelling the towel from her shoulder-length chestnut hair with one hand and shaking it free, while bringing up the Notes app on her phone with the other.

'Fifteen Beechwood Avenue. My satnav is telling me I should be there in twenty-five minutes. If you get there first, the mother's name is Naomi Bailey and the missing child is Cassie.'

'Right, I'll meet you there.'

'Are you sure you want to do this, Guv?'

'It's my job, Graham. A young girl is missing. We need to use everything at our disposal to find her.'

'Yes, Guv.'

Rachel disconnected the call and stood for a moment, her hands gripping the edges of the quartz work surface. It felt pleasantly cool to the touch and she had a sudden urge to rest her cheek against it. *Graham was right to ask the question. Can I do it? I've always known that a case like this may come my way one day. Can I be objective and not let my emotions cloud my judgement?* She closed her eyes and breathed deeply and slowly as she had been taught to do to calm herself. *I have to. A child is missing, and she needs my help. I wouldn't be able to forgive myself if something happened to her which my expertise and instinct could have prevented.*

Within minutes Rachel was dressed and out of the door, her first coffee of the day abandoned next to the toaster with two slices of untoasted bread sticking out of the top.

CHAPTER SIX

8.10 a.m. – Friday

That's not like Mum, Charlie thought, sleep still clouding his brain as he bent down to pick up the post from the grey doormat displaying the message 'PLEASE WIPE YOUR PAWS'. *She normally picks it up on her way to the kitchen.* Then he remembered. Over dinner, his mum had told him she was going to visit her sister, Sheila, in Devon for a few days. When he had questioned her seemingly last-minute decision, she had told him it had been arranged for months but that she was prepared to cancel if he needed her at home.

He knew the whole business between Naomi and him had put a huge strain on his relationship with his mum. At first, she had just been there to support him as he battled with the enormity of what he had done. She didn't bombard him with questions, instead encouraging him to eat and sleep, presumably hopeful that he would open up to her when he was ready. Charlie had always been able to talk to his mum about anything and everything, and she usually offered him the best advice, but this was different. How could he tell her how monumentally stupid he had been to risk everything for a drunken one-night stand?

Come on Charlie, wake up. He shook his head as though to remove the fog of sleep as he flicked the switch on the kettle and heaped coffee granules into his mug. *At this rate I'm going to be late for work, and that won't go down well on the back of the warning I've already had.* It wasn't surprising that he had slept through his alarm. Despite going to bed quite early, sleep had eluded him. All he had been able to think about was the laughter he had heard from his daughter and his estranged wife as they played together in the garden of his former home. It seemed so unfair that they should be having such a good time while he was going through such hell. He had heard his mum go out with Alfie and return a short while later, and he had heard her climbing the stairs and quietly opening and closing doors so as not to disturb him. An hour later, still wide awake, Charlie had got up and gone downstairs to make himself a cup of tea. He didn't put the television on for fear of waking his mum, so when he had finished his drink and sleep was still no closer, he had decided to go for a walk to try and tire himself out. It had been half past one in the morning when he had finally let himself back into the house, shivering from the freezing temperatures that had cut through the thin cotton of the pyjamas he was wearing beneath his winter coat, and gone back to bed.

He poured boiling water into his mug and picked up the note his mum had left on the countertop with instructions to feed the dog and water her plants. She had also reminded him to open the garage door for her return late on Sunday evening. Closing the up-and-over door wasn't a problem as she was working with the aid of gravity, but opening it was proving increasingly difficult for Hazel with her wrists getting progressively weaker. Not only was it heavy, it also made a grinding metallic noise, so they usually tried to avoid opening it too early in the morning or too late at night so as not to disturb the neighbours. He'd done it the previous evening before retiring to bed and had also reversed her car into the garage for her to make for a quicker getaway that morning. He'd even opened the boot to make it easier for her to slide her case in. *Maybe I'll put a drop of oil on the garage door while she's away*, Charlie thought, sipping his bitter black coffee, and I'll get on with all the other little jobs I've been promising to do for her around the house and never seemed to have time for when I wasn't living here.

Once Charlie was over the initial shock of Naomi throwing him out, he had tried to regain a semblance of normality in his life. He got up in the mornings and went to work, and came home for his dinner each evening after his ritual of observing the light in Cassie's bedroom being switched off. It was only a small thing but somehow it kept him feeling more connected to his daughter. The few times his mum had attempted to steer the conversation towards what had caused the break-up he had resolutely refused to speak to her, retreating to the sanctuary of his room. After one such occasion, she had followed him upstairs, tapped lightly on his door and let herself in.

'I only want to help,' she had said. 'I can't bear to see you hurting like this.' She had held out her arms, inviting him into a hug.

He had sent her away with the words, 'You can't help. No one can.'

The sound of his mum's sobbing had echoed through the house, and Charlie despised himself all the more for causing her such pain. One day he would make it up to her, but first he needed to be able to talk things through with Naomi – if she would only listen to his version of events.

Before he had slammed out of the house on that disastrous night, he'd shouted at Naomi, 'Maybe if we just made love when it feels right rather than when your charts and temperature tell you it's the best time for conceiving, I wouldn't feel so much like a sperm donor!'

He had got into his car and slammed the door so hard that the whole vehicle shook almost as much as his hands resting on the steering wheel. He realised he was in no fit state to drive, but he hadn't wanted to go back into the house until they had both had chance to calm down. Cassie was having tea at his mum's. He could hardly go barging in there ranting and raving. He desperately needed to talk to someone, so he had rung their best friend, Kate.

The three of them had been almost inseparable since the first day of senior school when Charlie had asked to share the girls' lunch table in the packed dining hall. She answered on the second ring.

'Hey, Charlie.'

'Hi Kate. Have you got a few minutes?'

'What's up? You sound stressed.'

'I've just had a shouting match with Naomi and stormed out of the house. I feel terrible about it.'

'Not in front of Cassie, I hope?'

'No, she's at my mum's. Naomi organised it so we could have a bit of "us" time, if you get my drift.'

'So, what's the problem? That's really thoughtful of her.'

'It probably seems that way, but she virtually leapt on me the minute I was through the front door.'

'Sorry, Charlie, am I missing something? Shouldn't you be ecstatic that she still fancies you so much after all these years?'

'If it was just that she fancied me I would be, but she had an ulterior motive. She always has an ulterior motive these days.'

'Trying to get pregnant, you mean?'

'She told you?'

'She tells me everything. It's really hard for her, Charlie. She's desperate for a little brother or sister for Cassie, and every month her body gives her the sign that she isn't pregnant feels like a massive failure for her.'

'I should have known you'd take her side. It's hard for me too, you know, being asked to perform when her flaming charts demand it.'

'I'm not taking sides, Charlie. We're not in school now.'

'Look, I probably shouldn't have called you, but I didn't know who else to turn to. I just needed to get out of there before we both said stuff we didn't mean.'

'Have you calmed down enough to have a sensible conversation with her?'

'No, not really.'

'Where are you?'

'Sat in the car outside my house.'

'Well, driving when you're in a bit of a state probably isn't the best idea. Why don't you walk down to the pub and have a beer? It'll give you both a bit of time to cool off. Do you want me to call her?'

'And say what? Your husband just rang me to say you've had a row? You can imagine how well that would go down. No, let's pretend this conversation never happened. I shouldn't have rung you.'

'I'm glad you felt you could turn to me, Charlie.'

'I guess that's what friends are for. Thanks for the advice.'

'Any time.'

Charlie had headed for the pub, forgetting that he normally avoided it on Thursdays and Fridays because those were the nights Jessica worked behind the bar. She and his wife had history from their schooldays, and the feud had continued into adulthood. Instead of a beer, he had ordered a large scotch and then another. Before long, the alcohol had loosened his tongue and he was telling the only person Naomi ever spoke ill of about the tension in his marriage. It was pure gold for Jessica, who had feigned sympathy and kept refilling his glass when the landlord wasn't looking. At closing time, when he was barely able to stand unaided, having consumed more than half the bar optic of Scotch whisky, she had offered to drive him home. When he finally dragged himself into consciousness the next morning, he was naked in her bed.

Accepting that lift was the biggest mistake of my life. The second biggest was not going straight home the next morning to try and explain to Naomi what had happened.

As it was, he had two text messages when he checked his phone during his lunch break. The first was from Naomi: *How could you? And with that bitch? I'm taking Cassie to stay with friends for*

*a couple of days. I want everything of yours out of the house when I
get back. I never want to see you again.*

The second message was from Jessica. It was a picture of him,
naked, accompanied by the words: *I thought Naomi had a right
to know.*

Charlie tipped the remains of his coffee down the sink; the
taste in his mouth was bitter enough.

He nipped back upstairs to clean his teeth before sticking his
head round the door of the spare room.

'You stay nice and quiet and I'll be back at lunchtime to get
you some food.'

CHAPTER SEVEN

8.53 a.m. – Friday

'Here, drink this.'

Detective Chief Inspector Rachel Hart handed Naomi the mug of sweet tea she had just fetched from the kitchen. It had given her the opportunity to have a quick exchange with her DI, who had arrived at the terraced house on Beechwood Avenue a few minutes before her. Both were only too aware that the hours following the initial call reporting someone going missing were crucial.

Naomi accepted the mug without speaking, wrapping her hands around it as though attempting to gain warmth.

'Is there anyone you'd like us to call?'

Naomi shook her head.

'What about your husband?' she persisted, gently.

'We – we're not together any more.'

'Yes, we know,' Rachel said, raising her eyebrows slightly at her DI. 'Your friend told us. Is there a possibility that your husband has your daughter? Maybe she was staying with him last night.'

Kate shifted uncomfortably from foot to foot and shot Naomi an apologetic look. She had arrived at the house before the police, after receiving a call from Barry, Naomi's neighbour, telling her that Cassie was missing. She had been trying to calm her hysterical friend when the police had arrived on the scene. While she was making the tea Naomi was now sipping, the DI had been asking her questions about the family. Kate hadn't realised just how much information she had divulged in the two minutes it had taken for the kettle to boil.

'She doesn't stay at her dad's. I put her to bed last night, just like I always do,' Naomi said, her voice flat and unemotional.

'And what time was that?'

'It was a bit later than usual, about half past eight, I think. We'd been carving a pumpkin for Halloween and then we lit some sparklers in the garden.'

'It's a bit early to be celebrating Bonfire Night, isn't it? Weren't you expecting her to be here on 5 November?'

'We weren't celebrating, we were making whiskers for the pumpkin – Cassie wanted to make it look like our ginger cat. Of course I expected her to be here with me on Bonfire Night. Where else would she be?'

'Well, I wondered if maybe her dad was planning on taking her to the firework display on the field across the road. I noticed the bonfire as we pulled up outside.'

Rachel had already made a mental note to have the huge pile of wood and broken furniture searched as a priority. It was the perfect place to hide a body, or somewhere to shelter for the night if the little girl had simply let herself out of the house and wandered off.

'The display is tomorrow night, and I've already told you she doesn't see her dad.'

'No. What you said was that she doesn't stay at her dad's.'

'It's the same thing.'

'Not necessarily. So, tell me a bit more about last night. You said you put Cassie to bed later than usual. Why was that?'

'I already told you that too. We were carving the pumpkin, but I've never done it before and it took longer than I thought.'

'She must have been quite excitable after carving the pumpkin and playing with the sparklers. Was she difficult when it was time to go to bed? Did you have to tell her to calm down – perhaps give her a little smack?'

'I've never smacked Cassie, and neither has Charlie.'

'When was the last time your husband saw his daughter?'

'Five weeks ago, the day before I found out he'd been cheating on me. I haven't allowed him in this house since.'

'Does he still have front door keys?'

'Yes. What are you getting at? Are you suggesting that Charlie let himself in here last night and took Cassie? Don't be ridiculous. He would never do anything to hurt me.'

Even as she spoke, Naomi realised how irrational her words must sound. Charlie had hurt her; he had broken her heart into a million pieces.

'Is that such a ridiculous suggestion? You must both be under a great deal of pressure and he must be missing his daughter. I think we need to speak to him and make sure that she is not with him before we instigate a full-scale search of the area. In any case, he has a right to know that his daughter is missing from home. Do you have his mobile number?'

'Why don't you ask Kate? She seems to have filled you in on everything else.'

'I'll get my phone from the kitchen,' Kate mumbled.

'I know Charlie. He wouldn't just let himself into the house. He wouldn't,' Naomi repeated, noticing Rachel's sceptical look. 'I never dreamed Cassie would open the front door without my permission. She's normally such a good girl. Why the hell didn't I put the key somewhere safer? If only I'd kept that damn pumpkin inside instead of putting it out on the doorstep. Oh, God, I don't know what I'll do if anything has happened to her.' Naomi curled forward in her chair, elbows tucked into her waist and both hands on her head, as she gently rocked back and forth.

Kate walked into the room with her mobile phone in her hand. She thrust it at Rachel and hurried to Naomi's side. 'It'll be okay, Noms,' she said, putting her arms around her friend. 'We'll find her. You told me she's sometimes woken up during the night since

Charlie left. Maybe that's what happened last night and she was a bit sleepy and confused and let herself out of the house and then couldn't get back in. She's probably curled up under a hedge fast asleep, as warm as a piece of toast if she's wearing her pink Puffa jacket. Speaking of toast, are you sure I can't get you a piece? You need to keep your strength up.'

Naomi shook her head, raising her tear-streaked face to look at her friend, a mix of hope, fear and desperation in her eyes.

'Do you really think so? What if she wandered onto the canal path? It's dark down there... what if she fell in? Oh, God, I can't bear it,' she sobbed. 'She's all I've got in the world.'

'Shhh, shhh,' Kate said, trying to soothe her distraught friend. 'We'll have her home in no time,' she reassured Naomi, raising her eyebrows questioningly in the direction of the policewoman who had her mobile phone to her ear.

Rachel shook her head. 'It's gone straight to voicemail.'

'He's probably already at work, and he puts his phone on silent so that it doesn't disturb him.'

'Where does he work?'

'Top Tech Solutions.'

'Graham, can you organise for one of the team to go to Mr Bailey's office to have a word with him? If he hasn't got Cassie, we'll have a better idea of how we need to escalate our enquiries. Naomi, do you think you are up to showing me some of the regular routes you and Cassie walk? School, the shops, friends – familiar places where she may have wandered if, as your friend suggested, she somehow got locked out of the house.'

Even in her distressed state, Naomi picked up a note of doubt in the policewoman's tone and fear clutched at her heart. *She doesn't believe Cassie has just wandered off. Either she thinks I've done something to hurt my own child or she thinks Cassie has been taken.*

For the first time since finding her daughter's bed empty that morning, Naomi was facing the real possibility that her daughter might have been abducted. *If she had wandered out onto the road half-asleep, there would have been no resistance from her if a car had pulled up at the kerbside and bundled her in. It would only have taken seconds and she could be anywhere by now.* As unlikely as it was, she began to hope that Charlie had come into the house and taken their daughter: the alternatives were unthinkable.

CHAPTER EIGHT

9.58 a.m. – Friday

Hazel glanced at the clock on the dashboard of her Volkswagen Jetta. It was almost 10 a.m. and she had barely moved in over an hour. *So much for leaving early so that I'd be at Sheila's for my lunch,* she thought, peering through the rain beating against her windscreen at the stationary traffic snaking ahead of her on the M4.

Shortly after dawn that morning, when Hazel had set off, it had been dry but the sky was filled with vivid shades of orange, red and pink. The old rhyme had flashed into her mind: 'red sky in the morning, shepherd's warning'. Sure enough, less than an hour into her journey the rain had started, gentle at first, but as she drove further west towards Devon, the intensity increased.

The weather conditions are probably the cause of the accident. Despite the delay, I should be grateful that I'm not involved in it. At least I'm warm and dry with the radio for company. She reached over to turn the volume up so that she could hear it above the noise of the rain hammering down on the metal roof. Lately, she had noticed that her hearing wasn't as good as it used to be. When she and Charlie watched television in the evenings, she struggled to hear some of the dialogue. *I should probably have a hearing test, but it will have to wait until this business with Naomi and Charlie is sorted out. The last thing he needs is something else to worry about. It's got to stop. I won't stand by any more watching him suffer, even if my interfering does make him mad at me for a while. Drastic situations call for drastic measures.* Hazel sighed. *That's the thing with children, much as they are a blessing, they are also such a worry.*

The car in front of her started to edge forward. Hazel put the Jetta in gear and inched forward too. She wasn't sure, but she thought she heard a faint knocking noise. *Don't tell me there's something wrong with the engine now?* She turned the radio down to listen more intently. *Maybe the poor old girl is just overheating in all this traffic? I'll get Charlie to give her the once-over when I get home, always assuming that he's still speaking to me.* As the traffic began to pick up pace, she listened out for the knocking sound again, but it appeared to have stopped. *With a bit of luck and no more hold-ups, I can still be at Sheila's for a late lunch.*

Unfortunately, luck was not on Hazel's side. She had driven less than two miles when the traffic slowed to a standstill again. Joining the back of the queue, she contemplated turning on her mobile phone and ringing Sheila, knowing her sister would be starting to worry about her lateness, but decided against it as she didn't want to risk getting a fine. As much as she loved her sister, if there hadn't been another very important reason to make this three-hundred-mile round trip, Hazel would have taken the next exit and headed home.

CHAPTER NINE

10.03 a.m. – Friday

While they were waiting to hear back from PC Drake, who had been sent to interview Charlie Bailey at work, DCI Hart decided it would be a good idea to walk across the field to where the bonfire was being constructed and check it out. They needed to be a hundred per cent sure that Cassie hadn't crawled inside it for shelter before it was set alight the following night. *If that means dismantling it and rebuilding it, then so be it*, Rachel thought. *We can't afford to leave any stone unturned.*

She cast a sideways glance at Naomi as they trudged across the field. Her head was down and her hands were thrust deep into her pockets, almost as though she wanted to be invisible. Rachel wasn't sure what to make of her. One minute she had seemed totally lacking in emotion, the next she was being sarcastic towards her friend, then defensive, before dissolving into tears. But it was the aggression that concerned Rachel the most. *Could Naomi have unintentionally harmed her daughter before reporting her missing to the police? Maybe she just lashed out and the child fell and now she's trying to cover it up? She's in a very stressful situation and there's no way of knowing what effect that level of stress may have on her. I have to keep an open mind to that possibility. Mistakes and assumptions cost lives, and there's no way I'm letting that happen on my watch. Whatever happened at the Baileys' house last night, I'm going to get to the bottom of it.*

There was quite a bit of activity around the base of the bonfire, which as they got closer, towered above them by some twenty feet. Balancing precariously near the top was a bearded man.

'You can't come any closer,' said one of the men piling wood around the base.

Rachel produced her warrant card. 'We've had a report of a missing child. We're going to need to check the bonfire to make sure she hasn't crawled inside. I don't suppose you've seen or heard anything?'

The man looked around to the other helpers at ground level, who all shook their heads or shrugged.

'What's going on?' the bearded man near the top of the construction called.

'A kid's gone missing, Guy. You haven't seen anything, have you?'

'Guy?' Naomi shrieked. 'Are you bloody joking? My baby's missing and you're pissing around. It's not bloody funny. She could be dead…'

All eyes turned to look at Naomi. Kate reached a protective arm around her shoulders.

'Sorry, love. We're not taking the piss. That's his name.'

Naomi was visibly shaking.

'I think it's best if we take her back to the house,' Rachel said. 'Graham, you supervise the dismantling of the bonfire for now and I'll ring the station to get you an extra pair of hands to help here, then you can move on to the house-to-house enquiries.'

'Okay, Guv.'

'Don't take any chances. She's a young child and could have squeezed herself into a much smaller space than you may imagine. The whole thing is going to have to come down. Sorry, fellas,' Rachel said over her shoulder, as she rushed to catch up with Kate and Naomi.

'I don't want to go back to the house,' Naomi was saying as Rachel approached. 'She's out here alone somewhere and I'd never forgive myself if I could have stopped something bad happening to her while I was at home drinking cups of tea. Let's try the towpath by the canal. Can we ask the neighbours to help?'

'For the moment, I think it's best if it's just us,' Rachel said, not adding that the last thing the police wanted, whatever the reason for the disappearance, was hordes of untrained people destroying potential evidence. 'I just need to organise for some extra officers to help out here and then we'll head down there. I was also wondering if you'd be okay if I ask PC Drake to bring your husband to the house. As Cassie's parents, anything you can spark off from each other in terms of where she may be sheltering could prove invaluable.'

'I don't really care as long as it helps me get Cassie home.'

An hour later, the trio were heading back towards 15 Beechwood Avenue, having uncovered nothing. It seemed to Rachel as though the energy that Naomi had displayed when she had instigated the search along the towpath had ebbed away with every passing minute. They had checked under every bush and shrub and in the two derelict sheds that were occasional homes for local tramps. The red-brick Victorian footbridge over the canal was another possible place under which Cassie might have sought shelter, but there was no sign of her. There had been a frightening moment when Naomi had stood right on the edge of the canal looking down into the greenish water inches below her feet. Rachel had exchanged a questioning look with Kate: *was she the type to throw herself in?* Naomi had turned back to face the two women with tears streaming uncontrollably down her cheeks.

'Do you think she is in there?' she had whispered.

Kate pulled her friend into a hug. 'Try not to worry. We'll find her, I know we will.'

Rachel was trying to decide at what point she would need to bring the team of divers in to drag the canal. *No point in being hasty. Too soon and Naomi could become hysterical, in which case she would be of no further use in the search. Not only that, but I could be accused of wasting police resources if the little girl turns up unharmed. No, better to wait a day. If Cassie is in the canal, she's already dead.*

As they walked up the path of number 15, the pumpkin cat, with his haphazard whiskers, seemed to be leering at them. Without warning, Naomi rushed forward, picked up the offending vegetable, raised it above her head and smashed it down onto the path with all the force she could muster, orange flesh splattering everywhere.

'This is all your fault!' she screamed hysterically, just as the police car containing her estranged husband pulled up in front of the house.

CHAPTER TEN

11.13 a.m. – Friday

She's lost weight, Charlie observed guiltily, watching Naomi being comforted by her best friend and wishing it could have been him with his arm around his wife. Although her fury had been directed at the pumpkin, the timing of his arrival at the house couldn't have been more appropriate. *It is all my fault. If I'd been here where I belong, taking care of my family, none of this would have happened.*

'Are you still okay with your husband coming into the house, Naomi?' Rachel asked. 'We can go back to the police station if you'd prefer.'

Naomi shrugged her shoulders. The angry outburst from moments earlier seemed to have deflated her as quickly as a sharp tack would a bicycle tyre.

'I really couldn't care less what he does. He's my husband in name only now.'

I deserve that, Charlie thought, following Rachel into the house, feeling like a stranger in the sitting room that he had painstakingly decorated as a surprise for Naomi and their newborn baby. Cassie had been born prematurely, at thirty-four weeks, and that had meant an extended stay in hospital for the pair of them until the tiny baby had gained sufficient weight to be discharged. He could remember gazing in wonder at the perfect little human they had created as he sat on the sofa feeding his

daughter expressed breast milk on her first night at home, while
his wife slept the sleep of the exhausted in their bed upstairs.
She had always been the most attentive mother to their daughter,
which made it seem impossible that she would allow anything to
happen to her. *What had happened?* Charlie had been told very
little when the police had come to his office building, other than
Cassie was missing.

'When did you last see your daughter, Mr Bailey?'

'Charlie, please call me Charlie. As I told your officer, I haven't
seen her since I moved out.'

'Have you spoken to her at all?'

'No. Naomi thought it would be best for Cassie to have a
clean break.'

'And what did you think, Mr Bailey? Did you think that was
the best thing for Cassie, to be kept away from seeing her daddy?'

'No. But I didn't want to hurt Naomi any more than I already
have, so I went along with it.'

'And you've made no attempt to see her in the past five weeks?
That must have been incredibly difficult for a loving father.'

Charlie lowered his eyes to the floor.

'Mr Bailey?'

*What should I say? It's going to be difficult explaining to the police
that I've been watching the house, hopeful for a glimpse of Cassie, but
if I don't, and they find out, it's going to look suspicious.*

'Well, actually,' Charlie said, 'I have tried to catch sight of her
from a distance.'

All eyes were on him now.

'Meaning?'

'I've been watching the house from across the road at around
Cassie's bedtime, in the hope that I might see her at the window
just for a moment.'

'What? Why would you do that?' Naomi demanded, addressing
Charlie for the first time.

'Because I miss her. However much you are hurting, I'm hurting too. I know I'm to blame for everything, but it doesn't mean I don't have feelings. It's been tearing me apart not seeing you and Cassie.'

'You should have thought about that before you shagged that tart,' Naomi shrieked.

Rachel cleared her throat. She had been conferring with her DI, who had been collating evidence gathered from the house-to-house enquiries along Beechwood Avenue.

'What time have you been watching the house in the evenings?'

'I usually stop off on my way home from work, about 6.45 p.m., and stay until her bedroom light goes off at around half past seven.'

Rachel was talking to Graham again in a lowered tone, nodding her head. Charlie stole a glance at Naomi. She was crumpled in the armchair, her head in her hands. The pain of seeing her like this was excruciating.

'Well, that's good news. One of your neighbours said she thought someone had been watching the house recently. We were worried that maybe this was a targeted kidnap, but hopefully that's now a line of enquiry we don't need to pursue, at least for the time being. It doesn't mean Cassie hasn't been taken. It could have been an opportunistic abduction if she was wandering along the road on her own.'

'What is she talking about, Naomi? Why would Cassie be wandering along the road on her own?'

'You can discuss that with your wife when we've finished, Mr Bailey. I need to know, and this is very important, what time you stopped watching the house last night.'

'Why do you keep calling me Mr Bailey when you're using her first name?' Charlie demanded, pointing his finger in Naomi's direction. 'You seem to think she's the innocent one in all this, when she's the one that allowed a five-year-old child, who is supposed to be in her care, to go wandering off in the middle of the night. I always thought you were a good mother, but now I'm not so sure!'

'That's totally unfair, Charlie,' Kate said, putting a protective arm around her friend. 'Naomi's had to be father and mother to Cassie since you moved out. She's barely slept in five weeks. She's exhausted, poor thing.'

'It was her choice,' Charlie railed. 'Me and Mum would have been only too happy to have Cassie for a few hours to give Naomi a break, but no, she was hell-bent on punishing us.'

'Is that really what you think, Charlie? You think I've been putting myself through all this stress and strain just to punish you? You must be out of your mind. My priority has been Cassie and what's best for her, and now you're trying to twist things and say that I'm an unfit mother.'

'I didn't say that, at least I didn't mean to. I just don't understand how she got out of the house. The door was locked when I checked it.'

'Hold on a minute,' Rachel said. 'You said you had been watching the house from across the road. You didn't mention anything about approaching it.'

'I don't usually, but Naomi had left a lit candle inside the pumpkin and I was worried that it might somehow set fire to the house. When I got closer, it turned out to be one of those fake ones. I must have just checked the door while I was there, out of habit. It was definitely locked, so how could Cassie have got out? Are you sure that's what happened?'

'What's that supposed to mean?' Naomi demanded.

'We're keeping all lines of investigation open Mr Bail— I mean, Charlie. No one is above suspicion at this point. You didn't answer my original question. What time did you leave the house last night?'

'It was much later than usual. About nine, I think. I heard them laughing out in the back garden way after Cassie's normal bedtime. What were you doing out there so late on a school night?'

'You gave up the right to question my decisions on bringing up my daughter when your sex life became more important than your family life. We were having a bit of fun, something that has been in precious short supply lately, thanks to you!'

'*Our* daughter. She's my daughter too, and if we find her safe and well after you allowed her to wander the streets at night on her own, I'm going to apply for custody.'

'You can't mean that,' Naomi said, a tremor in her voice. 'I only didn't hear her get up because I'd taken a sleeping tablet.'

'This just gets better and better. Alone in charge of a five-year-old, and you take a sleeping pill? For God's sake, what if she had been sick and needed you?'

'Stop trying to shift the blame. She's only started waking up in the night since you left. The doctor said stress can do that. If you think you've been suffering, what do you think it's done to her? Maybe she's run away because she's unhappy. This is what you've done to us, Charlie, you've smashed our little family to pieces.'

'You don't think she may actually have run away, do you?' said Rachel, interrupting the flow of pent-up anger and emotion. 'Could she have gone in search of her dad and found her way to her grandmother's house on her own? It's quite nearby, isn't it?'

'Hazel would have rung me if Cassie had just turned up there out of the blue,' Naomi said. 'I'm sure of it.'

'Would she?' Charlie said. 'After the way you've hurt her by stopping her from seeing her only grandchild? I wouldn't be so sure if I were you.'

'Are you saying that you think there is a possibility that Cassie might be at your mother's, Mr Bailey? I think we need to go and check it out.'

'She's not there,' Charlie said.

'How can you be so sure? A moment ago, you were suggesting your mother might not inform Naomi if her granddaughter had turned up unexpectedly.'

'Oh, of course she would! She'd understand the agony Naomi would be in if Cassie was missing from home. When I said she's not there, I meant my mum. She left this morning to go and visit her sister in Devon. She's away until Sunday evening.'

'And there's no chance that your mum may have taken Cassie with her? Is it worth ringing her to check?'

Was that a possibility? Could Mum have come across Cassie while she was out walking Alfie, and have taken her to Devon just to spend some precious time with her, without giving any consideration to the panic and anguish she would cause? But surely she wouldn't have done that without telling me, would she?

'I can try, but she doesn't usually have her phone switched on when she's driving, so she's not tempted to see who's calling if it rings. She doesn't want to risk getting a fine. She'll turn it on when she reaches Auntie Sheila's, and she always rings to let me know she's arrived safely.'

'And when do you expect that will be?'

'It depends on the traffic. The M4 near Bristol is always a bit of a bottleneck. She had left before I got up this morning, though, so it should be around midday.'

'Maybe try her number and if she doesn't pick up, leave a message asking her to call you.'

'Okay.'

'In the meantime, I still think we should check her house. Cassie may have gone there and been unable to get in. Perhaps she's fallen asleep under a hedge or maybe in an outbuilding. Does your mum's property have a shed or a garage, perhaps?'

'No shed,' Charlie said, holding his phone to his ear, 'but there is a garage at the side of the house. Hi Mum, it's Charlie. Can you ring me when you get this message, please?'

'I take it there was no reply?'

'No. The forecast was for heavy rain, so that's probably slowed her up a bit. It's nearly lunchtime and I've got to feed Alfie, my mum's dog. I put him in the spare bedroom when I left for work this morning. We may as well head there now.'

Naomi got to her feet.

'I think maybe you should stay here, Naomi, in case Cassie returns home,' Rachel said.

She slumped back into her chair.

'Graham, you stay here with Mrs Bailey. I'll let you know if we find anything.'

'Yes, Guv.'

As the front door closed, Pumpkin sauntered into the room and jumped up onto Naomi's knee.

'We were supposed to look after her, Pumpkin,' she said, salty tears spilling down her cheeks and plopping onto the cat's head. 'Where is she, boy? Where has Cassie gone?'

The cat looked up at her as though he had understood every word, made a chirruping sound and jumped down again, heading for the cat flap in the back door.

'Bless him, it's almost as though he understood you and he's gone to join the search. Those two are so close,' Kate said. 'Look, there's nothing much we can do until they get back. Why don't you have a lie-down upstairs? I'll hang onto your phone, and I'll come and wake you if they find anything. What do you say?'

'Will that be okay?' Naomi asked the DI, her voice once again flat and emotionless.

'It's probably a good idea,' Graham said, relieved that the situation was calmer. He had been a police officer for fifteen years, but it had still shocked him to hear Naomi and Charlie attack each other verbally in such a vitriolic manner. It would be a relief when the family liaison officer got there. They were trained to deal with situations such as this, and it would free him up to get more involved with the actual search for Cassie. 'We'll let you know as soon as we have any news.'

CHAPTER ELEVEN

'Down, boy,' Charlie said as Alfie jumped up at him, his big paws almost reaching shoulder height and his tail swishing enthusiastically from side to side. Hazel had taken to shutting Alfie in the spare bedroom upstairs when no one was in the house, after the golden retriever had worked out how to open the fridge door and help himself to the contents. 'Anyone would think he hadn't seen a human being for four days rather than four hours. Do you want to have a look around up here while I take him down to the kitchen to feed him? I'll get the key to the garage while I'm at it.'

Charlie was confident that Rachel and her police constable would find nothing in the house. He fished his phone out of his pocket to check the time. *Mum should be at Auntie Sheila's by now, so why hasn't she rung in response to my message? Is it possible that Mum has got Cassie with her?* He pressed his mum's name on his contact list, but it still went straight to voicemail. Keeping his voice low so that he wouldn't be overheard, he said, 'Mum, please call me. I'll understand if she's with you, but I just need to know she's okay.'

As Charlie poured out a bowl of dog biscuits, his eyes roamed the garden at the back of his mum's house and rested on the trampoline that his mum had insisted on buying for her granddaughter last summer. He could picture his daughter bouncing up and down on it, squealing in delight while Alfie barked encouragement.

Cassie was always laughing and smiling, and seemed happy enough with adult company and that of Pumpkin and Alfie, but it was a tragedy that he and Naomi had been unable to provide her with a younger sibling. *If things had been different, she would have been the best big sister ever.*

'Have you got those garage keys you mentioned?' Rachel asked, coming into the kitchen and interrupting his thoughts.

'Yes. They're on the hook with Alfie's lead. Have you finished up there?'

'Yes. Nothing untoward to report. Is there a key to the side gate as well?'

'No, it's just on a latch. I'll come out with you while Alfie's eating and open the garage door. It sticks a bit, so I always open it for Mum when she wants her car out.'

'But I thought you said she left before you got up this morning?'

'She did. I opened it for her last night and closed it this morning before I went to work.'

'Did you check the garage was empty before you closed it?'

'No. You don't think...?'

Without finishing his sentence, he pushed past Rachel, wrenched the front door open and ran the few paces to the up-and-over door.

'It's okay, Cassie, Daddy's here,' he said, struggling slightly to raise the heavy door, cursing himself that he hadn't oiled it before it got this bad.

The bright winter sunshine flooded the dim interior as Rachel arrived at his side. They were both met with a yawning space, empty but for a couple of half-used tins of emulsion paint and a pile of old bed sheets against the back wall. Hazel kept them to cover carpets and furniture when they were decorating. Charlie rushed over to the pile of sheets, scattering them in all directions before sinking down to his knees, his head in his hands.

'Where are you, baby girl?' he whispered.

'We'll find her, Charlie,' Rachel said, reaching out to touch his shoulder and swallowing down the lump in her throat. She knew exactly what he was feeling. The surge of hope followed swiftly by despair. It often happened in cases involving missing children, and not only from the point of view of the parents. Every time the cellar door had creaked open, Rachel had closed her eyes and prayed that someone had come to rescue them until she heard his gruff voice and her heart plummeted to her shoes once again. She pushed the memories away. 'It's early days yet. I'm going to expand the house-to-house enquiries as soon as we've heard back from the team at the bonfire. Come on, let's check the garden.'

'It's pointless. She can't reach the latch on the gate and we never leave it open,' Charlie said, struggling to regain both his feet and his composure.

'Let's look anyway. It's one more place to tick off our search.'

Rachel didn't add that the search wasn't merely for a place where Cassie could shelter; it would also include looking for freshly dug earth. Charlie had given a very convincing display of hoping to find his daughter in the garage, but Rachel had been a police officer long enough to know that emotional outbursts could sometimes be put on to provide a distraction from what was really going on.

CHAPTER TWELVE

1.08 p.m. – Friday

Naomi could hear the low mumble of voices from downstairs. She hadn't slept; she hadn't even closed her eyes because every time she did, all she could see was Cassie's happy, smiling face. It was like looking at a miniature version of Charlie; they shared the same sparkling blue eyes and dark, wavy hair with no hint of the red that had made Naomi the butt of jokes throughout her childhood. 'Ginge' had been the most common tease at primary school, but in her first year of the grammar school, one of the girls in her class had taken the teasing to a whole new level. She had embarrassed her in the playground just before Halloween by saying in a spiteful tone, 'We don't need to make a class pumpkin, we've already got one. Naomi's round face and orange hair fit the bill perfectly!' Most of the other girls in her class had laughed and begun chanting 'pumpkin, pumpkin, pumpkin', and the cruel nickname had stuck.

Kate was the only one not to join in, the same Kate who had stood by her through the drama of the split with Charlie and had rushed to be at her side this morning. She understood the magnitude of what Charlie had done. If he'd had his drunken fling with any other female on the planet, Naomi might have been willing to listen to his side of the story and possibly even forgive his infidelity, but he had sought solace in Jessica, the very person who had teased her so relentlessly throughout her teenage years.

It wasn't just the name-calling. That alone she could have coped with. It went much deeper. Jessica had always had a thing for Charlie. They had even dated a couple of times directly before Naomi and Charlie had started going out. Jessica had always maintained that she had dumped Charlie, and he had gone along with it, but shortly before he presented Naomi with a beautiful solitaire engagement ring, he told her what had actually happened.

'She's a nutter, Noms. We didn't even kiss on our first date and she was going around telling everyone that we were going to get engaged. I knew I had to break things off with her and pretty quickly.' He'd insisted that he only went on their second date so that he could tell her face-to-face that he didn't want to see her again and when she freaked out, he had told her that, to save face, he didn't mind if she said that she was the one doing the dumping. 'Honestly, Noms, I knew straightaway that I'd made a mistake in asking her out and I just wanted to be rid of her.'

Naomi had believed Charlie at the time because she was so in love with him, but now she wasn't so sure. *What if he was dumped by Jessica and had never got over it? Maybe my whole marriage has been based on a lie and this is what he really wanted all along?*

These were the irrational thoughts that had tortured Naomi in the weeks since her world had fallen apart. Unintentionally, her obsession with having another baby, a brother or sister for Cassie, had pushed her husband away. The moment things weren't running so smoothly in their marriage, Charlie had gone running to Jessica, the woman he really wanted, and had ended up in her bed. In her devastated state, Naomi convinced herself that there could be no other explanation.

There was a tap on the bedroom door. Naomi hoped it wasn't Kate with yet another cup of tea. Never a massive fan, preferring coffee or hot chocolate, she was starting to hate the stuff.

'Come in.'

It was Kate, but thankfully she was empty-handed.

'No news from Hazel's, I'm afraid.'

Naomi's heart sank. With every passing minute, the chances of getting her little girl back alive and unharmed seemed to be dwindling.

'DCI Hart just got back and asked if you feel up to coming downstairs. I think she's got some more questions she wants to ask you.'

Pumpkin had eased his way past Kate and jumped on to the bed where he was pushing his head under Naomi's hand, urging her to stroke him.

'Give me a few minutes, Kate. Is Charlie with her?'

'No. He went over to the search at the bonfire when there was no sign of Cassie at his mum's.'

'Do you think she's hiding there?'

'Honestly? I don't think so. She would have been awakened by all the shouting if she'd fallen asleep after crawling inside to shelter. I'm pretty sure she would have come straight out, particularly if she'd heard your voice this morning.'

'Then where is she, Kate?' Naomi asked, searching her friend's face for an honest answer.

'I think maybe she's trapped somewhere unable to get out. The police must think so too, because they're talking about widening the house-to-house search area and paying special attention to sheds, garages and other outbuildings. The DCI said they'll implement it once they've got the all-clear from the bonfire search.'

'Good. I can't bear the thought of her being alone and frightened overnight. She hates the dark.'

'Well, it's only a little after one, so there are still a few hours of daylight left. Oh, and don't be alarmed when you come down and see that they've dug up the sandpit.'

'What? Why would they do that?' Then it dawned on her. 'Do they really think I've killed my own child and then buried her beneath the sandpit? What kind of psycho do they take me for?'

'They're only doing their job, Noms. I guess they have to be thorough, whatever they think may or may not be the reason for Cassie's disappearance.'

'You don't think I've done anything to hurt her, do you?'

'Don't be ridiculous. I've never even seen you swat a fly. But they don't know you like I do. I overheard a couple of them saying that in missing children cases it usually turns out that family or close friends are involved, someone the child knows really well.'

'Has anyone actually spoken to Hazel yet? She hasn't been to see her sister since Easter and she usually plans these things months in advance. I'm sure she would have mentioned it to me before Charlie and me split up. Could she have taken Cassie, do you think?'

'It's possible, I suppose. You should speak to the DCI about it.'

'And Charlie?'

'I'd leave that to the police if I were you. It would be better if it seemed like it was them that are suspicious rather than you.'

'Why does it matter? Charlie and I are finished, so nothing either of us says or does now can make any difference.'

'Are you absolutely sure that's what you want, Noms? Isn't what you had worth fighting for?'

'What I thought we had, maybe. But what if it was actually Jessica he wanted to be with all along? The whole baby thing may have pushed him into her arms but he's a grown man, he could have said no. She's welcome to him.'

'But he hasn't been anywhere near her since that night. If you're so sure he wants to be with her, why isn't he?'

'Did he tell you that? Have you two been discussing things behind my back?'

'I wouldn't describe it that way. We've all been friends for such a long time, Noms, I think talking things over with me made him feel closer to you. He's so sorry for what happened.'

'It's a bit late for that.'

'Is there nothing he can do to change your mind?'

'Nothing. I'll never be able to trust him again after what he did. I can't stand the thought of him touching me with hands that have been intimate with her. It disgusts me. All I care about now is Cassie and getting her home.'

CHAPTER THIRTEEN

2.50 p.m. – Friday

It was almost 3 p.m. by the time Hazel finally pulled onto the driveway of her sister's bungalow in the tiny Devon village of Puddlington. *What an apt name for today. It's raining cats and dogs or, as Cassie and I always used to joke, Pumpkins and Alfies.* Her granddaughter's cheerful little face swam before her eyes and for the hundredth time since starting on her protracted journey, she wondered how on earth she was going to tell Sheila about the situation with Charlie and Naomi that had prevented her from seeing the little girl she adored. Absent-mindedly, she lifted the boot-release button in the driver's door and then remembered her overnight bag wasn't in there. Charlie had thoughtfully left the boot half-open for her after reversing her car into the garage, but Hazel had decided it would be easier with her dodgy wrists to slide the bag onto the back seat rather than lift it into the boot.

Her shoulders were aching from the tension of driving in such atrocious weather conditions for the best part of eight hours, and unsurprisingly she was bursting for the toilet. She had deliberately avoided drinking much en route because she didn't want to stop off at the motorway services, which would have made her even later arriving. Now she was paying the price for allowing herself to become dehydrated as a headache was starting to set in. As swiftly as she could, she got out of the car, pulled her bag off the back seat, closed the boot she had opened moments before and walked the few paces to Sheila's front door, hoping that her pelvic floor muscles would hold out just a little longer. Thankfully, her sister had seen the car pulling onto the drive and was already holding the door open.

'Sorry I'm late, sis,' Hazel said, squeezing past her sister's wheelchair in the narrow hallway, 'the traffic was a nightmare. Three accidents on the way. I don't know why people aren't more careful in this sort of weather,' she continued, slamming the door to the loo before Sheila had even had the chance to say hello.

Sheila was in the kitchen making a pot of tea when Hazel emerged a few minutes later, relief etched across her face.

'That's better – I was busting for the loo. I'm so sorry I'm late, I almost turned back at Bristol. I was stuck in a traffic jam between junctions 18 and 19 for over two hours. I think they must have closed the motorway to recover the vehicles. Anyway, I'm here now. How are you doing?'

'Oh, same old, same old. You know me, a bit of reading and a bit of knitting in front of the television of an evening keeps me busy. Speaking of which, I can't wait to show you the jumper I've knitted for Cassie. It's got a unicorn on the front. They're all the rage at the moment, apparently. How is my little darling?'

'Cute as ever, and she loves unicorns,' Hazel said, avoiding a direct answer. She had persevered with her terrible journey in order to tell Sheila about the situation with Charlie and Naomi, and to ask if she had any suggestions on how they could at least get the couple talking to each other, but there was no urgency to do it the moment she was through the door. 'Did you save me some lunch, or are we straight on to a Devon cream tea? I've missed your home-made scones,' she said, deftly changing the subject.

'Well, I've saved you half a cheese and vegetable pasty from lunch, so you can start with that while I do the scones.'

'This is lovely. Did you make it yourself, or need I ask?'

'Is the Pope Catholic? You know I love baking. Why would I buy something inferior when I can make it myself?'

'If it wasn't so good, I'd tell you off for being big-headed. I'm all right at dinners and stuff, but baking has never really been my thing.'

'Have you ever tried any of the recipes I send you home with?'

Hazel looked sheepish.

'No, I thought not. You might surprise yourself, and think how impressed Charlie and Naomi would be. Maybe you should offer to bake Cassie's birthday cake, I'm sure I'll have a recipe somewhere. It's hard to believe she's almost six. Where does the time go? Any plans for a little brother or sister for her? I would have thought those two would have wanted a big family as they were both only children.'

Although Hazel shared a lot with her sister, Charlie had specifically told her not to tell anybody about the trouble he and Naomi were having conceiving again, and she had respected his wishes. It was nobody's business but theirs, even if it did make it awkward when people innocently commented about it. Her usual answer was that they had plenty of time for that, but she wasn't going to deliberately lie to her sister. As things stood at the moment, there was no time and, if it stayed that way, it was probably a good thing that there was only one child to consider in the breakdown of their marriage.

'Perhaps they don't feel it's the right time,' she said elusively. 'Here, let me give you a hand with that tray. Shall I take it through to the lounge?'

'Actually, I've laid the small table in the conservatory. I like being in there when the rain is lashing down. It's like blowing a big fat raspberry to the heavens. We've had a few rumbles of thunder, so we may even be treated to a display of lightning. It'll be a bit like having some early fireworks.'

'Has anyone ever told you that you're weird?'

'Yes, you, on numerous occasions.'

'That's what sisters are for,' Hazel said, settling onto the squidgy cushions of the wicker chair. 'Oh, that's better. I hate to be antisocial, but I may need a lie-down after this, I'm shattered. And probably a couple of headache pills, too, if you've got any. I don't like getting old.'

'It's better than the alternative, though.'

Hazel could have kicked herself for her thoughtless remark. Sheila's husband, the love of her life, had passed away less than a year ago. *I definitely need a nap before I open my mouth and put my foot in it again.*

'Sorry. I wasn't thinking.'

'It's all right, I think I'm finally coming to terms with it. Your room is all ready – you take as long as you need.'

CHAPTER FOURTEEN

3.27 p.m. – Friday

Charlie arrived back at 15 Beechwood Avenue with PC Walsh after the search of the bonfire had proved fruitless. The timber tower had been carefully dismantled to avoid any larger pieces of wood falling through the structure and potentially injuring anyone or anything sheltering beneath. All that remained by the time they were finished was a scattering of twigs surrounded by a circle of an eclectic mix of different types of wood, from broken chair legs to tree branches. It had started to drizzle as Charlie walked away, leaving them to rebuild the bonfire in time for the firework display the following evening.

'Good luck, mate,' one of the men had said. 'I hope you find her.'

He was barely through the front door when DCI Hart asked him if he had heard from his mother and he had to admit that despite trying her number several times more, it was still going straight to voicemail. Charlie felt there was now a clear insinuation that the police officer suspected Cassie was with her grandmother. *I suppose it's inevitable she would start to think along those lines as we haven't been able to reach her, and in the DCI's eyes she has a clear motive. Naomi denying me access is in some ways understandable, but punishing Mum for something I've done is cruel.*

*

Charlie had waited almost a month before finally taking his mother's advice and making an appointment with Ray Brookes at Parker & Brookes solicitors. The last thing he wanted to do was antagonise Naomi by starting legal proceedings, but it was looking less and less likely that Naomi was going to grant him access to see Cassie unless there was an arrangement in place. The first question he had been asked, even before he had to give details about the circumstances of the separation, was 'How deep are your pockets?' He soon realised the answer was not deep enough. Ray had explained that the mother in separation or divorce cases was almost always awarded custody unless it was proven that she was unfit, in which case the courts would consider the father, although it was in no way cut and dried.

'The duty of the court is to protect the best interests of the child,' Ray had told him.

Charlie had left the solicitor's office feeling even more depressed than when he'd gone in. He didn't want custody, just a fair amount of access to Cassie, but Ray Brookes had seemed to suggest that it could be a long and expensive process.

*

'Mr Bailey?'

'Sorry?'

'I was asking if you have a phone number for your aunt,' Rachel said.

'She has a mobile, but she only turns it on when she's out and about, which isn't that often these days. She lives on her own now and she's in a wheelchair,' he offered by way of explanation.

'What about a landline number? Surely you've got that in case you need to contact your mum in an emergency.'

'I usually just ring Mum's mobile, so it's not stored in my phone. It's pinned on the noticeboard in Mum's kitchen. I should have rung while we were there, I suppose, but I was sure Mum would have returned my calls by now. Shall I go and fetch it?'

'I'll send DI Wilson, if that's all right with you, while you keep trying your mother's mobile number. I didn't want to get the Devon police involved unnecessarily, but it won't do any harm to have a police officer drop by the house as we're having such difficulty getting hold of her. Do you know your aunt's address, or is that on the noticeboard too?'

Charlie was pretty sure he detected a note of sarcasm in the police officer's tone. *Maybe she's beginning to suspect that Mum and I have planned this whole thing and that we're just stalling for time.*

'It's Butterfly Cottage, Puddlington, North Devon, but I don't know the postcode, I'm afraid,' he said, scribbling it down on a scrap of paper and handing it over to DI Wilson along with his house keys.

'I'm sure the local team will be able to find it, Mr Bailey. Shall I ask PC Walsh to step inside while I'm gone, Guv?'

'Thanks, Graham. While we're waiting for your aunt's number, I wanted to ask you a few questions about the young lady you have been seeing.'

Charlie bristled and there was a snort of derision from Naomi, who was huddled in the armchair in the corner. Kate had gone to pick her boys up from school, but had promised to come back once her husband was home from work to look after them.

'I'm not "seeing" her, as you put it. It was one night of poor judgement which I don't even remember.'

'Would you care to elaborate?'

'Not really.'

'It might be relevant to our investigation.'

Charlie sighed. 'I got very drunk one night after Naomi and I had an argument and Jessica offered me a lift home. I thought she meant a lift to *my* home, which was why I accepted. No one was more surprised than me when I woke up at her house the next morning.'

'Had you had sexual intercourse with her?'

Out of the corner of his eye, Charlie was aware of Naomi flinching at the question. The knuckles of her hands, which were gripping the chair, had turned white.

'I don't know. The naked photograph that Jessica sent to my wife would suggest that we did, but I honestly have no recollection of it, and I'm not even sure I would have been physically capable.'

'Why do you think Jessica sent the photograph to Naomi? What was she hoping to achieve?'

'Exactly what she has achieved. She's managed to come between me and my wife. She and Naomi have always had a strong dislike of each other. It's as though she was just waiting for an opportunity, and I presented it to her on a plate. I'm so sorry, Noms.'

'Don't you dare call me that. That's reserved for people I care about and who care about me.'

'But I do care about you,' Charlie said, approaching the arm-chair where Naomi was sitting, dropping down to his haunches and trying to take her hands in his. 'I love you, and I always will, whatever you think.'

'Well, you've got a funny way of showing it. Get away from me,' she hissed, pushing him backward, sending him sprawling across the patterned rug, his head narrowly avoiding contact with the corner of the wooden coffee table.

'I think you both need to try and stay calm,' Rachel said, as PC Walsh positioned himself between the two of them.

'Does he really have to be here? Can't you question him at his mother's, or the police station?'

'We can, but for the moment I'd rather keep you two together. One of you may say something that sparks a memory in the other. Try to remember that we all want the same thing here. This is about finding Cassie, even if that means opening up old wounds.'

Naomi grunted and Charlie picked himself up off the floor and moved to the far end of the sofa, while PC Walsh resumed his position by the lounge door.

'In your opinion, Mr Bailey, would this Jessica be satisfied with the damage she had already inflicted, or would she be prepared to go even further?'

'Are you saying you think she may have taken Cassie?'

'I'm asking the questions here, Mr Bailey.'

'I don't know. I barely know her.'

'Really? Your wife told me that you dated her before you two got together.'

Charlie shot a glance at his wife. *Why would Naomi tell the policewoman that?*

'I went on two dates with her when we were seventeen. I asked her out because she flirted with me and I was flattered. I knew more or less straight away that I'd made a mistake.'

'So why take her on a second date?'

'I wanted to let her down gently, but she turned nasty. She said I'd led her on, that she thought we were made for each other and that one day I'd realise what a big mistake I'd made finishing with her. But that was a long time ago. I've barely seen her in the eleven years since Naomi and I got married.'

'Even though she works in the pub at the end of your street? Don't you go into your local?'

'She's only been working there for a few months, and only on Thursdays and Fridays. I choose not to go in there on those days.'

'So it would be fair to say you've deliberately avoided her?'

'I suppose. Naomi doesn't like her, so why would I want to have anything to do with her?'

'But you did, Mr Bailey. In her eyes, she'd been led on by you once before. It's possible that she's feeling aggrieved because you haven't attempted to see her since the split with your wife. I think we need to talk to her. Do you remember where she lives?'

'Not really, but it's Friday, so she may already be at the pub.'

'Good point. I'll head down there once we've made contact with your mother.'

Right on cue, Charlie's phone rang. He answered it on speakerphone. 'Mum, thank God. I've been trying to call you. Why didn't you turn your phone on when you got to Auntie Sheila's, and why didn't you ring like you normally do?'

'I'm sorry, love, I didn't mean to worry you. I had the journey from hell. I didn't get here until almost three and I was so shattered that I had to have a lie-down. I must have dozed off. I've only just turned my phone on now.'

'So you haven't listened to your messages?'

'No. I'm so sorry if you've been worrying unnecessarily.'

'Listen, Mum, I need to ask you something and you have to tell me the truth.' Despite having tried his mother's number repeatedly, Charlie hadn't really planned what he was going to say once he eventually got through.

'What is it, Charlie? What's wrong?'

'Have you got Cassie with you?'

'What are you talking about? Why would Cassie be with me? She's at home.'

'I'm at Naomi's and Cassie's not here. She's missing, Mum.'

The strangled cry that came from the other end of the phone shocked everyone listening in.

'Mum, are you okay? Mum?'

It was his Auntie Sheila's voice that they heard next.

'What on earth's going on, Charlie? Your mum's as white as a sheet and shaking. What's happened?'

'I was hoping that maybe Mum had taken Cassie with her to visit you, but clearly she hasn't. We don't know where she is. It looks like she may have been taken.'

'Oh, dear God. That poor little mite. Naomi must be in pieces. Is there anything we can do?'

'The police are here, and they want to ask Mum a few questions. Is she up to it?'

'I think she needs a few minutes. I'll make her a cup of tea and call you back when she's recovered from the shock. Is that okay?'

Charlie raised his eyebrows in question in Rachel's direction and she nodded agreement.

'Of course.'

He ended the call and put his phone on the coffee table ready for the return call.

'Is there anything else we can be doing while we're waiting to speak to Mum?'

'How do you two feel about getting the media involved? An appeal for witnesses can help in certain circumstances, but if we're going to do anything along those lines it needs to be sooner rather than later.'

Charlie tried to make eye contact with Naomi, but she was staring straight ahead, gently rocking herself backward and forward in her chair.

'Sooner as in when? Tomorrow?' he asked.

'Or maybe even later tonight. Once we release this to the news channels, they could have film crews on site within an hour. I'd rather wait until we've spoken to your mother and Jessica, but I think we could still make the late evening news.'

'What do you think, Naomi?'

'I think I want to kill you,' she said, launching herself across the room and pummelling his chest with her fists as hard as she could.

PC Walsh made a move as though to pull her away, but Charlie shook his head. *I deserve this*, he thought, making no attempt to stop his distraught wife from venting her anger on him. Gradually the pounding lessened, then her arms fell limp at her sides and the racking sobs began. He reached one arm around her shoulders and the other beneath her legs and lifted her off the floor.

'I'm taking her up to our room. She's had enough for now.'

'Do you want me to call a doctor and get her something to calm her down?'

'No. She doesn't like taking medication. That's why I was so shocked about the sleeping pill.'

Naomi was clinging to her husband's neck.

'It was only a herbal one, Charlie. Kate said it would just make me drowsy. If I hadn't taken it, I would have heard Cassie get up. Oh God, I'll never forgive myself if anything bad has happened to her.'

'Shhh, shhh, try to relax. We're going to get her back, I know we will,' he whispered into his wife's hair.

'How can you be so sure?'

'I just am. You need to trust me, okay?'

'I want to, but I don't know if I can after what happened.'

'Don't think about that now. Once we get Cassie home, we can put the past five weeks behind us and try to start rebuilding our lives together. It's going to be all right,' he said, stroking his wife's forehead, 'I promise.'

As Charlie left the room carrying his distraught wife, Rachel made a note in her notebook.

How can he be so sure that they are going to get Cassie back? Does he know where she is? Did he fake the kidnap to try and get back with his wife?

CHAPTER FIFTEEN

Charlie's phone started to ring while he was upstairs tending to his wife. Rachel pressed the green button to answer the call, assuming it was his mother.

'Hello,' she said, 'is that Mrs Bailey?'

There was a moment of silence, then the person on the other end of the call disconnected.

That's odd, Rachel thought, *but maybe it threw her with me answering the phone.* She was about to put the phone back on the coffee table when it rang again. The screen read, *mum mob.*

'Hello? Mrs Bailey? Is that you?'

'Yes,' Hazel said, in a voice so quiet she could barely be heard.

'This is DCI Rachel Hart. I'm heading up the investigation into your granddaughter's disappearance. Did you ring a couple of moments ago?'

'No. I'm sorry if I kept you waiting, but I'm still trying to come to terms with the situation. How long has Cassie been missing?'

'We don't really know. She was last seen when her mother put her to bed last night at around 8.30 p.m.'

'That's late for a school night.'

'Yes, so we believe, but apparently your daughter-in-law was carving a pumpkin and it delayed the normal routine.'

'It was very good. I saw it on the doorstep.'

'You were near the house last night?'

Rachel could have sworn she heard a sharp intake of breath.

'Yes. I passed it when I was out walking Alfie, my dog.'

'I see. Is that a regular route for you, or did you just happen to be passing last night?'

'I've started going that way recently, since… since…'

'Since Naomi and Charlie have separated?' Rachel asked, sensing the other woman's reluctance to finish her sentence. 'Is this something you have yet to tell your sister about?'

'That's right.'

'Okay. I'll try and phrase my questions so that she won't suspect anything. What time were you out walking your dog?'

'It must have been around 10 p.m. Dinner was later than usual, and then I did the washing-up before I took Alfie out. I was in bed by 10.30 p.m. though, I remember checking, so yes, it would have been just after ten.'

'Did you notice anything unusual, apart from the pumpkin, of course?'

'No, I don't think so.'

'Please think carefully, Mrs Bailey. Any clue you can give us might be vitally important in finding Cassie.'

'Well, there was a speeding car.'

'Go on,' Rachel urged.

'Don't tell Charlie, but I'd been admiring the carved pumpkin, thinking what a good job Naomi had done, when I was dazzled by some really bright car headlamps. Then a car pulled away from the kerb at speed just ahead of me. I remember it clearly because I was grateful that I'd kept Alfie on his lead and not let him run on the field opposite like I normally do.'

'Did you get a good look at the car? Colour? Make? Model?' Rachel asked as Charlie came back into the room.

'No, I'm sorry. The lights had blinded me and by the time I turned to try and catch the number plate it was already rounding the corner.'

'So you can't tell me anything about it?'

'Well, I'm not a hundred per cent sure, but I think it might have been red. My next-door neighbour has a red car and I remember wondering if it had been stolen, but when I got home his car was sitting on his drive. I assumed it was more likely to be a teenager showing off to his girlfriend, or perhaps I disturbed them having a bit of a kiss and cuddle.'

'And you've no idea of the make?'

'No, I'm afraid not, but it I think it was a hatchback rather than a car like mine with a separate boot. It's funny, I thought I couldn't tell you any details about it but it's surprising what registers without you realising.'

'So, just to confirm, you think the speeding car was red in colour and may have been a hatchback?'

'Yes.'

'That information could be very useful. I'll have my team check the CCTV cameras in the vicinity and trace the vehicle and its owner. Even if it's nothing to do with Cassie's disappearance the driver may have seen something. You've already been really helpful, but there is one more thing I'd like to ask. Did you happen to notice if the pumpkin had sparklers stuck in it, to look like cat's whiskers?'

'I honestly can't remember. Is it important?'

Vitally, Rachel thought. *It would determine whether Cassie had already opened her front door to add the finishing touches to the pumpkin or not, which would give me a better idea of what time she went missing.*

'Not really, but if you do remember, perhaps you could let Charlie know. He's here if you want to speak to him.'

'Yes, please.'

Rachel handed the phone over to Charlie.

'Mum, it's me. Are you okay?'

'This is just the worst news, Charlie. Do the police think she's been kidnapped?'

'It's one of their theories, although Naomi says Cassie has been waking in the night since I moved out. There's a possibility that she let herself out of the house, wandered off and got lost or trapped somewhere.'

'She must be so frightened. Do you need me to come home?'

'I don't think you should drive back tonight after your terrible journey down there, but maybe come home tomorrow instead of Sunday?'

Rachel signalled to Graham, who was standing just inside the front door having returned from Hazel's house with the phone number they now no longer needed, to join her in the kitchen.

'My gut reaction is that the grandmother is telling the truth,' she said. 'I don't think we need to alert the Devon force at the moment, and by the sound of things, she's coming back tomorrow anyway.'

'It's too late, Guv, they're already on their way. They don't hang about when a young child is missing.'

'Well, it won't hurt to make absolutely sure that Cassie is not with her grandma, I suppose. Have you organised the dog handlers for the morning?'

'Yes, Guv.'

'And the divers to search the canal?'

'At first light.'

'How is the list of known paedophiles in the area coming along?'

'They're working on it back at the station. It should be complete by the morning, too, and then we can start working our way through it.'

'Good work, Graham. Did Kate say what time she would be back to sit with Naomi?'

'Between six and half past, she said.'

'Right. Well, I want you to stay until she gets here and then head back to the station for a debrief at 7.30 p.m. We'll keep PC Walsh on the front doorstep, but for the moment I think it's better to have a third person in the house rather than just Charlie and

Naomi. Her moods are understandably very unpredictable, and I don't want to be responsible for her grabbing a knife and doing him some harm. If we'd been able to persuade Naomi to have the family liaison officer stay with her, you wouldn't have to babysit.'

'They both came across as a bit unhinged earlier.'

'I suppose any of us would be if our only child had gone missing.'

'Yes, Guv. Sorry, Guv, I wasn't thinking. Are we going to break this story to the media?'

'Not until I've spoken to this Jessica person. I'm going to head to the Golden Lion now and see what she's got to say for herself. I know Charlie's a good-looking chap, but she appears to be obsessed with him. I can't see it myself. There are plenty of fish in the sea. Why would she be so hell-bent on destroying a happy marriage? I feel there's more to this than childhood nicknames, but whatever it is, would she really take it out on a five-year-old child?'

Rachel picked up her car keys and was about to walk out of the kitchen when she remembered the call that had come through on Charlie's phone directly before his mother rang. 'One more thing, Graham. See if you can get a look at Charlie's phone if he leaves it lying around. Check the call log and make a note of the number that rang him directly before his mother's call. If you get it, I want to know who it belongs to. Who hangs up without saying anything just because an unexpected person answers the phone? I'll tell you who – someone with something to hide.'

CHAPTER SIXTEEN

5.35 p.m. – Friday

'I thought you told Charlie you were going to drive back in the morning,' Sheila said, watching her sister pile the clothes and toiletries that she had only unpacked a couple of hours previously back into her overnight bag.

'I did, but I can't stand not being there with him.'

'He'll be all right, he's got Naomi.'

Hazel took a deep breath.

'No, that's the point, he hasn't. There's something I haven't told you because Charlie asked me not to. Part of the reason I persevered with the dreadful traffic today and didn't just turn around and go home is because I wanted to tell you face-to-face rather than over the phone: Naomi and Charlie have been living apart for the past five weeks.' Hazel registered her sister's shocked expression and decided it was best to carry on and get it all off her chest. 'It gets worse. Naomi has stopped both me and Charlie from seeing Cassie. Neither of us have had any contact with her since Charlie moved out.'

Sheila gasped. 'That's awful. I can't believe Naomi would do something like that. She's been like a daughter to you, and me for that matter. Why would she be so heartless?'

'Because she's hurting. I don't know the whole story but it's something Charlie did, and she can't, or won't, forgive him for it.'

'Is it another woman? Surely he hasn't been having an affair behind her back? They always seemed like the perfect couple, well, the perfect family, really. That can't be right, not Charlie of all people.'

'It's something along those lines, Sheila, but he won't even tell me exactly what happened. All I know is that it nearly destroyed him when she threw him out. For the first few days I was afraid he might do something to hurt himself.'

'I can't believe you didn't tell me what was going on. All of this must have been a huge burden for you too.'

'Like I said, Charlie asked me not to say anything to you. I guess he was hoping that they would be able to sort things out, but that's never going to happen if Naomi won't even talk to him. No one would wish for something like this to happen to Cassie, but if Charlie and Naomi are under the same roof and speaking to each other, some good may come from it so long as they find our little angel safe and well.'

'Don't go, Hazel. If he's at Naomi's you'll just be in the way. Let them lean on each other for support.'

'If I thought she would let him stay at the house tonight that's exactly what I'd do, but if she sends him away and he starts spiralling downwards again, I can't trust him to be on his own. You didn't see him those first two weeks. He didn't eat, he didn't sleep, and he wouldn't even fuss Alfie. I was terrified. I thought I was going to lose him, Sheila.'

'Do you want me to come with you?' Sheila asked as Hazel opened the front door and the ferocity of the weather became apparent. 'I hate the idea of you driving all that way on your own in these conditions, especially as you must still be so tired from your horrendous journey down.'

'I'll be fine. I'll stop at the services for a coffee to have with one of my scones when I get to the motorway,' Hazel said, patting the bulge in her handbag. 'And once this nightmare is over, I'll come and stay for a week or two, if you'll have me.'

'I've told you many a time, you can come and stay permanently if you want to.'

'I may take you up on that one day. You know how much I love it here. Now, are you sure you don't need any more logs bringing in? I can get them before I go.'

'Don't fuss,' Sheila said, reaching up to hug her sister. 'I've got plenty of logs to keep me going for a few days. The rain's bound to let up eventually. You did pack the unicorn jumper for Cassie, didn't you? When they find her, it will be something to take her mind off whatever has happened to her.'

'Yes, I've got it.'

Neither sister needed to voice their hope that the little girl would get to wear it.

'You drive carefully. Ring me when you stop at the services and the minute you get home. I shan't go to bed until you do.'

From the cover of the porch, Hazel pressed the button on her key to unlock the car then made a dash through the drenching rain. She quickly slid her case onto the back seat, got in the front and buckled her seat belt. Turning on the engine, she gave Sheila a little wave and put the Jetta in reverse gear, but before she could move a police car parked up across the driveway, blocking her exit, and a uniformed officer got out.

Hazel's heart started thumping in her chest as she watched him walk up the drive through her rear-view mirror. *Was he here to tell her that they'd found Cassie? Please God*, she prayed silently, *please let her be alive.* He signalled for her to wind her window down.

'Mrs Bailey?' the policeman asked.

Hazel nodded, not trusting herself to speak.

'I need to ask you a few questions. Is it all right if we get inside out of this rain?'

Hazel looked back at the house where Sheila was still outlined in the doorway.

'It's my sister's house, but I'm sure it will be fine,' she said, getting out of the car and following him up the drive. 'Did they find Cassie?'

'Not yet. That's why I'm here. I need to talk to you about her disappearance.'

They reached the doorway, and Sheila looked up at her sister and then at the policeman. 'Surely you don't think Hazel has anything to do with it? I was with her when she heard the news and she almost fainted from the shock. That's right, isn't it, Hazel?'

'It's all right, Sheila, they're just doing their job, and I have nothing to hide.'

The policeman was direct but considerate with his questioning, ascertaining when the trip to Devon had been planned and seemingly satisfied when Sheila showed him her wall calendar in the kitchen with the date circled in green pen. He asked the sisters' permission to have a quick look around the bungalow to make sure that Cassie was not being hidden there. He left a mere fifteen minutes after arriving, and was able to report that there was no sign of the missing five-year-old.

CHAPTER SEVENTEEN

6.03 p.m. – Friday

There were only a handful of cars in the car park of the Golden Lion when DCI Hart pulled in. The light drizzle from earlier was becoming more persistent and looked likely to turn into full-on rain by the morning.

It's not the sort of weather for a young child to be sleeping rough, but at least it's a few degrees warmer than the sub-zero temperatures last night, Rachel thought. In terms of Cassie's survival, a lot depended on what time she had let herself out of the house to stick the sparklers in the pumpkin. If she was outside all last night, even with her Puffa jacket on, Rachel doubted that they would find the little girl alive, unless she had managed to get inside an outbuilding of some sort. The extra officers that had been drafted in after lunchtime to search all outbuildings within a one-mile radius of Cassie's home had found nothing, apart from a stash of illegally imported cigarettes which had been confiscated pending investigation.

Rachel knew that a mile was quite a distance for an adult to cover, let alone a five-year-old, but she had approved the extended search anyway, not wanting to leave anything to chance. Once the media became involved, her every decision would be scrutinised. She didn't want to be accused of not doing everything possible to find Cassie while there was a chance that she was still alive. Missing children cases always stirred up a lot of emotion with the general public, and she knew offers to help with the search would come flooding in as soon as the story was broadcast. But she also knew, only too well, that sometimes the 'information' they gave muddied the waters and the real clues were buried until it was too late. *It's all about the timing. Getting it wrong could cost Cassie her life.*

She hadn't wanted to pressurise Hazel on the phone when she had asked about the pumpkin 'whiskers', but she was intending to question her about it again, in person, when she was back from Devon the next day. *If I can coax her into visualising the pumpkin, her powers of recall may be improved and, if it turns out the whiskers weren't in place when she was passing the house, it could potentially rule out the possibility of the speeding car having anything to do with Cassie's disappearance.*

In the house-to-house enquiries which had revealed that someone had been watching the house, a different neighbour said she had noticed an unfamiliar car parked outside her house a couple of times in the past week. No description of the car had been logged, so it was high on Rachel's list of priorities to question the residents of Beechwood Avenue further the next morning. If it turned out to be the red car that had dazzled Hazel with its headlights the previous evening, they needed to trace it and interview the owner as a matter of urgency.

So many different lines of enquiry and so far, nothing, but all we need is one break for the pieces to start to fit together, and maybe that break will come from Jessica.

Rachel pushed open the half-glazed door and found herself in a virtually deserted bar area which even ten years ago would have been packed out at this time on a Friday night, with people winding down after the working week. It was little wonder pubs were closing down at the rate they were. Some of the fall in the popularity of local pubs could be attributed to the smoking ban, but Rachel imagined that the availability of cheap alcohol in supermarkets must play its part, too. Pubs might have cleaner air these days, but unless landlords made more of an effort to attract customers there would be nobody around to appreciate it.

The Golden Lion was a traditional establishment, stuck in the 1970s and desperately in need of a revamp. The lighting was harsh and the garish patterned carpet smelled of the many sloshes of beer it had been treated to over the decades. There was a pool table and a dartboard at one end of the bar, but that appeared to be it in terms of entertainment. Rachel looked around. There was no 60-inch flat-screen television offering Sky Sports, no raised stage area to suggest occasional live music or karaoke, and seemingly no restaurant.

That's what brings customers to pubs these days, good pub grub and entertainment. No wonder this place can only attract a handful of customers; it has absolutely no appeal. She approached the bar and waited while the dark-haired barmaid attended to an elderly man at the far end who looked like he had already had a skinful even though it was only a little after six.

'Yes, love, what can I get you?'

She looks a lot older than her early thirties, Rachel thought, as the barmaid approached.

'Jessica?'

'Who's asking?' the barmaid said, immediately wary.

'I'm Detective Chief Inspector Hart. I need to ask you a few questions. Is now a good time?'

'I'm Mandy. Jessica didn't show up for work, so I'm just holding the fort until Debbie, our Saturday barmaid, gets here. I'm the landlord's wife,' she offered. 'I don't normally work behind the bar.'

'Right,' said Rachel, doubtful that they would take enough cash to cover the barmaid's wages. 'Is she sick?'

'I've no idea. She hasn't rung to say why she's not in, she just didn't show up again.'

'Again?'

'Yes. She was a no-show yesterday as well. It's not like her, she's been with us for a few months and she's usually the most reliable of all the girls.'

'Have you tried to contact her?'

'Not me. Pete might have. He's out the back, I'll go and ask him.'

'Can you also get me her phone number and an address if you have one?'

'Sure.'

Rachel reached into her pocket for her mobile and tapped on Graham's name. He answered on the second ring.

'How's it going with Jessica?'

'She's not here. She wasn't in yesterday either, and hasn't rung them with any explanation.'

'That's a bit odd.'

'Very. Something doesn't feel right. I can't put my finger on it at the moment. A couple of things. Is Kate back?'

'Yes, she arrived about ten minutes ago. Naomi is still upstairs, so Kate's taken her a cup of tea.'

'Good. Did you manage to have a look at Charlie's phone?'

'I wasn't able to access that information, I'm afraid.'

'I take it Charlie's in earshot?'

'That's right.'

'Okay, we'll have to leave that for now. So, a slight change of plan. I'm going to need you to meet me at Jessica's so that I'm not on my own when I question her, and then we'll head down to the station for the debrief. Can you let everyone know it might be slightly later than I thought and apologise for ruining their Friday night? Once I've got Jessica's address off the landlord, I'll text it to you,' she said, terminating the call as a whippet-like man approached her.

'Pete?'

'That's right.'

'Did your wife fill you in on who I am and what I need?'

'Jessica's not in any trouble, is she?'

'We're hoping she may be able to help us with an ongoing investigation. Have you been in contact with her?'

'No. I've tried to call her but she's not answering her phone. If you get hold of her, you can tell her from me that next time she wants a couple of days off she'd better ring to arrange it first or there won't be a time after that, if you get my drift,' he said, pushing a piece of paper across the bar with an address and a mobile number.

'I'll tell her how concerned you were for her well-being,' Rachel said, unable to keep the sarcasm from her voice. 'Thanks for your cooperation,' she added, wafting the piece of paper in the air as she headed towards the exit. 'Oh, actually, Pete, one more thing. Does Jessica usually drive to work?'

'She does.'

'Do you know what car she has, by any chance?'

'She did have a Fiat 500 but she changed it a week or so ago for a flashy BMW. I said to Mandy that she must have won the lottery or something. You don't buy a car like that on barmaid's wages. Hey, maybe that's why she didn't come to work. Perhaps it was a big win, and she's just going to be a lady of leisure now.'

'Is it red, by any chance?'

'It is, as it happens. She didn't nick it, did she? Is that what you need to question her about? I don't want no thieves in charge of my tills.'

'Innocent until proven guilty, Pete,' Rachel said over her shoulder, her voice lacking conviction.

CHAPTER EIGHTEEN

'Were you planning on staying here tonight?' Charlie asked.

'Well, I've brought some stuff over in case Naomi wants me to,' Kate replied. 'Alan's with the boys so it wouldn't be a problem, but I don't have to if you'd rather it be just the two of you. I mentioned it to her when I took her tea up, but she shrugged her shoulders as though she wasn't bothered either way.'

'Don't take it personally. She's been up and down all day. One minute she's angry and shouting, the next she's tearful and then she retreats into a trance-like state. I don't know if my being here is helping or not. She's physically attacked me twice, but I think maybe it's good to release the anger that she's been holding onto after what happened. Has she said any more about it to you since we last spoke?'

'Not really. She showed me the text she received from Jessica. I know it's none of my business, but what were you thinking? And with that nasty bitch, too. I thought we always presented a united front when it came to her.'

'We do – or we did – oh, I don't know. If only I'd remembered it was one of her working nights when you suggested I go to the pub to calm down, none of this would have happened.'

'You didn't have to speak to her, apart from to order your drink. You could have just holed up in a corner with your nose stuck in your pint.'

'It was whisky actually, but I suppose you're right. I needed to get a few things off my chest or I would have exploded. She was very sympathetic, and I guess the more I drank, the more I talked, and she seemed happy to listen.'

'I'll bet she was. I don't suppose you asked her how she came to be working in a pub at the end of the street you live on? I couldn't believe it when Alan and I went in there for a drink back in the summer and there she was behind the bar. I had to act all friendly with her so I could find out which days she was working. Can you imagine Naomi's face if it had been you two instead of us?'

'She really can't stand Jessica, which makes what I did even more difficult for her to forgive.'

'She'll come around eventually. You just need to give her time.'

'I'm not so sure. As time has gone on, it feels less and less likely that we'll ever be able to get back what we had.'

'Don't give up hope. You know, when Barry rang me this morning to say Cassie was missing, I half wondered if you'd finally cracked under the pressure of not seeing her and had taken her.'

'You don't really mean that, do you? I could never do that to Naomi, no matter how much I miss Cassie.'

'It's amazing what we're capable of when we want something badly enough. Did Jessica say what happened to the rich bloke she married? You remember the wedding, don't you? She had the nerve to invite us, along with most of the rest of the school, just so that she could have the biggest reception party ever. I'm so glad we didn't go.'

'To be honest, I did most of the talking, but she obviously did pretty well out of the divorce settlement judging by the size of her house. It makes you wonder why she needs to work as a barmaid in a crappy pub.'

'For company? It must be pretty lonely living on your own when you're used to having someone else around. That's why I've made myself so available to Naomi. I don't think she's been coping that well since you left. She's been forgetful and struggling to sleep.'

'I heard about the sleeping pills. I'm surprised you suggested them, but even more surprised she took one.'

'They were only the herbal ones I take sometimes. I've been trying to get her to buy some for a couple of weeks, but she said she hates going into shops because she thinks everyone is talking about her behind her back, poor thing. I had a couple left in a pack in my bag, so I gave them to her yesterday morning. They're only meant to relax you so you can drop off to sleep naturally. Maybe they had more of an effect because she hasn't been eating much.'

'I noticed how thin she looks. I feel terrible for putting her through all this. She has been looking after Cassie properly, hasn't she?'

'Well, obviously, I'm not here all the time, but when I have been, Cassie has always seemed fine. I think having Pumpkin to cuddle has helped.'

'They're inseparable. Do you know what reason Naomi gave Cassie for me not living here?'

'I think she was a little economical with the truth. Cassie seems to think it's a temporary situation and that you'll be coming home.'

'And you don't think that's the truth?'

'Of course, I hope it is, but I honestly don't know, Charlie. I've been friends with you both for such a long time, and I wouldn't have imagined that either of you could do anything of this magnitude to hurt the other. I know you've had a few rows about the baby situation, but we all have rows and then make up, that's part and parcel of being married. Couples survive, and are sometimes even stronger after one of them has a casual fling, but this is different. As you just said, it's your choice of partner that's the problem here rather than the act itself. I don't know if she'll be able to get past that.'

'Neither do I,' Naomi said.

'I didn't know you were there,' Charlie said, spinning round to face his wife, who was standing in the doorway to the lounge.

'Obviously. I'm sorry to interrupt your cosy little chat, but I just wondered whether the police have decided to involve the media or not?'

'No one's been in touch one way or another, but it's probably getting a bit late to do it tonight,' Kate said. 'Come and sit down and I'll get you another cup of tea.'

'I don't want any more bloody tea! I feel like I'm drowning in the stuff,' Naomi snapped. She sank onto the sofa, massaging her forehead with her fingertips. 'I'm sorry, Kate, I know you're only trying to be helpful. It's just that today has felt like the longest day of my life and it doesn't feel as though any progress has been made.'

'It feels like that for all of us,' Charlie said. 'I think today has been more about ruling out possibilities before they escalate things. I overheard them say they're bringing in the dog handlers first thing in the morning. If she's lost somewhere close by, they'll find her.'

'And if she's not? What then? She's my life, Charlie, she's all I've got left. Without her, I might as well just curl up in a corner and die.'

'You don't mean that.'

'Yes, I do. She's the only thing that has kept me sane these past few weeks. Her earnest little face fills my mind every time I close my eyes. I will never forgive myself if anything has happened to her.'

Kate shuffled her feet awkwardly. 'Look, maybe I should leave you two to talk. Why don't I pop home and get the boys to bed and come back later?'

'We've got nothing to say to each other.'

'Please, Noms, can't we at least try?'

'I've told you before, only people I love are allowed to call me Noms, and you don't qualify in that department any more, remember? As you pointed out earlier, this wouldn't have happened if you'd been here. But you weren't here, Charlie, and we all know why.'

'Won't you just let me try to explain what happened that night?'

'What is there to explain? You stormed out of the house leaving me in a state of near hysteria while you went to the pub to get pissed. And if that wasn't bad enough, you aired all our dirty laundry to Jessica and then shagged her.' Naomi's voice had increased in volume the angrier she became. 'From where I'm sitting, there really is nothing more to say.'

'But that's just it, Naomi,' Charlie said, trying to remain calm. 'You've only ever looked at the whole situation from your point of view. You've never put yourself in my position and the way you made me feel every time I wasn't man enough to get you pregnant. You and Cassie were my world. You two were enough for me, but seemingly we weren't enough for you. If we'd been blessed with another baby I would have been over the moon, and I would have loved it the same way that I love Cassie, but I didn't *need* it. I had all I needed with my two girls.'

Kate moved over to the door.

'I'll be back in an hour but I'm at the end of the phone if you need me, Noms,' she said as she left the room.

CHAPTER NINETEEN

6.55 p.m. – Friday

DCI Hart was already parked opposite Jessica's house when DI Wilson pulled up to the kerb behind her. The rain was sheeting down now, and Rachel rummaged around in her glove compartment for the compact umbrella she kept in there for such times. It was pink with navy-blue cats and dogs on it, a gift from her most recent boyfriend, who thought she should have something more 'girly' than the plain black one she normally carried. The umbrella had outlasted the relationship by a considerable amount, but that wasn't unusual. Every time Rachel started to feel an emotional connection with a boyfriend rather than a purely physical one, she ended things. It was as though she didn't have enough love left inside her to share with anyone else. Her therapist had said that she needed to learn to love herself again first before she could even think of loving anyone else. *She's right, and I'm not there yet,* Rachel thought, swinging her legs out of the car and pressing the button for the umbrella to unfurl. She offered it in Graham's direction, but he shook his head and pulled the hood of his coat up in preference.

'Well, I've got to be honest, this wasn't what I was expecting,' Rachel said, surveying the large detached house in front of them.

'Me neither.'

'I don't know why, but I'd pictured her living in a grotty flat above a row of shops. It doesn't make sense that she would work for peanuts in a dingy pub on the other side of town if she doesn't need the money.'

'She must have her reasons.'

'Well, let's find out, shall we, although to be honest, it doesn't look like there's anyone home.'

As the pair approached the front door the security lights flooded the block paving driveway, illuminating the topiary box bushes in their cast-iron containers either side of the front door. Beneath the shelter of the porch, Rachel rang the bell. They waited for a few minutes before ringing the bell again and then rapping the door knocker. There was still no response.

'Let's have a nosy around the back, Graham. Have you got a torch in your car?'

'Yep. I won't be a tick.'

It was as Rachel watched Graham splash through the puddles on the way back to his car that she noticed the *For Sale* sign for the first time, the wording of which was partially obscured by the diagonal *SOLD* sticker. *That's something else to get on to first thing in the morning*, she thought, making a note of the estate agent's name and number. *Did the house go on the market before or after the infamous night with Charlie Bailey? Jessica was clearly in the process of moving, but where was she moving to? A new life in a different area where if she arrived with a young child in tow, no one would ask any questions because they would think it was her daughter? It would be easy enough to get fake papers for Cassie if money was no issue.*

But if all this was planned, why not just hand her notice in at the pub rather than attract attention by not showing up for work? And what about the little girl? It wouldn't be like taking a baby and bringing her up as your own. Cassie would have memories of living with a different mummy and daddy. She would most likely let something slip at some point, if she was able to settle at all, unless... unless Charlie has been playing us all along. Maybe there was more to his one night of indiscretion with Jessica. Perhaps the two of them had been secretly seeing each other for years, with Charlie promising to leave his wife. Jessica could have got tired of waiting, so forced the issue by sending Naomi the photo and text. Leaving his wife might not have been a problem for Charlie, but perhaps life without his daughter was unthinkable. Once Naomi had thrown him out, he'd lost Cassie anyway. Maybe that was when he devised a plan for the little girl to go missing. Jessica could take her away somewhere and then he would join them as soon as the coast was clear. It's a possibility, Rachel thought as she watched Graham make his way back across the driveway, directing the beam of light from his torch from side to side like the beam from a lighthouse illuminating treacherous seas. She shivered. It was hard to believe that one human being could fall out of love with another so completely that they would punish them by taking their child, but she had been in the police force long enough to know it was entirely possible. She was no longer shocked by people's behaviour towards one another.

'What are we looking for, Guv?' Graham asked.

'We won't know until we find it, and we can't actually go in unless a door or window has been left unsecured. Let's just shine the torchlight through the windows for now and if anything doesn't look right, we can try and get a search warrant for the morning. Let's start with the garage. You check whether the door is locked while I go round the side and see if there's a window. I don't suppose Jessica's car will be there, but if it is, we'll be able to cross-check the number plate with the CCTV footage when we get it.'

Rachel started to head around the side of the garage with the torch, but stopped abruptly when Graham called out to her.

'We're in luck, Guv, it's open and her car is here.'

She made her way back to the front of the garage.

'Well, for the second time tonight, I wasn't expecting that.'

'I know. I was pretty surprised when I turned the handle and it just opened.'

'That too, but I was meaning the car. The landlord at the pub said Jessica had recently been arriving at work in a red BMW. I presumed she had sold her old car, but clearly not.'

They both stood looking at a pale blue Fiat 500.

'Maybe she was having trouble selling it, or perhaps it's broken down and that's why she got the new car?'

'Or perhaps she needed an easier car to bundle a young child into the back of? I haven't met Jessica, but I get the feeling that she is involved with Cassie's disappearance in some way. I just haven't figured out how or why yet. We need the CCTV footage from Beechwood Avenue ASAP. We have to find the red car, and when we do, I'm pretty sure it will somehow be connected to our missing barmaid. Come on, let's check the rest of the house. You never know, we may get lucky and find another door unlocked.'

CHAPTER TWENTY

7.07 p.m. – Friday

'You made it clear to Kate that you don't want any more tea, but how about I make you a milky coffee? Or better still, a cup of hot chocolate?'

Naomi wanted to refuse but at the mention of the hot, sweet drinks her stomach rumbled, giving the game away that she was really hungry. She had rejected various offers of food all day, but now she was starting to feel a bit faint and that wouldn't do at all if, by some miracle, Cassie turned up on the doorstep needing her mum to look after her.

She nodded, the anger of a few minutes earlier subsiding as quickly as it had flared. Just like a tropical downpour, her outburst had been over in a few minutes, leaving an uneasy sense of calm and the feeling that the next one might arrive at any moment.

'Coffee or chocolate?' Charlie prompted.

'You decide.'

'I'm going to make you a hot chocolate, just the way you like it, with two spoons of sugar and some squirty cream on top. You have got squirty cream, haven't you?'

'Of course. You know how much Cassie loves it on fresh fruit.'

Charlie did know how much his daughter liked her favourite dessert, but he hadn't been there to see her enjoy it for over a month. They locked eyes for a moment, connecting, feeling each other's pain, before Charlie dragged his gaze away and headed into the kitchen to warm the milk in the pan they had bought specially for that job. Everything felt so familiar as he tipped a little of the warming milk onto the cocoa powder and sugar, mixing it to a smooth paste before pouring the rest of the milk onto it just before it reached boiling. As he pulled the can of cream from the fridge, he glanced at the clock. It was a little after seven. It jolted him back to reality. If Cassie was here, it would be time for them all to head upstairs for her bath and a bedtime story.

'Oh, God. What a mess.'

'Charlie?'

He spun around.

'Nearly ready,' he said, forcing a smile. 'It smells so good, I wish I'd made myself one. I just need to add the swirl of cream. Do you want a biscuit with it?'

'We will get her back, won't we?' Naomi asked, her eyes wide with fear. 'You said we would.'

He turned back to finish the sickly creation and avoid eye contact with his wife. 'We have to think positively. If the police stop treating me and Mum as suspects and focus all their efforts on finding Cassie, it might help. Here, drink this, you look as though a puff of wind would blow you away,' he said, handing Naomi her favourite mug, which had a picture of a ginger cat wearing sunglasses on it.

She took the mug and sipped the hot milky liquid, leaving a small moustache of cream on her top lip. 'Have you seen Pumpkin?' she asked, casting her eyes around the kitchen. 'He's usually asleep on the chair before we go up for bath time.'

'No. I get the distinct impression he's avoiding me. You always were his favourite, despite me being the one who saved him.'

'Can you claim that?' Naomi asked, the merest hint of a smile twitching the corners of her mouth.

In truth, it had been Charlie's friend Mike who had taken a shortcut to work along the canal path and spotted a cloth bag on the bank that appeared to be wriggling. On closer inspection, he'd discovered five tiny kittens, clearly destined for a watery grave until the perpetrator had had a last-minute change of heart, or more likely lost their nerve. In the freezing temperatures, the kittens wouldn't have lasted more than a few hours anyway if he hadn't stumbled across them. There were two black kittens, two grey and one ginger, and by lunchtime they had all found homes among the staff in Charlie and Mike's office.

'Well, let's say I saved him from going to live with a family who probably wouldn't have loved him as much as we do.'

'No one could love him as much as we do. Earlier I told him to go and look for Cassie, and he disappeared out of the cat flap as if he was going to do just that. I think I'll call him in,' Naomi said, crossing to the back door, 'I don't like him being out this late at night. 'Pumpkin,' she called, 'come on boy.' She waited several minutes, the cold, damp air creeping into the kitchen, before calling again, but the ginger tom didn't appear. 'That's odd,' she said, shivering as she closed and locked the door. 'I wonder where he can be?'

'He'll be back when it's his supper time,' Charlie said. 'He's not stupid. Come on, let's take your chocolate through to the lounge before it gets cold.'

Naomi huddled in the corner of the sofa, hands around the mug, and took small sips of her drink.

'Charlie, why did you want to call him Pumpkin?'

Naomi had been incredulous when Charlie suggested they call the tiny kitten by the rather cruel nickname she had been saddled with at school.

'I told you at the time. I thought by calling something as cute and adorable as a kitten Pumpkin, it would banish all unhappy memories of your being bullied at school. It worked, didn't it?'

'I thought it had, but since... well, since you and she... you know, I've been wondering if she was the one you wanted all along, and if you've been seeing her behind my back all through our marriage. Maybe calling the kitten Pumpkin was a cruel joke that you two shared at my expense.'

Charlie was staring at his wife, open-mouthed. 'You don't really believe that, Naomi? I can't stand the woman, and I went out of my way to avoid her at all costs, you know that.'

'No, I only know what you told me. What if it was all a lie? What if my happy little life was built on a big fat lie?'

'You must know you're only thinking like that because of the trauma we're going through. A missing child is probably the worst thing that can happen to parents, maybe even worse than losing a child to a terminal illness. At least they have time to prepare for the inevitable, devastating though it is. The feelings we're experiencing are as much to do with shock and fear of the unknown as guilt that we have let this happen to our little girl.'

Naomi's head shot up.

'I said "we", Naomi. I'm not blaming you. All you did was leave the keys in a place where a resourceful five-year-old could reach them. She wanted to help her mummy by finishing off decorating the pumpkin cat, which should have been my job in the first place. I'm the one who has messed everything up. If anyone should be feeling guilty, it's me. And trust me, I'm drowning in guilt. What stupid idiot risks ruining his whole life because he can't handle a few drinks? The truth is, you and Cassie are my world. How could you even entertain the idea that I would choose Jessica over you?'

'But you did, Charlie, even if it was only that one time. You refused to make love to me and rushed straight off into her waiting arms.'

'It wasn't like that.'

'Then what was it like, Charlie? You keep saying you want me to hear your side of the story, well, now I'm ready to listen because I have to know what has led us here.'

Charlie wasn't sure that now was the best time to try and explain himself, with them both in such a vulnerable state, but he knew it might be the only opportunity he would get, the only chance to try and get his wife to see things from his point of view. He dropped his gaze to the floor, unable to look her in the eyes.

'I – I was upset after storming out of the house. I felt guilty for getting so angry with you when I knew how desperately you wanted another child, but it just made me feel so inadequate. I wanted to come back in the house and tell you how sorry I was, but I was afraid it would just cause another row. I needed to talk to someone. I couldn't ring Mum because she had Cassie with her, so I rang Kate. She told me I shouldn't drive as I was so agitated, and she suggested cooling off in the pub before coming home to apologise. We must have both forgotten it was one of Jessica's nights behind the bar. The minute I walked in she was completely attentive, getting me a drink and coming back to offer a refill when I had downed that one. She asked me if I was okay, and I just started talking to her. It was like the steam being released from a pressure cooker. Once I'd started, I just couldn't stop. I genuinely have no idea if I slept with her or not, and please believe me, that's the truth. But I actually feel worse for revealing our inability to get pregnant again to her, of all people. I knew I was betraying your trust, but I couldn't seem to stop myself.'

Charlie looked across at his wife for the first time since he had begun speaking, but she was resting her head on the back of the sofa with her eyes closed.

'The drinks kept coming and I knew I should stop but I didn't. It was as though I wanted to drink until I couldn't remember any of the pain of the argument and the hurtful things I said to you. I wanted to disappear into the bottom of my whisky glass. When she offered to take me home, I thought she meant bring me back here. I was so drunk, I have no idea how I thought I was going to explain it to you, but I was beyond making a reasonable decision. I can't remember arriving at her house, going inside it with her and undressing, but I know that's no excuse. I don't believe I was capable of having sex with her even if I'd wanted to, which I absolutely didn't, but I shouldn't have let myself get into that kind of a state. It felt horrible waking up in her bed.'

Charlie was aware of Naomi flinching, but she still had her head back with her eyes closed.

'That's when I made the second biggest mistake of my life. I should have come home to face the music. God, why didn't I just take the day off work and come home to try and explain things to you? I'm a selfish, thoughtless idiot, and I'm so sorry for everything about that night: the argument, getting drunk and whatever did or didn't happen with Jessica. But I'm an idiot that loves you with every fibre of my being, and I always will.'

The silence was deafening. Charlie waited for some kind of response, but none came.

'Naomi?'

'I'm tired. I'm going to bed,' she said eventually, hauling herself up off the sofa with an almighty effort.

'Do you want me to stay...? Obviously down here,' he added.

'You or Kate, I don't really care. I just need to go to sleep, and with a bit of luck I'll never wake up.'

Charlie watched his wife slowly climb the stairs, using the banister for support. *What have I done to her, to us?* he thought, burying his face in his hands, but not before he noticed a flash of orange streak past her and into the bedroom they used to share.

CHAPTER TWENTY-ONE

8.38 p.m. – Friday

'Right, can I have a bit of hush, please. I know it's late,' DCI Hart said, her eyes flicking to the large clock on the end wall of the incident room, 'so I'll try and keep this as brief as possible.'

She and DI Wilson hadn't found any of the doors to Jessica's house unlocked. They had shone the torch through the windows but there was no sign of life and nothing seemed out of place. They'd eventually arrived back at the police station shortly after 8.30 p.m., having been held up in the football traffic heading towards the Madejski Stadium for Reading's 8 p.m. kick-off. As Rachel's car had inched forward in the rain, she had to contend not only with vehicles but also rival sets of fans spilling across the roads with little thought for their own safety. She had considered putting the blue light on, although how effective it would have been was anyone's guess, but she decided against it as it could possibly be deemed improper use. Technically, she wasn't on her way to deal with an emergency, but every minute lost in the traffic jam was wasted time in their search for Cassie, whose earnest face was currently gazing out at the gathered police officers from the centre of the whiteboard at Rachel's side. A hush fell over the room.

'So, what do we know? Cassie Bailey,' she said, pointing to her photo, 'disappeared from her home at some point last night or in the early hours of this morning. Her mother, Naomi, claims she put her to bed at around half past eight and retired to bed herself less than an hour later,' she said, writing Naomi's name on the board. 'She discovered her daughter was not in the house this morning at around seven thirty when she went to wake her for school, meaning there is approximately a ten-hour window during which Cassie went missing. We need to narrow that down, which we should be able to do once we get the CCTV footage from the camera on the corner of Beechwood Avenue. How are we doing with that, Errol?'

'We requested it at 2.12 p.m. but there seems to be some delay. I'll chase them up.'

'Maybe just remind them that we are dealing with a missing child here, not someone doing thirty-four miles an hour in a thirty-mile-an-hour zone.'

'Yes, Guv.'

A hand shot up at the back of the room.

'Yes, Eleanor.' PC Eleanor Drake was new to the team and very keen to prove her worth. Rachel could see a lot of her younger self in the constable.

'Actually, there was a speeding car yesterday evening at around 10 p.m. One of the neighbours said she remembered it, during the course of my house-to-house enquiries.'

That would confirm Hazel Bailey's story, Rachel thought.

'Did she get the number plate, or make and model?'

'No. The witness said she heard it rather than saw it, unfortunately,' Eleanor said, consulting her notebook.

'So, we don't even have a vague description or a colour?'

'No, Guv.'

'We really do need that CCTV footage urgently. Cassie Bailey's grandmother, Hazel,' she said, adding her name to the whiteboard, 'also reported a speeding car at around 10 p.m. She thinks it was a red hatchback of some description. It may not be connected, but the sooner we can rule it out the better. Speaking of Hazel Bailey, she drove down to Devon this morning to see her sister.'

There was a buzz around the room.

'Apparently it was a planned visit. The local team called on her at her sister's house and reported back that there was no sign of Cassie. That doesn't mean to say she's not there, but my gut feeling is that the grandmother is telling the truth when she says she hasn't got her. She is driving back here tomorrow, so we will have the chance for further questioning if we feel it's necessary. We have also questioned her son Charlie, Cassie's father, and at the moment I don't have a reason to bring either him or Naomi into the station for formal questioning. There is, however, a person of interest who I would like to trace as a matter of urgency: Jessica Toland, a barmaid in the pub at the end of the Baileys' road. She knows them both from their schooldays and there is no love lost between her and Naomi, particularly since she had a one-night stand with Charlie Bailey a few weeks ago which led to the Baileys' separation. She didn't show up for work on the night of the abduction, nor again tonight. DI Wilson and I went to interview her at her house but there was no one home, and her mobile phone went to voicemail. The house has a 'For Sale' board outside with a sold sticker across it. I want to know when that house went on the market. The estate agents are Framptons. PC Drake, I'd like you to follow that up first thing in the morning. Who has been assigned to work on the known paedophiles list?'

A couple of hands were raised.

'We need that list ASAP. Focus your attention on those with a known history involving very young girls.' Rachel swallowed hard. An image of her six-year-old self, holding her sister Ruth's hand as they sat on the sofa in their next-door neighbour's house having an orange squash after he had invited them to pick apples from the tree in his back garden, flashed before her eyes. 'I... I'll let DI Wilson fill you in on plans for the morning. Please remember a young child's life is at risk here. Anything, no matter how inconsequential it may seem, needs to be investigated.'

Rachel left the incident room and headed for the toilets. She locked herself in a cubicle and sat down on the closed toilet seat. Her hands were shaking and there were beads of perspiration on her forehead. *Can I do this? Is it just too close to home?* She breathed deeply for a few minutes, feeling her pulse rate gradually returning to normal, before sliding the bolt open and moving towards the washbasins. She turned on the cold tap and cupped her hands before closing her eyes and splashing the water on her face.

'Are you all right, Guv?'

It was Eleanor Drake.

'Yes, of course, why wouldn't I be?' she replied, a little more harshly than she intended.

'You just looked a bit pale when you left the incident room.'

'Thanks for your concern, but I'm fine. I needed to freshen up before taking a look at all the collated information. It looks like it might be a late one for me.'

'Anything I can help with, Guv?'

She examined the young constable's face, wondering if someone had made her aware of what Rachel had experienced as a young child. *Is she asking if I need help on a personal level, or is she volunteering to stay even later and work on the case?*

'No. You get yourself home. I need you fresh for the morning. Good night.'

CHAPTER TWENTY-TWO

8.54 p.m. – Friday

Charlie was in the kitchen making himself a coffee and some toast when he heard the front door open. It was Kate.

'Where's Naomi?'

'She was totally exhausted, so she's gone up to bed to get some sleep.'

'I've got some more of the herbal sleeping pills if she needs them.'

'She doesn't. I checked on her a few minutes ago and she was dead to the world. She looked so peaceful lying there with her hand resting on Pumpkin. We had a bit of a scare earlier. He wasn't asleep in his usual place and didn't come in when she called him. That would be all she needs, for the cat to go missing too. I wish we could both wake up tomorrow morning to find this has all been a horrible nightmare.'

'This whole thing has been incredibly hard for both of you, but especially her. She was already in a highly emotional state because you guys couldn't get pregnant, and then your indiscretion with Jessica almost tipped her over the edge.'

'Tipped her over the edge?'

'I didn't want to mention it, but she's been a bit flaky and forgetful, and I'm pretty sure not being able to sleep properly hasn't helped. That's why I gave her the sleeping pills. I thought a decent night's sleep would ease the pressure a bit. I was thinking about what was best for Cassie, too.'

'What do you mean? Naomi's a great mum.'

'Of course she is, but without you around to share the load, little things have been starting to get on top of her. I just don't think Naomi's cut out to be a single mum.'

'She isn't a single mum, Kate. I'm here for her whenever she needs me.'

'She does need you, Charlie, but it's whether or not she wants you back in her life. It's the whole trust thing. Do you think she will ever completely trust you again?'

'I hope so. We were talking earlier, and at least she listened to my side of the story, something she refused to do before.'

'Really? How did she react?'

'She didn't. She just said she was tired and went to bed.'

'Well, at least she didn't get hysterical. That's something else I've been worried about. She hasn't been as patient as usual. I even heard her raise her voice to Cassie on one occasion, something she never did when you lived here. You don't think Cassie has become a little bit scared of her mum and has simply run away, do you?'

'No, I don't, and I'm surprised you would even suggest it, if I'm honest.'

'Maybe I'm just hopeful that Cassie has wandered off, rather than thinking someone's taken her.'

'I know there are some seriously messed-up people in this world but taking a child – why would anyone do that?'

'Have you heard anything more from the police, or have they called it a day?'

'DCI Hart rang just before you got here. It's too late to do a press conference tonight, and apparently Jessica wasn't at the pub when she arrived to interview her.'

'Why would they want to interview Jessica? They don't think she's got anything to do with Cassie going missing, do they?'

'I don't know. Perhaps they are merely eliminating her from their list of suspects. We're all on it at the moment it seems, me,

Mum, even Naomi. Maybe they were checking to see if Jessica drives a red car.'

'A red car?'

'Yes. When they spoke to Mum on the phone, she told them she'd seen a red car drive away at speed last night while she was out walking Alfie. It's probably not connected, but the police will no doubt want to find the owner.'

'Of course. It could be an important lead.'

Before Charlie could answer, his phone started to ring.

'Hi Mum. Are you feeling a bit better now?'

'I'm on my way home. I've stopped at the services to get a coffee, but I wanted to let you know I should be back in a couple of hours.'

Charlie frowned. 'I thought we agreed you should come home tomorrow after a decent night's sleep.'

'I couldn't bear the thought of you being in the house alone worrying about Cassie. There's no news, is there?' she added, making Charlie's heart contract at the hopeful note in her voice.

'No, still nothing. I was going to stay over at Naomi's, I – I mean ours, but Kate's just showed up, so she can stay instead,' he said, raising his eyebrows in question.

Kate nodded her response.

'No, you stay, Charlie. I'll be fine with Alfie. If you two are under the same roof, you'll have a chance to talk about… stuff,' she finished, lamely.

'We've already talked, Mum, and she's sleeping now. After everything that's happened today, she was exhausted. I can't see her waking until morning. I'll come back and relieve Kate early enough for her to get her boys off to school.'

'It's Saturday tomorrow,' Kate whispered, 'so no great rush, just swimming at 10.30 a.m and Alan can take them if needs be.'

'Shall I make you something to eat?' Charlie offered.

'I'm not really hungry,' Hazel replied. 'Sheila gave me some of her buttered scones to have with a coffee, but when I took a bite of one it tasted dry and got stuck in my throat, and you know what a great cook she is.'

'We're all feeling a bit like that, but I'll make you something anyway. Drive carefully.'

'I will. See you in a bit.'

'Thanks for agreeing to stay, Kate,' Charlie said, heading out into the hall, grabbing his coat from the banister and unlocking the door. Will you be able to feed Pumpkin?'

'Of course, I know the drill. Half a sachet of wet food, a small handful of dry and check his water bowl. I've done it often enough when you guys have been away on holiday.'

'I don't know what Naomi and I would do without you, you've been such a good friend.'

'Likewise. We're the three musketeers, always looking out for each other in good times and bad.'

CHAPTER TWENTY-THREE

10.02 p.m. – Friday

Rachel raised her head at the sound of a knock on her office door. She was surprised to see it was past 10 p.m. as she signalled for Graham to come in.

'I'm heading home now, Guv, if that's all right?'

Something in his voice suggested to Rachel that he thought she should do the same. It had been a long and emotionally charged day for all of them.

'Can we just have five minutes, Graham? The football traffic won't have cleared yet so you might as well be here with me as sat in a jam.'

He closed the door and moved across the room to sit down at the other side of her desk. 'What's on your mind, Guv?'

'I just wanted to get your thoughts on the Baileys.'

'Fire away.'

'Let's start with Naomi. She's obviously been under a lot of stress since the breakdown in her marriage. It can't be easy, coming to terms with your husband's infidelity and trying to keep everything as normal as possible for your child. I should imagine five-year-olds can be quite demanding at the best of times, but Naomi's probably been trying to compensate for Charlie not being around, particularly as she is the one who is keeping them apart. Do you think she could have snapped and done something to harm Cassie?'

'Well, judging by the violent outbursts directed at her husband, I'd say she has a bit of a temper when provoked, but I'm not sure whether I believe she would direct that towards her daughter,' Graham said, 'at least, not intentionally. She was in a hell of a state when I got to the house this morning, shaking and wailing and white as a sheet. She would need to be one heck of an actress to pull that off.'

'She was in a similar state down by the canal. I actually thought she was considering jumping in at one point. But this business with the sleeping pill is bothering me. I'm not sure I would take a sleeping pill if I was the sole adult in charge of a very young child who often wakes up during the night.'

'I hear what you're saying, Guv, but those herbal ones usually only have a very mild effect. If she's been struggling to cope she probably thought she was doing the best thing for Cassie.'

'She's been coping looking after Cassie on her own for over a month, so I'd have thought she would be getting used to it by now, and might have less of a need to take a tablet to make her sleep.'

'Not necessarily,' Graham said. 'I remember when my two were newborn babies. You get to a point where sleep deprivation makes you do things you would never normally consider. Maybe she just hit a wall.'

'Or maybe she hit her daughter? Just supposing, as you suggest, that she was exhausted, and Cassie was playing up at bedtime, what if she lashed out in anger and accidentally killed her? The story of taking the sleeping tablet and being out for the count would make a pretty good alibi.'

'But what would she have done with the body? We checked the sandpit and the garden for signs of freshly dug earth, and none of the neighbours said they saw or heard her car leave the driveway. I can't imagine she would have got very far carrying the child, there's absolutely nothing of her.'

Rachel thought for a moment. 'I know we had a bit of a look around the house this morning when we first got there, but I think a more thorough search is justified. We should check the loft tomorrow.'

'We can do it when the dog handlers arrive. They can take the dogs up to Cassie's room to get her scent and lift one of them up to the ceiling hatch on the landing. The dogs would soon let everyone know if she's up there, dead or alive.'

'I don't know why,' Rachel said, tapping her pen absent-mindedly on her notepad, 'but I don't believe she's dead, at least not yet. Maybe it's just wishful thinking. What do you make of Charlie Bailey?'

'He looks like a bloke who seriously regrets getting pissed and shagging the local barmaid. His life has unravelled as much as Naomi's, in fact more so because she won't let him see their daughter.'

'Don't you think it's strange that he's been watching the house every night?'

'Not really. As a dad myself, I'd probably do anything to catch a glimpse of my kids if they were being kept from me.'

'But isn't it a bit weird that he would try the door handle?' Rachel persisted. 'If it had been left unlocked, what would he do about it? He could hardly call out to Naomi, could he?'

'True, but he probably still has a key, so I guess he could have locked it in order to make sure his daughter was safe.'

'That's another thing. I wonder why Naomi hasn't changed the locks? I think it would be the first thing I would do in similar circumstances.'

'Maybe she's hopeful that they will somehow end up back together?'

'It didn't seem that way earlier.'

'No,' Graham agreed.

'And didn't you think it was a bit odd that it took so long to get hold of his mum? I know she said she had a terrible journey down to Devon, but I'd have thought that would have been all the more reason for her to ring Charlie the moment she got there. Surely she must have realised he'd be worried to have not heard from her.'

'He left her a message to call him, didn't he?'

'Yes, but apparently she didn't turn her phone on straight away, so she hadn't heard it. That's possible, of course, or they could be in this together. If one of them took Cassie at some point last night, they could have used the trip to Devon to give them a window of a few hours to hide her somewhere on the way.'

'But who would she be with, Guv? Cassie's only five. I can't imagine a loving dad or grandma leaving her on her own.'

'Jessica?' suggested Rachel. 'Maybe Charlie enlisted her help to look after Cassie for a few days until he could go to her himself. It would tie in with her not showing up for her shifts at the Golden Lion. We really do need to speak to her as soon as possible, if only to eliminate her from our enquiries.'

'You don't think Hazel took her without Charlie's knowledge, do you, Guv? Not seeing the grandchild she dotes on could have affected her judgement. Maybe she just wanted to spend a few hours with the child, and didn't realise the seriousness of what she had done until the police turned up to search her sister's house.'

'If that was the case, where was Cassie when the Devon police searched?'

'That blows that theory, I guess.' They both fell silent for a moment, before Graham said, 'I'm shattered, Guv. I reckon the football traffic will have cleared by now. We'd both benefit from a good night's sleep, and then we can view things with fresh eyes in the morning.'

'You're probably right,' Rachel said, doubtful that she would get much sleep while a young child was missing from her home. 'It's just that I can't shake the feeling that someone knows a lot more than they're telling us, but at the moment I can't work out who.'

'It's only been a few hours, Guv. It'll all start falling into place.'

'I hope so, Graham, for Cassie's sake.'

CHAPTER TWENTY-FOUR

10.03 p.m. – Friday

The rain had started to come down quite heavily again as Hazel pulled the VW Jetta back onto the M4 after her short stop at the services. For a while she needed to have the wipers on top speed to clear the windscreen of the deluge. She kept her speed below 50 mph and stayed in the inside lane because of surface water lying on the carriageway. As it was, spray from other vehicles was being thrown up as cars and the occasional lorry passed her in the middle lane, exceeding what she considered to be a safe speed.

No wonder people have accidents, she thought, reacting to the brake lights illuminating on the car in front by applying gentle pressure on her own brake pedal to avoid aquaplaning. *Maybe Sheila was right and I should have stuck to my original plan of driving back in the morning, but I can't bear the thought of Charlie being on his own with all this extra worry heaped on top of the separation.* That was one of the problems of being a single parent: there was no one to share the burden of the lows or the euphoria of the highs, as Hazel knew only too well.

She reached to turn the radio on and pressed one of the preset buttons for Classic FM. She usually enjoyed listening to talk radio, in particular Radio 4, on her long journey to and from Devon, but she was fearful of concentrating too intently on the conversation or the short stories rather than the road ahead. The strident, crashing chords of Gustav Holst's 'Mars', from *The Planets Suite*, instantly filled the interior of her car and seemed an appropriate accompaniment to the weather conditions. He wasn't normally one of her favoured composers – she preferred the gentler offerings of Chopin or Franz Liszt – but she was glad of the raw energy of the piece in her fight against the tiredness that was growing with every passing mile. Holst transitioned to Beethoven, followed by a choral offering that Hazel didn't recognise and didn't really enjoy. She was about to turn the radio off when the presenter announced that coming next was Rachmaninoff's 'Rhapsody on a Theme of Paganini'. It had been her father's favourite piece of music and was played at his funeral. Instead of turning the radio off, she increased the volume to immerse herself in the sound and was surprised when big fat tears began to roll down her cheeks and drop into her lap. It wasn't only Charlie who had been feeling the pressure of the past five weeks. She had needed to be so strong for him that she had rarely allowed herself to show any emotion. Alone in her car with only Rachmaninoff and the drumming of the rain on the roof for company, the enormity of what life without Cassie would be like completely overwhelmed her. Since her birth almost six years ago, Hazel's whole world had revolved around her granddaughter; a future without her was unthinkable. *Come on, Hazel, pull yourself together, woman. You're no good to anyone in this state.* She took several deep breaths and her tears subsided along with the ferocity of the rain.

By the time her car headlamps illuminated the large blue road sign informing her that hers was the next junction, it was twenty to eleven. The rain had virtually stopped, allowing her to have the wipers on intermittently. It was just as well, as the hypnotic backward and forward motion had begun to have a soporific effect on her. A few miles back she had experienced the jolt of the chin suggesting that she had nearly fallen asleep at the wheel. Instead of pulling off at the nearest exit and taking a break, as she knew she should, Hazel had wound her window down hoping that a blast of fresh air would be equally as effective. *Only a few more miles now*, she thought, pulling her car to a halt at the red traffic lights after exiting the motorway. Suddenly, there was a squeal of brakes and a flash of bright lights in her rear-view mirror before the deafening crunch of metal on metal flung her forward towards the steering wheel.

'Don't try to move,' a voice said, 'the police and ambulance are on their way. What's your name?'

Hazel opened her eyes and panicked initially when all she could see was white. Then she remembered the lights bearing down on her moments before the crash and realised that the driver airbag must have inflated on impact. She tried to ease back slightly to see who was talking to her, but her seat had her pinned forward.

'I'm Hazel,' she said. 'What happened?'

'You've been involved in an accident, Hazel. A lorry went into the back of you at the traffic lights.'

'Is the driver all right?'

'Just a bit shaken up, I think. He jumped straight down from his cab, shouting and swearing after the impact, but I managed to persuade him to go and sit on the grass verge with my wife and another of the motorists who witnessed the crash until the police get here. Are you hurt?'

'I don't think so. I can't move much at the moment, so I can't really tell.' Hazel could hear the wail of sirens getting gradually louder. 'Was it my fault?'

'That's for the police to decide. I think the lorry driver was probably travelling too fast in the wet conditions, but in his defence, the lights had changed to green and he probably expected you would pull away more quickly than you did. Technically, though, he went into the back of you.'

Hazel closed her eyes. *Did I fall asleep for a few seconds? Am I to blame?* She tried to picture the traffic lights changing, but she couldn't. *Oh God, what if someone had been killed because of me not being as alert as usual! It doesn't bear thinking about.*

'The police are here now, so the ambulance shouldn't be far behind. They'll want a statement from me, I guess, but then I'll be on my way. I hope everything turns out all right.'

'Thank you for stopping and for staying with me. Some people would have just driven off, not wanting to get involved.'

'It's the least I could do.'

'We'll take it from here, sir. Do you know how many people are in the vehicle?'

'Just the driver as far as I can see. Her name is Hazel. I'll be over on the verge with my wife if you need to take statements from us.'

'One of my colleagues will be with you shortly, sir. Hazel, can you hear me? We'll soon have you out of there. Was there anyone in the car with you?'

'No. I'm on my own.'

'Okay. Well, I'm going to try and open your door, so you just stay nice and calm.'

Hazel could hear the sound of the handle being lifted and then released a couple of times and a bit of huffing and puffing before a grating sound, which she presumed was the door opening.

'Right, I'm going to reach across you, Hazel, and undo your seat belt so that I can try and push the back of your seat away from you. I want you stay leaning forward on the airbag. Is that okay?'

'Yes, fine.'

Moments later, the officer had freed Hazel from the restraint of the seat belt just as the paramedics arrived on the scene. Together, they were able to gently lift her from the car onto the waiting gurney and move her into the back of the ambulance to carry out some on-the-scene checks. Amazingly, she had escaped injury. Her only issue was that she couldn't hear properly with her left ear, but the paramedic put it down to shock. By the time he had finished his examination and was happy that she didn't need to be taken to the hospital, the tow truck had arrived to remove the vehicles. Despite minimal damage to the front of the lorry, the whole of the back of the VW Jetta was totally crushed. The police told her that if anyone had been travelling in the back of the car, they would almost certainly have suffered life-threatening injuries.

Hazel was sitting in the back seat of a police car, a blanket around her shoulders, waiting to be driven home. She hadn't rung Charlie, even though she knew he would be starting to worry at her lateness. *It'll be better to explain what happened in person so he can see I'm not hurt, unlike my poor car.* She watched as the tow truck started to lift the Jetta off the carriageway, water dripping from its boot despite the rain having stopped. *I hope it's only water and not petrol from the fuel tank.* One of the lights that was being used to help the police clear away debris from the collision illuminated the drips momentarily. They weren't water, nor were they petrol; the substance was thicker, and it was red in colour.

Hazel could feel her heart pounding in her chest, and it felt as though the blood in her veins had turned to ice. She pictured herself closing the car boot much earlier that morning after she had decided it would be easier to put her case on the back seat. *I didn't check it before closing it, I had no reason to.* She remembered the faint knocking sound she thought she had heard when she was stuck in the traffic jam and what Charlie had said on the phone about Cassie possibly having locked herself out of the house. Hazel could feel her throat tightening. She was struggling to breathe. *Oh my God, what if she found her way to my house and climbed in the boot to escape the bitter cold?*

All eyes turned in Hazel's direction as she let out a blood-curdling scream, pointing in horror at the puddle collecting beneath the crushed boot of her car.

CHAPTER TWENTY-FIVE

11.15 p.m. – Friday

'Guv, I didn't wake you, did I?'

'No, I've only been in a few minutes. I stopped off at the petrol station to get myself a fresh loaf of bread. I'm just making myself some toast. I thought we decided to call it a day?'

'We did, but there was an accident on my way home.'

'Shit. Are you all right? I probably shouldn't have kept you so late.'

'Thanks for your concern, but I wasn't involved in the accident. It had just happened and there was only one police vehicle on the scene, so I pulled over to help.'

'As if you haven't had a long enough day already. Honestly, Graham, in some ways you're more of a workaholic than me.'

'My wife would probably agree with you on that. Anyway, the reason I'm ringing is that I was taking a witness statement from a woman whose husband was helping one of the drivers who was trapped in her car. When he came over, I asked if the driver was all right and he mentioned her name was Hazel.'

Rachel, who had gone back to concentrating on spreading butter on her toast once she knew Graham wasn't involved in the crash, was instantly alert.

'Hazel? That's not a very common name.'

'Exactly what I thought, Guv, so I ran the licence plate and it turns out that the vehicle the lorry had ploughed into the back of belongs to Hazel Bailey, as in Charlie Bailey's mum. How's that for a coincidence?'

'I don't believe in coincidences, Graham. She's supposed to be at her sister's in Devon, driving back tomorrow. I wonder what made her change her plans?'

'It gets better. I was getting into my car after handing over the statement I'd taken to the traffic boys, and there was an almighty scream. Honestly, Guv, it was like someone was being murdered. Hazel Bailey was pointing to her car as the tow truck was lifting it up off the carriageway. There was red liquid dripping from the smashed-up boot that looked alarmingly like blood.'

Rachel's grip on her phone tightened.

'And was it?'

'No. It was brake transmission fluid, and the boot was completely empty when the team prised it open, but judging by her reaction, Hazel Bailey clearly thought it was.'

'Where is she now?'

'On her way home. The paramedics checked her out at the scene and miraculously she was completely unharmed physically, just shocked, unlike her car, which looks as though it's a write-off.'

'Have they taken it to the pound?'

'Yes.'

'I want forensics on it first thing in the morning. Maybe I was wrong to believe she had nothing to do with Cassie's disappearance.'

CHAPTER TWENTY-SIX

Day Two – 8.02 a.m. – Saturday

'There's been a development, Mr Bailey.'

'Have you found her? Is she… is she…' Charlie's voice tailed away.

'We haven't found Cassie, but we have found Jessica,' DCI Hart said.

'Where?'

'After circulating her details, naming her as a person of interest in a missing child investigation, a border control officer apprehended her in Portsmouth about to board a ferry to Spain.'

'But Cassie wasn't with her?'

'No. Jessica's being driven here from Portsmouth now for questioning.'

'You think she has something to do with it?'

'Not necessarily, but her actions do seem a little suspicious. She may well have a perfectly convincing explanation.'

'Does everything else wait until after you've interviewed her?'

'We'll hold off on releasing anything to the press, but the sniffer dogs are on their way to your house now and my officers have already started working through the list of paedophiles. How is your wife this morning? Do you think she will be able to do a television appeal this afternoon, if we still haven't found your daughter?'

'She's not up yet. Kate stayed with her overnight. She checked on her in the night and again just before I arrived at seven, but she was sleeping. All I need to do now is locate the cat. He seems to have gone missing again.'

'We had a cat when I was a child that used to disappear for weeks at a time. It turns out he was being fed by a family on the next street, and used to split his time between the two households. Very smart creatures, cats. People don't give them enough credit. I'll be in touch later, once we've interviewed Mrs Toland.'

'Who?'

'Mrs Toland. It's Jessica's married name, and she's kept it even though she's divorced. Just one question: the night she took you back to her house, do you remember if she had a problem starting her car?'

'I can't say with any certainty, but I don't think so. Why do you ask?'

'It seems she drove down to Portsmouth in a red BMW which we've now discovered is a hire car. The landlord from the pub says she's been driving around in it for the past couple of weeks, which is odd as her Fiat is parked in the garage of her home.'

'Hold on a minute. Do you think it might be the car my mum saw parked on the street outside here the night Cassie went missing?'

'Possibly. We'll have a clearer idea once we're able to check the number plate against CCTV footage. DS Green and the dog handlers should be with you shortly, and I'll be in touch with any further developments. If you need anything in the meantime, PC Harman is on your front doorstep.'

'Who was that?' Naomi asked sleepily from the top of the stairs where she was standing wrapped in her fleecy dressing gown, which now seemed two sizes too big for her.

'It was DCI Hart. They're going to question Jessica about her movements on Thursday night.'

'Do they think she has something to do with Cassie going missing?' Naomi said, gripping the banister.

'At the moment they just want to know her whereabouts on Thursday night. She was due at work but didn't show up, and the same again last night. She was stopped at Portsmouth about to board a ferry to Spain but there was no sign of Cassie,' Charlie said, in response to his wife's hopeful expression.

'I hope they pull her fingernails out, although they're probably fake just like the rest of her.'

'They're questioning her, not torturing her, although I do take your point,' he said to Naomi's retreating back as she headed into the bathroom.

His wife was spot on in her assessment of Jessica. Her hair was dyed blonde, her bust size had increased enormously since they had all left school aged eighteen and her sweeping eyelashes certainly weren't her own. *It's all as fake as the compassion she showed me the night she plied me with enough drink to sink a battleship. The question is: why? Why did she deliberately set about getting me drunk? Looking back, it almost seems as though she planned it, and yet she couldn't have. She had no way of knowing I'd be in the pub that night. It must simply have been an opportunity to get one over on Naomi. Who would have thought that a schoolgirl grudge could continue so far into adult life? Women, I'll never understand them*, he thought, as he watched Naomi pad carefully down the stairs.

'Have you been here all night?' she asked.

'No, Kate took over for me. Mum decided to drive home from Devon, so I went back to hers to make her some supper. There didn't seem much point in coming back in case I disturbed you. You were fast asleep when I left.' He deliberately didn't mention the accident his mum had been involved in. Naomi was already struggling to cope, so there seemed little point in adding more drama, particularly as his mum hadn't been injured. 'Did you manage to sleep through?'

'Yes, I did, surprisingly.'

'Maybe having Pumpkin on the bed with you helped. I saw him go streaking up the stairs after you last night,' Charlie said, smiling.

'Well, he's not there now. He obviously deserted me when he realised it was breakfast time. Have you fed him, or did Kate do it before she left?'

'She must have done. I haven't seen him this morning. Talking of food, can I get you some toast?'

'I don't know if I can face anything solid, but I could probably manage another hot chocolate.'

'I think I might join you.'

Before Charlie had even poured the milk into the saucepan to warm up, there was a knock at the door.

'I'll get it,' Charlie said. 'It's probably the dog handlers. DCI Hart said they were on their way. I expect they need to let the dogs have a sniff round Cassie's room to get her scent before they start their search.'

Less than thirty minutes later, after the dog handlers had left, Naomi and Charlie were sitting hugging their mugs of hot chocolate at the kitchen table.

'Before I fell asleep last night,' she said, 'I was thinking over what you told me about the night of the argument. I'm finding it very hard to come to terms with what you did, but I can see how my constant pressurising to try for another baby might have pushed you too far.'

Charlie started to speak, but Naomi raised her hand.

'No, let me finish. Until Cassie went missing, I didn't appreciate just how precious she is. When you said yesterday that she and I were enough for you, it set me thinking. If I was forced to make the kind of decision that Meryl Streep's character did in the film *Sophie's Choice*, choosing between Cassie and getting pregnant with a new baby, it would always be Cassie, of course it would.

I love every dark hair on her beautiful head. I love the smell of her when she cuddles me before her goodnight kiss. I love the little jokes she makes and the earnest look in her eyes when she's asking me a question. It doesn't mean to say that I wouldn't like to have another baby, it simply means I recognise that I was wrong for that to be my primary focus. She is such a special little girl, and a gift that for so long we were denied. I should have been satisfied with what I had, and not greedy for more. I'm not being overly dramatic when I say my life will be over if anything bad has happened to her.'

Charlie put down his mug and reached out across the table to take her hands in his.

'You'd still have me. If you want me, that is?'

'No. I mean, yes, I still want you, but if anything has happened to Cassie I don't know if I'd be able to be with you, looking each day at the grown-up version of the little girl I didn't take proper care of.'

'That's not true, and you know it. Nobody could have done more for our little girl than you. Even with the emotional turmoil you were suffering, constantly asking your body why it was letting you down and not allowing you to create a brother or sister for Cassie, you still made every moment of her day a joy. You're a natural mother, and it's so cruel that you've been denied a host of children to care for. I'm the selfish one for not understanding how strong your maternal instinct is. When we get Cassie back, we'll go and get specialist help if we need to. I'm just so sorry that it has taken something so monumental to make me see reason,' Charlie said, tears coursing down his cheeks.

Seeing her husband in such a state made Naomi struggle to keep her own emotions in check. She swallowed hard before saying, 'I've never seen you cry before, not even when Cassie was born.'

'Because I've always tried to be the big strong man. The hunter-gatherer who looks after his woman. The person who can make everything right for the most important people in his life. But I can't make this right. It's out of my control, and with every passing minute I'm more and more fearful of what the outcome will be. Please, Naomi, please tell me that whatever happens, we'll have each other. I couldn't bear to lose both my girls.'

'I love you, Charlie. I've always loved you from the moment you asked Kate and me if you could sit on our dinner table on the first day of senior school. Never in my wildest dreams did I think you would choose me, the funny little ginger pumpkin, to be your girlfriend and then your wife, and I almost let you slip through my fingers. I never want to be without you again. I'm only whole when I'm with you.'

They were both crying as Charlie moved around the table to take his wife in his arms, and they clung to each other as though their lives depended on it. When Charlie's phone rang, he almost didn't answer it, but Naomi pulled away from him, a tense expression on her face.

'Maybe they've found her.'

Charlie picked up his phone. 'Hello? Mum, is that you? What's wrong, you sound as though you're crying.'

He listened for a few moments, his face a study of shock and fear. 'Okay. Okay, I'm coming.'

'What?' Naomi almost screamed at him. 'What's happened?'

'It's Mum. She's at the police station. She says she's been arrested.'

'What are you talking about?'

'Look, I wasn't going to tell you because I didn't want to worry you, but Mum was involved in an accident last night on her way back from Devon.'

'Oh my God, is she all right?'

'Physically, yes, but she was very badly shaken, and now this. I've got to go to her.'

'Do they think she was responsible for the accident? Did someone else get hurt? Is that why they've arrested her?'

'No, it's nothing to do with the crash. They towed her car to the police compound last night, and during preliminary examinations this morning the forensic scientist found some evidence that they think suggests Mum may have had something to do with Cassie's disappearance.'

CHAPTER TWENTY-SEVEN

11.12 a.m. – Saturday

Charlie sat bowed forward on an uncomfortable orange plastic chair in the reception area of the police station, his elbows resting on his thighs, while his legs jiggled up and down nervously. It was hard to take in that a few hundred yards away two different people were being questioned about Cassie's disappearance, and even harder to comprehend that one of them was his mother.

He had been waiting for over two hours since leaving Naomi in the bathroom of the house he had formerly called home. Her reaction to the news that his mum had been arrested, suspected of having something to do with Cassie's disappearance, had shocked him. Moments earlier they had been hugging each other and talking about getting back together, but her mood had swung to the polar opposite and she had begun hurling accusations at him, along with the mug she had recently drunk her hot chocolate from.

'Your mum couldn't have done this on her own,' she had accused. 'Are you in this together? Did she take Cassie somewhere, to stay with a friend or something, in the hope that her going missing would bring us back together? Is she at Sheila's? Were they hiding her when the police called? It's sick. No, it's worse than that, it's evil. How could you do this, Charlie? You've got to tell me where she is,' she had ranted.

No amount of denying any collusion with his mum over Cassie's disappearance had any effect on Naomi's uncontrolled outburst.

But it was the physical violence that worried him the most. *If this is how she behaves when she's under extreme stress, is it possible that she could have done something to harm Cassie?* Kate had mentioned that she had heard Naomi raise her voice to Cassie, which Charlie had dismissed at the time, but now he was afraid she might have a point. *If Cassie had been misbehaving, maybe Naomi raising her voice wasn't enough to calm her and she lashed out and accidentally hurt her.* Charlie didn't want to believe that his wife would harm their little girl, but if she was at the end of her tether, he was starting to wonder if it was a possibility. Unable to calm Naomi, who repeatedly screamed, 'GET OUT OF MY HOUSE' at him before locking herself in the bathroom, he had called Kate.

'I'm sorry to bother you, Kate, but Naomi has flipped. She thinks Mum and I have got Cassie hidden away somewhere.'

'Why on earth would she think that?'

'The police found something in the boot of Mum's car that apparently suggests Cassie may have been held prisoner in it.'

'That's ridiculous. Your mum would never harm Cassie.'

'Well, the police think otherwise. They've taken her down to the station for questioning. I need to go to Mum, but I can't leave Naomi on her own. She's hysterical. She's locked herself in the bathroom and she's making a weird wailing sound. I'm scared she might harm herself. Can you come?'

'Of course. Alan can take the boys swimming. I'll be there in five minutes.'

'You're an angel. One day we'll be able to pay you back for everything you've done for us.'

Charlie waited until Kate arrived before leaving for the police station. Much as he hoped he wouldn't see Jessica, he was resigned to the fact that he probably would. Sure enough, she arrived at the police station about ten minutes after he did and shot him a withering look.

'Pathetic,' she mumbled as she walked past him, deliberately swinging her hips.

For once Jessica is right. I've been pathetic from the start of all this. Rowing with Naomi because I couldn't understand the intensity of her feelings, unable to control my motormouth because of a few drinks, and possibly misreading the enormity of the impact this has had on my mum. 'What a bloody mess,' he muttered under his breath.

'Mr Bailey? Can you come this way, please?'

Charlie followed the officer down a corridor that smelled vaguely of disinfectant to a small office at the end where DI Wilson was sat at a desk next to a man Charlie didn't recognise. His mum, looking confused and frightened, sat opposite.

'Mum,' Charlie said, 'are you all right?'

'Yes,' she said, quietly.

'Mr Bailey, we've questioned your mother regarding the disappearance of your daughter. We did ask her if she wanted a lawyer present, but she declined. We're satisfied with the answers she has given us so far and, having checked with the traffic police, they corroborate your mother's story about being held up in several traffic incidents, which would have delayed her arrival at her sister's house. The Devon police are on their way to Mrs Sheila Flaherty's house to confirm what time your mother arrived and to have a more thorough search of her property, if she is agreeable,' he said, checking the notes in front of him on the desk. 'If the timescale would make a detour to take Cassie elsewhere highly improbable, we are prepared to let your mother go for now. She has offered no explanation for the piece of pink fabric that forensics found in the boot of her car this morning. We are currently running tests to establish whether or not it is a piece of your daughter's jacket. As such, we may need to call her back in for further questioning. Do you understand this, Mrs Bailey?'

Hazel nodded.

'I'll go and check if the Devon police have been in contact with Mrs Flaherty yet. Please wait here.'

'Is it possible to have a few moments with my mother in private?' Charlie asked.

'I don't see why not.'

As soon as the two men had left the room, Charlie turned to his mum. 'You haven't done anything crazy have you, Mum? I know this business with me and Naomi has really upset you, but please tell me the police have got this all wrong.'

'Charlie, you know I absolutely adore Cassie. I would never do anything to hurt her. But she is my granddaughter and you are my son. The feelings you have for Cassie are the feelings I have for you. You are, and always will be, my priority. I would never knowingly do anything that would cause you pain. I hope that answers your question.'

'But what about the pink fabric? How did it get there?'

'I honestly don't know. All I can think is that at some point Cassie's coat was flung in the boot of my car and a piece of the lining, somewhere that went unnoticed by you and Naomi, got caught on something sharp.'

'But you told me last night that there was a moment after the accident when you thought the leaking brake fluid was blood. Why did you think that?'

'Like I said, I wondered if maybe she had climbed into the boot to shelter from the cold and got trapped in there. If I had taken her, do you really think that I would lock my granddaughter in a car boot when I could just as easily lay her down on the back seat? We both know she always falls asleep within minutes of the start of a car journey.'

Charlie breathed a sigh of relief. His mum's explanation seemed perfectly reasonable to him; now they just had to hope it would satisfy the police.

CHAPTER TWENTY-EIGHT

11.22 a.m. – Saturday

Two doors down, the interview being conducted by DCI Hart was also coming to a close. Jessica Toland had been quite cocky at first, denying any contact with Charlie and Naomi since their schooldays, but when the police officer had produced a printout of the text message and photograph that had been sent to Naomi, she had changed her story and her tone became more aggressive.

'All right, so I sent the text message to Naomi. What of it? I thought she had a right to know that her precious Charlie had been playing away.'

'And that was your only motivation? You were being considerate towards someone you have despised since you were all at school together? I find that hard to believe. Please remember that anything you say during this interview is being recorded and could be used at a later date if this matter should go to court.'

'Well then, no, that wasn't my reason for telling Naomi. That smug bitch had it coming to her. All the girls at school fancied Charlie, and he ends up with the pumpkin…'

'So it was a vindictive act on your part?'

'I suppose so.'

'And what were you hoping it would achieve?'

'I was hoping she'd kick him out for being a cheat. Job done, I'd say.'

'On the night in question, would it be fair to say that you deliberately plied Mr Bailey with alcoholic drinks in an attempt to get him drunk?'

'He's a grown man. He knows how to say no.'

'But he didn't say no because he was in an emotional state.'

'How would I know? I'm a barmaid, not a shrink.'

'It's my understanding that you engaged Mr Bailey in conversation once he'd had a few drinks, and that he confided in you that he and his wife were having problems conceiving a second child.'

'I don't remember.'

'You do remember that we're recording this?'

'Okay, so he told me his issues. It's not so unusual. We get drunks in the bar all the time wanting to share their life story.'

'And do you offer them all a lift home? Are you running a minicab business as well as working behind the bar?'

'Of course not, although I could use the money. Pete pays peanuts, and it turns out my wonderful, rich ex-husband had bought everything on credit. I'm skint, but then you probably already know that if you've been snooping around.'

'I'd prefer to call it conducting enquiries. So why did you offer Mr Bailey a lift?'

'Charlie and I are old school friends. I didn't want to be responsible for him getting mugged on the way home.'

'But instead of dropping him up the road at his house, you drove him across town to your house. Why was that?'

'Because the stupid bugger passed out before he could tell me his address. What was I supposed to do, guess where he lives?'

'Are you telling me you don't know where Mr and Mrs Bailey live?'

'That's right.'

'So when we get the CCTV camera footage from Beechwood Avenue, the red vehicle that was seen parked close to their home on several occasions won't be a match for the rented BMW that is currently being transported from Portsmouth to our police compound for investigation?'

There was a slight pause that didn't go unnoticed by Rachel Hart.

'You've confiscated my hire car? What for?'

'Like I said, it's part of our police investigation.'

'And my Fiat? Have you taken that too?'

'Not at the moment, but we may have cause to depending on how our investigation progresses. Back to my question: was it the red BMW you hired that was parked near the Baileys' house on Beechwood Avenue two nights ago?'

'Absolutely not. I'm not a stalker, you know.'

'So, you're not a psychiatrist, you're not a minicab driver and you're not a stalker. What exactly are you, Mrs Toland?'

'A barmaid who's getting pissed off with your questions. Have you finished with me yet?'

'Not quite. Did you know Mr and Mrs Bailey's first child is a daughter?'

'Yes. He told me all about her when he was pissed.'

'She is missing from home. She disappeared on one of the evenings that you failed to turn up for work. Were you responsible for her abduction?'

'You're kidding, right? That's something else I'm not, a child-snatcher. What would I want with a kid, anyway?'

'I don't know, Mrs Toland, but I believe yours was a childless marriage? Maybe that wasn't of your choosing?'

'That shows how little you know about me. I've been on the pill since I was sixteen. I have no desire to be a mother.'

'Then is it possible that you thought taking the child would lead to the total breakdown of the Baileys' shaky marriage, and that maybe Mr Bailey would turn to you for more than just a one-night stand?'

'That's crap, and you know it. I didn't take the kid. And as for wanting Mr Bailey, as you keep calling him, I'm not interested. He's not all that downstairs, if you get my drift. I couldn't get him a stiffy despite my best efforts. It nearly ruined the bloody photo. As far as I'm concerned, Mrs Bailey can keep her precious little Charlie – pun intended.'

'Interview concluded at 11.32 a.m.,' Rachel Hart said, pausing the recording equipment. 'You're free to go, Mrs Toland, but I would request that you remain in this area and make yourself available for further questioning if required. Please don't attempt to leave the country, as you are still very much part of a police investigation.'

Jessica scraped her chair back along the floor, muttering, 'Bloody police harassment.'

Rachel waited until she had left the room before turning to PC Drake.

'I want her movements tracked. I'm pretty sure she's involved in this somehow.'

'Then why did you let her go, Guv? Couldn't we have held her for further questioning?'

'We could, but I'm mindful that a young girl's life is at stake here. If Mrs Toland has got Cassie hidden away somewhere where she is exposed to the elements, it's highly likely that she wouldn't make it through another night if the temperatures drop below freezing. If there's the slightest chance that releasing Jessica leads us to finding Cassie, I'm prepared to take the risk.'

CHAPTER TWENTY-NINE

11.45 a.m. – Saturday

Jessica was breathing heavily when she left the police station, despite everything going as well as she could have hoped. She'd known that she would be a person of interest to the police as soon as it was revealed that she had been responsible for the breakdown of the Baileys' marriage. Failing to go in to work at the Golden Lion the previous evening had been a master stroke. It immediately cast suspicion on her and, exactly as expected, they had circulated her photograph to the airport and port authorities. When she handed her passport to the customs officer in Portsmouth, she had noticed a flicker of recognition in his eyes. He kept her talking by asking her questions about her trip: was it for business or pleasure? Who was she visiting in Spain? How long was she planning on staying? By the time he had finished, she was aware of two officers flanking her and was not surprised when they asked if she would accompany them to their office. She had been suitably outraged by their preventing her from leaving the country, and had sat sullen and silent in the back of the police car on the journey to Reading earlier that morning.

So far, there is only one thing I would have done differently, she thought. *I should have left collecting the second half of my payment for kidnapping Cassie until after the inevitable police interview. I didn't bank on them asking to search my bag, and I could hardly refuse as it would have aroused suspicion. Thank God they weren't that thorough. Explaining why I had fifteen grand hidden under the lining in the bottom of my bag would have been tough, even with my powers of invention.*

As she made her way towards the taxi rank at the station, Jessica once again reflected on her good fortune at having a brother living in Spain who had spent the whole of his adult life on the wrong side of the law. Without Joel's contacts, she would never have been able to source anyone who could produce fake documents. It was he who had put her in contact with the forger, Antonio, a few months previously when she had rung to ask for his help.

'I can't believe you're finally seeing sense and joining me in a life of crime,' he had said. 'What's the point of working all the hours God sends, getting paid peanuts and still having to pay tax, when you can live here with me on the Costa del Crime? Life's too short, sis.'

Jessica couldn't resist a smile. She and Joel had never been particularly close, but over the past few weeks, she had completely fooled him into thinking that she was intending to go and join him in Spain, when it couldn't be further from the truth. The police would also be pretty certain that she was intent on a new life at her brother's, after picking her up when she was about to board the ferry to Bilbao. When she disappeared again, Spain would be the first place they would look, and by the time they realised they were barking up the wrong tree, it would be too late.

It's a bonus that they didn't confiscate the Fiat. That will get me to London within an hour and then I can just dump the hateful little heap and head to the flat on public transport. Jessica could feel the increase in her pulse rate just thinking of seeing Antonio again, and they had only been apart for a few hours.

*

She had been instantly attracted to the Venezuelan the moment the door to his Gunnersbury flat had swung open. He was tall and dark, but not in a swarthy way, and his eyes were an intense shade of green. Before she had even stepped inside, clutching the envelope with the photographs needed to produce the fake documents, she had felt a fluttering in her chest that she hadn't experienced since Charlie had asked her out on a date all those years ago. Her former husband had been short, fat and twenty years older than her, but he had only ever been a means to an end. She wanted to live in the lap of luxury, and he had provided it, until he had admitted he was almost penniless after trying to keep her in the style she had grown accustomed to for almost ten years. When he had finally broken the news that he was going to file for bankruptcy, she had instantly countered that she was filing for divorce. For all those years, the only way she had been able to tolerate the touch of his pudgy, clammy hands pawing at her body was by picturing Charlie's face. If she had still been with her husband, she had a feeling that Charlie's image would have been replaced by this handsome South American.

After going through all the documents that she needed and agreeing on a price, Antonio had asked her if she was interested in art. She had shrugged non-committally, so he opened one of the doors leading off the living room and stood aside to let her pass. The walls were covered with paintings of nude or semi-nude women.

'I love painting beautiful women,' he had said, 'and you would make a perfect addition to my gallery.'

Within hours she was in his bed, and within days Jessica knew she had met the person she wanted to spend the rest of her life with, but not in a grotty flat in Gunnersbury. Lying together in the afterglow of sex one afternoon, she had asked him why he had come to England. He had told her about his hopes of gaining recognition for his paintings in Europe and how, when that hadn't happened, he had turned to forgery to pay the rent and keep food on the table. 'But,' he had said, 'things are looking up. Some of my early works are now selling for good prices at home. I was thinking of jumping bail and going back. Why don't you come with me?'

That was when they had come up with the plan to make the extra money they would need to buy a small art gallery in Caracas. They would be at least ten thousand pounds better off and possibly twenty, on top of the thirty grand payment for taking Cassie, if both of their targets fell for it. Best of all, if the police did finally unravel the ins and outs of Cassie's disappearance, they wouldn't be able to touch them in Venezuela, as it had no extradition treaty with the UK.

*

As Jessica got into the back of the cab to take her home to pick up the Fiat, there was one tiny seed of doubt niggling at the back of her mind. It was something Antonio had said to her the previous afternoon as she was leaving to pick up the money before driving to Portsmouth.

'How do you know you can trust that woman? What if she tips the police off and they are waiting at your house for you instead of the money?'

It had made her nervous collecting the package from under the front passenger seat of the Fiat, but it had all passed off without a hitch. Yet it had played on her mind, and she had made what she now realised was a mistake by dialling Charlie's number from her own mobile rather than the pay-as-you-go phone that was back at the Gunnersbury flat, with the intention of bringing the plan forward by a day. It had been a hell of a shock when a woman answered his phone.

'Forty-seven Pemberton Road, please,' Jessica said. She could sense the driver's gaze on her through his rear-view mirror, so she fiddled around in her bag with her head down. The last thing she wanted to do was strike up a conversation with a nosy cab driver. She pulled out her phone and pretended to make a call, throwing in the occasional, 'really?' and 'you're kidding' for authenticity, while keeping her gaze firmly out of the window.

When they arrived at her house, she paid the driver with a £20 note and while he was rooting around for change, she pushed the phone firmly into the gap between the seat and the seat back. *If they're planning on keeping tabs on my whereabouts by using the GPS on my phone, they'll think I've done as asked and stayed in the Reading area. Following a load of taxi journeys should keep them pretty busy before they realise my phone and I have parted company,* she thought, smiling to herself.

CHAPTER THIRTY

11.46 a.m. – Saturday

'Naomi? Can you still hear me? Why don't you come out of there and I'll make you a nice cup of tea, or coffee if you'd rather?' Kate added hastily, remembering the outburst from the previous day. She had been sat at the top of the stairs, outside the bathroom door, trying to coax Naomi to come out since she had arrived at the Baileys' house more than two hours ago.

'Go away. I already told you I don't want to talk to anyone.'

'You'll have to come out sometime.'

'Why? I might just stay in here until I die,' Naomi said, the utter desperation of her situation evident in her voice.

'Don't be silly. You're only saying that because you're upset.'

'I've every right to be upset. Just when I thought Charlie and I were making up, it turns out that he and his mum planned this whole thing. I don't know who to trust any more.'

'You can trust me, Naomi. We're like sisters, you and me. Come on, open up.'

There were a few moments of silence and then Kate heard a shuffling noise before the bolt was pulled back on the door.

'Don't look at me, Kate,' Naomi said between sniffs, 'I know I look terrible.'

'It doesn't matter to me what you look like,' Kate said, although she couldn't help noticing her friend's appearance. Her cheeks seemed to have sunk into her face and her eyes, already shadowed with dark circles due to lack of sleep, were swollen and red-rimmed. 'Do you want to go back to bed and I'll bring you a hot drink up, or do you want to come downstairs?'

Naomi shrugged.

'Let's go downstairs. What shall I get you to drink?'

'I don't really care so long as it's not sweet tea.'

'Maybe try a chamomile if you've got any. It's supposed to be soothing and calming.'

'I think it's going to take more than that, although at the moment I haven't got the energy to be anything but calm. I feel beaten, Kate. It feels as though the universe has got it in for me for some reason, and won't let up hurting me until I curl up and die.'

'Don't keep talking about dying, it's not healthy. You'll get through this even if you have to have a little help from the doctor.'

'What do you mean?'

'Well, I know you don't like taking medication, but I was wondering whether you should think about taking some antidepressants or something. You've had two huge shocks in such a short space of time, anybody would be struggling to cope.'

'You could be right. There are times over the past five weeks when I've wanted to walk over to the canal and throw myself in. The only thing stopping me was Cassie, and now I haven't got her there's no reason not to.'

'You're doing it again.'

'What?'

'Talking about dying.'

'Well, no one would miss me if I was gone. Since Mum and Dad's accident, I've only had you, Charlie, Hazel and Cassie, and now it's down to just you, and I'm not sure you'd miss me that much after the burden I've been lately.'

'You're talking absolute nonsense, of course I'd miss you. You don't know for certain that Hazel and Charlie had anything to do with Cassie's disappearance, and I'm sure the police will find her now they have the sniffer dogs out. It's only been a day and a half, and if she's locked in somewhere out of the cold, she'll be fine. Hungry and thirsty and probably pretty scared, but she'll be fine. What she will need is her mum firing on all cylinders, so you should give some serious thought to what I said about getting some medication to help you be there for Cassie when you get her back. Here, drink this,' Kate said, sliding the mug across the table, 'while I clear up that mess. What happened?'

'I threw my mug at Charlie.'

Kate raised her eyebrows.

'I just lost it. I was so angry at the thought of him and his mum taking Cassie away from me. She's my world.'

'She's Charlie's world too, you know. Not being able to see her has been killing him. Did you know he's been to see a solicitor regarding access?'

'No, I didn't. Why should he have access to her after what he did?'

'Because he's her dad, and Cassie must miss him terribly. Does she ask about him?'

'Sometimes. I've overheard her telling Pumpkin not to worry about her daddy being away because he'll be home soon. Oh God, what have I done? If I'd given Charlie the chance to explain himself instead of reacting the way I did, none of this would have happened. It's all my fault… all of it.'

'Stop being so hard on yourself. I've no idea what I would do if I found out Alan had been sleeping with someone else,' Kate said, sweeping pieces of broken crockery from the dustpan into the bin. *Probably celebrate, and wait for the big fat divorce settlement*, she added silently.

Unlike Charlie and Naomi's relationship, Kate's was not a happy marriage, and even her boys brought her little pleasure. What she would have liked was a daughter like Cassie to buy pretty clothes for and take to ballet class, but that wasn't going to happen now that Alan had secretly had the snip. *Selfish bastard*, she thought, scrubbing at the chocolatey stain on the wall with renewed vigour. *But I suppose it's no surprise he doesn't want any more children. He knows I don't love him, and he probably knows I never have.*

'Thanks, Kate. I wish I was more like you. You always seem to be able to see both sides of the story. When Charlie gets back, I promise I'll give him a chance to explain what went on at the police station, and I won't throw any more cups around.'

'That's more like it. Now, why don't you go and have a shower and get dressed? It will make you feel better.'

'I think I will, not that any of my clothes fit me any more, they're all hanging off me.'

'Right, so when you come down, I'll have some cheese on toast ready for you.'

'Our favourite. I remember your mum always used to make it when I came round to your house after school for tea.'

'Yes, we used to sit on my bed listening to music, trying not to drop crumbs, with Daisy walking backward and forward across our legs, wanting a treat.'

'She was such a funny cat. Which reminds me, have you seen Pumpkin this morning?'

'Not since I fed him just before Charlie got here. He's probably over on the field checking out the bonfire, you know how inquisitive he is.'

CHAPTER THIRTY-ONE

12.35 p.m. – Saturday

After dropping his mum back at her house, Charlie walked round to Beechwood Avenue. He decided against letting himself in, reasoning that he didn't want to upset Naomi again, if in fact she had calmed down after her outburst that morning. He rang the bell and waited, exchanging pleasantries with the young constable on the doorstep. The remnants of the shattered pumpkin had been swept to the side of the small front garden, underneath the camellia bushes with their shiny evergreen leaves. There was rain in the air again, which meant the temperature was milder, but that was of little consequence now that the police believed Cassie was not out in the open.

Before leaving the police station, Charlie had been called into DCI Hart's office.

'Take a seat, Charlie. I wanted to talk to you about the possibility of doing a press conference with you and Naomi this afternoon.'

'I'm not sure whether that will be possible. She had a bit of a meltdown this morning after you guys arrested my mum. She got it into her head that we'd conspired to hide Cassie away somewhere. After screaming and shouting at me, she locked herself in the bathroom and she was still there when I left to come here. If she's in that frame of mind, I don't think she would want to be in the same room as me.'

'It was unfortunate that we had to bring your mum in for questioning, but we wouldn't be doing our job properly if we didn't follow up on all leads. The interview with Jessica Toland was inconclusive. I think we need to release the news of Cassie's disappearance to the press today. The sniffer dogs didn't come up with anything definite, but after leaving your house as though they were hot on Cassie's trail, they stopped and barked a little way along the street.'

'What do you think that means?' Charlie asked, fear evident in his voice.

DCI Hart's response was measured. 'I don't want to speculate, but I think the appeal should be for any witnesses to come forward who may have seen a child fitting Cassie's description being bundled into a car.'

It was the stuff of nightmares. Someone had his little girl and could be doing unspeakable things to her at that very moment.

'Perhaps if you ring the house and speak to Kate, she'll be able to tell you whether or not Naomi is up to doing an appeal. If not, is it something I can do on my own? It feels like we've wasted precious time questioning Mum and Jessica when we could have appealed for witnesses earlier.'

'I know it must be very frustrating for you, Charlie, but trust me, once this gets out, we will receive all sorts of false information. Some of it will be malicious and some will be from genuine callers who think they've seen something they haven't. It takes a lot of manpower to answer all the phone calls we'll get from all over the country. There will no doubt be positive sightings in Manchester, Edinburgh, Norfolk, you name it, and probably none of them will turn out to be Cassie. But, and it's a big but, it could lead to that one piece of information that will get your daughter back alive.'

Rachel knew only too well how vitally important that one piece of information from a witness who had seen something out of the ordinary could be. She could still visualise the look of relief and gratitude on the faces of her parents when they arrived at the hospital to find her unharmed. *Maybe physically unharmed, but the mental scars live on forever*, she thought, closing her eyes momentarily before continuing.

'So, to answer your question, it would be better to have you both there, particularly as the general public always seem to empathise with and respond better to a grieving mother, but if Naomi can't or won't do it, then you alone would be preferable to not doing it at all. As you suggest, I'll ring the house now to assess the situation while you take your mother home.'

Charlie had been at the front door for several minutes before it was finally opened by Kate.

'Sorry,' she said, letting him past her, 'Naomi was in the shower when DCI Hart rang. I was just upstairs explaining to her what the police want to do this afternoon. She's a bit shaky after this morning's histrionics, but she says she wants to do it, so I need to call back to give the go-ahead. I was going to make Naomi some cheese on toast, but maybe you could do it now that you're here, to try and get back in her good books?'

'How has she been?'

'Up and down, to be honest. I suggested that maybe she needs to see a doctor to try and get her mood swings under control.'

'How did she react?'

'Let's just say she didn't object. I think she knows she can't go on like this, Charlie, or she'll make herself really sick. I'll ring the detective chief inspector back, call Naomi down and then I'll head home if you don't mind, to give Alan a break. Three boys under ten can be very hard work when you're not used to it, and he's probably been giving them loads of sugary treats to keep them quiet. They're going to be hyper at the bonfire tonight.'

'Is that tonight? I've completely lost track of time. How things have changed since we all went last year.'

'I feel a bit bad about going when you guys have got all this stuff going on, but the boys have been really looking forward to it and I didn't want to let them down, especially as I'm away for a few days next week.'

'Don't be silly, of course you should go to the bonfire, you've got your own family to take care of and they've barely seen you over the past two days. Are you going anywhere nice?'

'Not really. Alan volunteered me to house-sit for one of his work colleagues who has a couple of cats that won't go into a cattery while he's away. He said I've earned a break from him and the boys.'

'It's a good job you've had some practice with Pumpkin.'

'True, but a spa day would have been more to my taste, if I'm honest.'

Charlie was putting the cheese on toast under the grill when he became aware of someone standing in the doorway behind him. He could smell 'The One', his wife's fragrance, but decided not to turn and face her, hoping that she would be the first to speak.

After a few moments, she said, 'I'm sorry about this morning. I – I don't know what came over me.'

'Let's not talk about it.'

'I want to. I'm sorry I doubted you, and Hazel. Kate told me that the police were satisfied with Hazel's explanation about why the piece of pink fabric was in the boot of her car. It makes perfect sense. We always put all our coats in there when we're going out together. This whole business is really messing with my head. Kate thinks I should see someone. What do you think?'

'I think we should have our lunch and get this afternoon over with first, and then if you still feel like talking things through, we can do it tonight.'

'That sounds like a plan, although I was wondering if your mum might like to come round rather than sitting at home alone.'

'Do you mean that?'

'Yes. I've been pretty awful to her, and I honestly didn't mean to be. I was so wrapped up in feeling mad at you and sorry for myself, I didn't give a thought to how not seeing Cassie might be affecting her. Do you think she would come?'

'Like a shot, but she'll have to come quite early. She won't leave Alfie on his own with fireworks going off, so she'd want to bring him and get here before the display starts.'

'I'd forgotten that was tonight. We'll need to get Pumpkin in too. You remember how terrified he was even of our sparklers last year. He hasn't been in the house at all today. I wonder where he can have got to?'

'Someone else's kitchen, probably. Whoa, only just caught it before the cheese started to burn. I must be losing my touch,' Charlie said, concentrating on pulling the pan out from beneath the grill, all thoughts of Pumpkin instantly forgotten.

CHAPTER THIRTY-TWO

3.30 p.m. – Saturday

Charlie and Naomi arrived at the police station at half past three, with the press conference scheduled for 4 p.m. They were met by DI Wilson and taken into the same office where Hazel had been interviewed earlier that day.

'If you'll hang on here for a few moments, DCI Hart will be with you shortly. We've just received some new evidence regarding Mrs Toland that I believe she wants to talk to you about, Mr Bailey, prior to the press conference.'

'What evidence?'

'I'm not at liberty to say. The detective chief inspector will be able to fill you in.'

'Please tell me you haven't been keeping anything from me, Charlie. I don't think I can cope with any more nasty surprises.'

'I have no idea what it could be, I promise. You are going to have to start trusting me again.'

'I'm trying, Charlie, really I am.'

'Ah, Mr and Mrs Bailey, thank you for agreeing to come down to the station to do this,' Rachel Hart said, sweeping into the room. 'I always think it's better to do this type of thing somewhere official, if possible. I think the general public believe that guilty people steer clear of police stations, so they tend to believe what they are being told if it's in this kind of environment.'

'Why wouldn't they believe us?' Naomi said. 'Nobody would lie about a thing like this.'

'You'd be surprised. Before we go through, I've got a new development I wanted to ask you about, Mr Bailey.'

'Go ahead, I've got nothing to hide.'

'Yesterday afternoon, when we were waiting for your mother to call us back, there was a call to your mobile phone which I answered, believing it to be her. The person on the other end of the line hung up after hearing my voice, which I thought was quite suspicious. I asked DI Wilson to check it out and we've now traced the number that called you. It was Jessica Toland.'

'What?'

'Can you think of any reason why she would have called you yesterday?'

'Of course not. How would she even have my number?'

'Well, obviously she had your number, and Naomi's, because she sent you both text messages. I couldn't put my finger on it yesterday because I was so focused on making the best decisions around trying to find Cassie, but when I got home last night something was bugging me and that was when I remembered the texts. How did she get your mobile phone numbers? Did you give them to her, Mr Bailey, or could she have gained access to them from your phone while you were passed out in her bed?'

Naomi stiffened.

Charlie glared at the police officer. *Why did she have to mention him being in Jessica's bed? She knew how fragile Naomi was; the slightest little thing could trigger another emotional outburst, and that wouldn't be very helpful just before the witness appeal.*

'I have a security code,' he said through gritted teeth. 'I often leave my phone on the desk at work, and I wouldn't want people having access to my private messages and emails. That woman couldn't possibly know my code, and I certainly didn't give her our numbers.'

'Which leads me back to how she got hold of them? Any thoughts?'

'I have no idea. Why don't you ask her?'

'Oh, we will, as soon as we can trace her.'

Rachel was annoyed with herself for not guessing that someone as smart as Jessica would realise that the police could track her movements with the GPS signal on her mobile phone. She had assigned Eleanor Drake to the job of keeping tabs on her, and it hadn't taken long for the young PC to voice her suspicions that all was not as it seemed after more than a dozen short journeys were registered within the Reading area in under two hours. The traffic police had pulled the taxi over as requested, much to the driver's annoyance, and recovered Jessica's phone from where she had hidden it down the back of the seat a couple of hours previously. Once they knew they had been wrong-footed, PC Drake was sent to Jessica's house where she found the garage doors open and the Fiat 500 missing. It was discovered an hour later on double yellow lines in front of a shopping arcade in Richmond, where it had been clamped. *Was my decision to let Jessica go the right one, when I could have held her without charge for up to twenty-four hours?* Rachel wondered.

'I thought you had her here for questioning?' Charlie said.

'We did, but there wasn't enough evidence to hold her.'

As the finger of suspicion was once again pointing in Charlie's direction, following his inability to explain why Jessica might have been calling him the previous afternoon, Rachel chose not to divulge that they had now received the all-important CCTV footage. The camera on the corner of Beechwood Avenue had malfunctioned or, as she suspected, had been tampered with, which was why there had been such a delay. Two of her officers were currently going through the footage from other cameras in the area from around the time Hazel had seen the speeding car.

We need to chase the car hire company again to confirm it was Jessica's name on the rental agreement. Everything has to be done by

the book so that we can bring her back in for further questioning
without being accused of police harassment. How long can it possibly
take to check details on a computer? I should have put Eleanor Drake
on it. I bet she would have had answers by now.

When Rachel had arrived for work that morning, shortly after
9.30 a.m., there had been a note on her desk from the young
constable with a detailed breakdown on the sale of Jessica's house.
Exchange of contracts had taken place three weeks previously and
the completion date was just days away. Again, she was reminded
of the thoroughness of her younger self when she had joined the
police force after finishing her degree in psychology, fuelled by
her desire to catch the bad guys.

Everything pointed to Jessica embarking on a new life in Spain,
but what had prompted the sudden desire for a change of lifestyle?
Was it just the divorce from her husband, or did she need to start
afresh somewhere where no one knew her because she would have
a young child in tow? Following the discovery that Jessica had
tried to call Charlie the previous evening, Rachel was forced to
consider the possibility that he had removed his daughter from
her bed and was planning a new life with his mistress. But if that
was the case, where was the little girl now? At the moment, there
were far more questions than answers, and time was running out.

CHAPTER THIRTY-THREE

4 p.m. – Saturday

There was a low hum of chatter as DCI Hart entered the room that had been set aside for the press conference. Half a dozen television news crews had their cameras trained on the raised area at the front of the room, where a table was set up with microphones and two chairs behind it. There were also around twenty print journalists, some with notebook and pen, and others with their mobile recording equipment set to capture every word of the press conference along with still photographs. Rachel raised her hands and the room fell silent.

'Thank you all for coming at such short notice. As you know, a young girl is missing from her home and we need your help in trying to find her. Her name is Cassie Bailey and she's five years old. As yet the exact time of her disappearance is unclear, but we do know it was after 9 p.m. on Thursday night and before 7.30 a.m. on Friday morning. Despite an intensive search of the area surrounding her home using police tracker dogs, we have been unable to locate her. At the time she went missing it is believed she was wearing a bright pink Puffa jacket over her pyjamas and pink-and-white spotted wellington boots. You should all have been given a photograph of Cassie along with our official police statement when you entered the room. Her parents, Naomi and Charlie Bailey, are going to appeal for witnesses, but I would request that you do not ask them any questions as I'm sure you can appreciate that this is a very distressing time for them.'

There was a mumbling among the gathered journalists.

'If you do have any questions, please direct them to me or my DI at the end of the appeal.'

Rachel moved to stand at one side of the table. Naomi and Charlie were ushered into the room by DI Wilson before he took up his position at the other side of the table and the couple sat down in the chairs between them. There was a lot of shutter-clicking as the gathered press took photographs to accompany their front-page story, and then total silence as Naomi, her face as white as the sheet of paper in her hands, began to read.

'On Thursday evening, after her bath, I read my daughter, Cassie, a bedtime story and turned her light off at around half past eight. When I went to wake her on Friday morning to get her ready for school, she wasn't in her bed. At first I didn't worry too much as she sometimes wakes up in the night and goes downstairs to curl up on the sofa with our cat, but she wasn't there either. I checked the back garden and searched the rest of the house, but I couldn't find her. That's when I noticed the key was in the front door, and when I tried the handle it was unlocked.' Naomi's voice started to tremble and tears began to roll down her cheeks. 'She'd gone, my beautiful little girl had gone.'

Charlie put his hand over his wife's hand as she let the piece of paper she had been reading from drop to the table. He continued, 'We'd like to ask anyone who was in the area of our home on Beechwood Avenue to come forward if they saw anything even remotely suspicious. Perhaps a person or people hanging around late on Thursday evening, or maybe a car stopping for a few moments before speeding off. If our daughter was taken in a vehicle, she could be anywhere by now.' Charlie swallowed hard. 'Please take a good look at the photo of her and let your local police force know if you think you've seen her, or respond to the incident number or email address. Please help us get our little girl back. She's our world.'

As Charlie put his arm around his wife's shoulders and ushered her out of the room, Rachel overheard a male journalist say to a colleague, 'Who's your money on? I reckon it was the wife, she looks unhinged.'

'No, the dad looks shifty to me,' she replied.

Rachel raised her eyebrows in Graham's direction, and he responded by shaking his head. She shot the journalists a withering look, but found herself unable to completely dismiss their opinions.

'Any questions?' she asked, and was immediately bombarded.

CHAPTER THIRTY-FOUR

4.55 p.m. – Saturday

Naomi had barely spoken a word on their journey back from the police station. Once they were in the house, she excused herself, saying she needed to have a lie-down.

'Can you give Pumpkin another call, please?' she asked Charlie, disappearing into her bedroom and closing the door firmly behind her. Having started to believe Charlie's version of events, she was now in turmoil once again. Why had Jessica tried to ring her husband the previous evening if, as both Charlie and Kate had maintained, he'd had nothing to do with her since the night of the argument? And, although she hadn't thought about it previously, how had Jessica got her mobile phone number? *Charlie must have given it to her, but why?* Naomi's doubts concerning her whole marriage were returning. She lay on her back, eyes wide open, staring up at the ceiling that she and Charlie had painted. He had done the majority of it with the paint roller and she had done the cutting in, the neat line where the edges joined the walls, with a half-inch angled brush. They had always done everything as a team, but now she had to face the possibility that Charlie had been acting, waiting for an opportunity to move on to the life he really wanted. Naomi didn't want to believe it, but she simply didn't know any more.

She turned onto her side and hugged her knees to her chest, curling herself into a foetal position. *Will I ever fully trust him again?*

How on earth are we going to move on from this? A sob caught in her throat, but she forced it down, trying to breathe deeply and stay calm. *If only Mum was still alive, I could ask her what I should do, but she's gone; I've got no one. Charlie was always the first person I turned to in a crisis*, she thought, reaching for a crumpled tissue on the bedside table to wipe her eyes. Next to it was her mobile phone. She picked it up and selected Kate's home number. After several rings, it went to voicemail.

'Hi, you've reached Kate and Alan. I'm sorry we can't take your call at the moment, but leave a message and we'll get back to you as soon as possible.'

'Kate… it's Naomi, are you there?'

She waited for a few moments, hoping that her friend would pick up. She didn't. She disconnected the call but before she had time to put her phone back on the bedside table, it rang.

'Sorry, Noms, I was just putting a casserole in the oven for after the firework display. Are you okay? Well, when I say okay, I mean… well, you know what I mean.'

'I just needed to hear a friendly voice, Kate.'

'Isn't Charlie with you?'

'He's downstairs.' Naomi paused. 'I'm not sure I trust him, Kate.'

'What makes you say that?'

'Before we did the appeal, the police inspector asked Charlie why Jessica would be ringing him last night?'

There was a sharp intake of breath from the other end of the phone line.

'She's got a bloody nerve. What did he say?'

'He said he had no idea, but I don't know if I believe him. You told me they haven't been in contact since that night. I just wanted to check that you weren't lying to me to protect me.'

'Well, I'm only going by what Charlie told me. Obviously, I have no way of knowing if he was telling the truth, but I assumed he was because he seemed to be so upset about losing you. I wonder why she was ringing him?'

'Precisely. Do you think maybe she took Cassie? Perhaps they are planning on running away together. The police are trying to track her down so they can bring her in for questioning again.'

'Again?'

'Yes. Didn't Charlie tell you? They found her last night, about to get on a ferry to Spain, so they brought her back to Reading this morning for questioning.'

'And she didn't have Cassie with her?'

'No. But maybe she has hidden her somewhere and the plan was for Charlie to pick her up before joining Jessica in Spain.'

'I think you're letting your imagination get the better of you. You're stressed because of what you're going through, under-standably, but I doubt Jessica or Charlie has anything to do with Cassie's disappearance. I watched the press conference and he was very convincing... you both were,' she added quickly. 'Have you mentioned any of this to him?'

'No.'

'Well, don't. He's already starting to think you're going a little crazy, I wouldn't give him any more ammunition if I were you.'

'He's not the only one who thinks I'm going crazy, Kate. I'm not sure how much more of this I can take. I feel like I'm teetering on the edge of an abyss. In a strange way, I hope the two of them have cooked all this up together. At least then I could be sure Cassie is safe. Charlie would never do anything to hurt her. He loves her so utterly and completely – he loves her more than he loves me, I think.'

'That's rubbish and you know it. He loves both his girls, and would do anything for you. I would keep these thoughts between us two, at least until after the police have questioned Jessica.'

'Okay.'

'Promise?'

'Brownie's honour.'

'Let me know when they find Jessica. It will be interesting to hear why she was bothering Charlie when his little girl had just gone missing.'

'In fairness, she wouldn't have known that.'

'No, of course not. Sorry, Noms, but I'm going to have to go and get the boys ready for the bonfire party and the fireworks display. Try not to get yourself into too much of a state. When they find Cassie, she'll need her mummy to be strong.'

'Have a good time,' Naomi said, but Kate had already ended the call.

There was a light knock on the door before Charlie opened it.

'I thought I heard voices,' he said.

'I was speaking to Kate on the phone.'

'Oh?'

'Telling her to enjoy the fireworks.'

'Right. It's gone five, and Mum will be here soon. I was rummaging through the fridge and you don't seem to have much in, but I found some potatoes in the vegetable basket. I thought maybe we could have jackets with grated cheese if you fancy?'

'I'm not really hungry, but you go ahead and do them for you and your mum.'

'I'll put an extra one in for you in case you change your mind.'

'Okay,' Naomi said, wondering why they were having a conversation about baked potatoes when what she really wanted to ask him was why Jessica had called him the previous evening.

'That sounds like Mum now. I'll go and let her in. You come down when you're ready,' Charlie said, smiling at his wife encouragingly as he pulled the door closed behind him.

CHAPTER THIRTY-FIVE

5.25 p.m. – Saturday

Naomi could hear the low mumble of voices as she made her way silently down the stairs a few minutes later. She had intended to stand outside the lounge door and listen to Charlie and Hazel's conversation for a few moments, but Alfie was having none of it. She could hear him whining and jumping up at the door, his thick claws clattering down the paintwork, and she could imagine his long tail wagging manically from side to side, endangering any delicate objects in the vicinity. *If only people were as uncomplicated as animals*, she thought, pushing the door open and succumbing to a face wash from his lolling tongue.

'Alfie, get down,' Hazel said sharply.

The dog responded by leaning back on his haunches, his bottom in the air with his tail still wagging furiously and his front paws outstretched.

'Come here, Alfie. Let Naomi into the room. I'm sorry, love, he's just so excited to see you after all these weeks,' she added, as Alfie obediently retreated from the doorway and settled on the floor next to the armchair where Hazel was sitting.

Naomi noticed the warning look that Charlie shot in his mother's direction.

'How are you, Hazel?' She'd never felt comfortable calling Charlie's mother 'Mum'.

'Well, worried sick, like you two must be, if I'm honest.'

And she looks it, Naomi thought. Hazel's normally ruddy complexion had a hint of grey to it and she had huge dark circles under her eyes that clearly weren't only the result of her long day of driving.

'I'm glad you agreed to come. I wanted to say I'm very sorry for not letting you see Cassie these past few weeks. I thought I was doing the right thing for her, but I didn't take anyone else's feelings into consideration. It was selfish and thoughtless of me,' Naomi said, her words tumbling out, so anxious was she to get her apology off her chest.

There was an awkward pause.

Hazel, always one for speaking her mind, didn't respond. She couldn't bring herself to say everything was all right when, obviously, it wasn't.

Charlie stepped in to break the silence. 'I don't think we should discuss this now. When we've got Cassie back, we can all sit down and talk things through and try to put these past few weeks behind us. Let's just make tonight about breaking the ice and feeling comfortable in each other's company again. Agreed?'

'If that's what you think is for the best,' Naomi said, glancing over at Hazel, who nodded her agreement.

'I do. Now, I need to get those spuds in the oven. Do either of you want a hot drink? Tea for you, Mum?'

'I'll do the drinks,' Naomi offered. 'It will give me something to do. It's the waiting for news that's so excruciating. This past day and a half has felt like months. Time seems to have passed so slowly.'

'Have the police been in touch at all since the television appeal?' Hazel asked.

'Not yet, but it's only been an hour or so. DCI Hart did say they would be overwhelmed with calls from the public to begin with, and it would be a case of picking through all the information for anything relevant.'

There was a loud bang and Alfie immediately started barking.

'Here we go,' said Hazel, 'the worst night of the year for us pet owners. I'm not arguing about how pretty they are to look at, but do they have to make them so damn loud? Shush, boy, you're safe in here.'

'Did you get Pumpkin in?' Naomi said, casting a worried look at the old club chair where he would normally be curled up sleeping.

'No. I tried calling him just before I came up to the bedroom, but he didn't come. Like I said earlier, he's probably been accepting treats from one of the neighbours and they've gone over to watch the display on the field without realising that he's still in their house,' Charlie said, trying to reassure Naomi by making light of the situation. 'He'll saunter back in through his cat flap later on and settle down to clean himself, totally unaware of all the worry he's caused.'

'I hope you're right, he's terrified of fireworks,' Naomi said, gazing anxiously out of the window, mindful that if Cassie was trapped somewhere, unable to see the colourful explosions overhead, she would be very frightened too.

The official firework display had started at 6.30 p.m. and lasted for only half an hour, but the occasional swooshes and bangs from back garden celebrations had continued until almost 10 p.m., by which time Hazel felt it was quiet enough to head home with Alfie.

'I'll walk you back, Mum, in case there are any rogue fireworks and Alfie gets spooked. I'm not sure you're strong enough to hang onto him with your dodgy wrists.'

Hazel didn't protest.

'I'll come too,' Naomi said. 'I feel like a prisoner in this house at the moment. The walk will do me good. Do I need my brolly?'

Charlie opened the front door, nodding a greeting in the direction of the police constable who turned to see who was leaving the house. The acrid smell of gunpowder hung in the air.

'It looks like it's stopped raining, but I think a scarf would be a good idea to put across your mouth. You too, Mum, all this smoke will tickle your throat and make you cough. It always lingers longer when the air is damp and still.'

After they'd said their goodbyes to Hazel and Alfie, Charlie suggested going to the field on their way back home to call Pumpkin.

'If he's been outside with all this racket going on, he'll probably respond better to hearing your voice than mine.'

'True. We all know he prefers me to you.'

'Only because you usually feed him.'

'And brush him and clean out his litter tray.'

'Fair point.'

Charlie looped his arm through Naomi's, grateful for a sense of normality between them for however short a period of time it might last, and the pair trudged onto the field, their feet sinking in the squelchy mud. The towering bonfire, hastily rebuilt following its dismantling the previous day, had burnt out but was still smouldering, a wisp of smoke rising from its centre. The area was deserted after the earlier merrymaking.

'What are you thinking?' Charlie asked.

'I was just remembering last year. We had such a good time with Kate and Alan and the boys, watching the fireworks and eating toffee apples and marshmallows toasted on the fire. Cassie will be sad she's missed this. We'll have to make it up to her next year.'

Charlie slid his hand down his wife's arm and squeezed her gloved hand.

'Maybe we can go on holiday somewhere at New Year and she can watch a firework display there to make up for it.'

'I hope she wasn't frightened.'

'She's a tough little cookie. She wouldn't let a few fireworks scare her.'

'But if she couldn't see them, only hear them, she may not have realised what it was. I can't bear to think of her alone and scared.'

I'd rather think of her alone and scared than consider the alternatives, Charlie thought, squeezing his wife's hand even tighter.

They had reached the bonfire, and Naomi rested her head against Charlie's chest. 'You are telling me the truth about you and Jessica, aren't you, Charlie?'

'Yes,' he said, gently raising her chin so he could look into her eyes. 'You are the only girl I've ever loved. What we have is special. I can't believe I almost lost you.'

He leaned forward, intending to kiss her gently on the lips, but Naomi dropped her head forward, so he only made contact with her hair. He felt her body stiffen.

'What's that?' she said, pointing towards the bottom of the bonfire.

Charlie's eyes followed to where her finger was indicating. He squinted, trying to see through the dark and the lingering smoke. It was something green and sparkly. A sick feeling started in the pit of his stomach.

'Is it what I think it is?' Naomi said, a hint of hysteria creeping into her voice. 'It is, isn't it?' she said, letting go of Charlie's hand and moving towards the smouldering fire.

Charlie grabbed her shoulder. 'Don't go any closer. The whole lot could come toppling down and bury you. Let me find a stick to reach for it.'

Naomi began shaking violently while Charlie searched frantically around for a piece of stick long enough to reach into the base of the bonfire. He was already pretty sure what it was but hoped against hope that he was wrong.

'This should do it,' he said, trying to keep his voice calm while edging closer to the bonfire. After a couple of attempts, and at full stretch without getting too close, he managed to drag the green object along the ground with the end of his stick and retrieve it.

It was badly burnt, only the area around the buckle surviving, but there was no mistaking that it was the remains of an animal collar. Pumpkin's collar.

Naomi screamed, a shrill, primeval sound that cut through the night air, before she sank to her knees sobbing hysterically.

'No, no, no,' she wailed.

Oh God, why is this happening? Charlie thought. He took the still-warm piece of Pumpkin's collar and shoved it in his pocket, his eyes straining to see if he could see the charred remains of their family pet, before realising that even with some of his nine lives intact, there was no way Pumpkin could have survived that inferno. Charlie tried to haul Naomi to her feet, but she just kept collapsing like a rag doll. He gently lifted her slight frame and started walking back across the field. Her crying had stopped, but she was shaking so hard that Charlie could hear her teeth chattering. He had no idea what to say to try and console her.

Suddenly, a bright light temporarily blinded him.

'Who's there,' he asked, staggering backward a couple of steps.

'It's PC Walsh. I heard a scream. What's going on here?'

'It's me, Charlie Bailey. My wife needs help. I think we've just discovered our cat burnt to death in the bonfire.'

CHAPTER THIRTY-SIX

11.45 p.m. – Saturday

'I've given Mrs Bailey a sedative,' Dr Moss said, pulling the bedroom door closed behind him. 'She's sleeping now, and will probably be out for several hours. Honestly? I would rather have her in the hospital for observation, but if she insists on staying here you must make sure she gets total bed rest. Is that clear?'

'Yes, yes of course. It's just that with our daughter missing, Naomi wants to be here in case she should find her way home. She would never forgive herself if she wasn't here to comfort Cassie.'

'That's understandable. But she is in a very fragile state. She'll need a member of the medical profession with her if it turns out to be bad news about Cassie.'

Charlie caught his breath.

'I'm sorry, I didn't mean that to sound so brutal,' Dr Moss said, placing his hand on Charlie's forearm. 'It goes without saying that I hope you and your wife get your daughter back unharmed. The injection I've given her should see her sleeping through until seven or eight in the morning, but I would suggest someone sitting with her to be on the safe side. I've written the dosage she is to have on the prescription, but basically, it's just a case of making sure she has the tablets every four to five hours throughout the day with food.'

'How long will she need to stay on them for? She hates taking any kind of pills,' Charlie said, looking down at the instructions he had been handed.

'It's difficult to say, and it really does depend on the outcome concerning your daughter. I've given you enough for the next three days, and I'll come back to see her on Tuesday morning unless circumstances change in the meantime.'

'Thank you, doctor.'

'One more thing. I saw Mrs Bailey a few weeks ago when she was concerned about your daughter's disturbed sleep pattern. I told her not to be unduly concerned, and that it was probably down to the change in living arrangements and should soon settle down.'

Charlie felt a flush of embarrassment colouring his cheeks.

'I notice that she has lost a lot of weight in the interim period. You need to try and make her eat. She's very thin and weak, which won't help her recovery.'

'I'll try, doctor, but neither of us have felt much like eating.'

'I understand, but for Mrs Bailey it's essential that she has proper meals. The drugs I've prescribed are powerful and can cause unpleasant side effects if taken on an empty stomach.'

'I'll do my best,' Charlie said. 'My mum might be able to tempt her with some of her favourite dishes.'

'Good. And make sure you eat when she does,' the doctor added, 'to give her some encouragement.'

'Thanks again for coming out to see Naomi, Dr Moss. When I said I was going to call an ambulance, she really freaked out.'

'It was my turn to be on call tonight, and for once there weren't many minor casualties to deal with pertaining to fireworks and bonfires.'

At least, not human ones, Charlie thought as he closed the front door. *Poor old Pumpkin, what a horrible way to end his life.*

He wandered through to the kitchen and flicked the switch on the kettle. He would need a few black coffees if he was going to stay awake all night. Before he had a chance to add the boiling water to the coffee granules in the bottom of his mug, his mobile phone started to ring in his coat pocket. He glanced at the kitchen clock.

It was almost midnight. *Who on earth would be ringing at this time of night?* He hurried out to the hallway to answer his phone before the noise disturbed Naomi. It wasn't a number he recognised.

'Hello,' he snapped, half wondering if it was Jessica again.

'Mr Bailey? It's DI Wilson here. I'm sorry to disturb you so late, but DCI Hart asked me to call you to let you know we located Jessica Toland. She checked into a Travelodge near Heathrow, which suggests she may have been planning to leave the country, despite being asked not to as she's part of our ongoing investigation. She's being brought to the police station tonight for questioning first thing in the morning.'

'What's that got to do with me? I couldn't care less about Jessica Toland, unless she has Cassie with her or knows where she is.'

'I quite understand, but I'm just doing as asked. How is your wife, by the way? PC Walsh contacted the station to tell us that she had collapsed.'

'She's sleeping. At least I hope she's still asleep and that the phone didn't disturb her.'

'Awful news about your cat.'

'Yes, it truly is. Pumpkin was like a second child to Naomi.'

'Well, at least when she's over the initial shock you'll be able to get her another kitten, so it's not really like losing a child – they're irreplaceable... Sorry, that all came out a bit wrong. I wasn't suggesting that anything bad has happened to Cassie, or that you didn't love the cat. No offence intended.'

'None taken. This whole situation has got us all on edge, and you can't have had much rest if you're still at the station now.'

'I'm just about to hand over to the night team. We've been inundated with calls from the general public since the appeal this afternoon, and we've also been trawling through the CCTV footage from Thursday night in the area close to your house. We've got a positive ID on the red BMW.'

Charlie gripped his mobile phone tighter.

'It was the car that Jessica Toland hired, and on a couple of pictures you can clearly see it is her behind the wheel. That's why we're bringing her back in.'

'Was there anyone else in the car with her?' Charlie asked, his heart racing.

'Not as far as we can tell. The passenger seat was definitely empty, but it was impossible to tell from the angle the footage was taken whether there was anything or anybody on the back seats. Hopefully we'll be able to extract that information from Mrs Toland tomorrow. It's surprising how quickly suspects begin to confess, particularly if they're working with someone else and they've only played a minor role. It's called passing the buck.'

'Do you think Jessica was working with someone?'

'Well, we don't even know for sure that she has anything to do with Cassie's disappearance, but evidence is mounting against her. Mind you, most of it is circumstantial, unless the forensic report we're waiting for on the car gives us anything conclusive. My question has always been what would Mrs Toland have to gain by taking your child? It doesn't really make much sense unless she was simply being vindictive. I can't think of another explanation, can you, Mr Bailey?'

'No, I can't, unless… you don't think she was intending to blackmail me, do you? Maybe that was what the phone call yesterday was all about, and she got spooked when DCI Hart answered my phone.'

'It's a possibility, but I would have thought she would have tried to contact you again if that was the case. She hasn't called you again, has she?'

'No. I would have told you.'

'Even if she threatened to harm your little girl?'

'She hasn't called me. You do believe me, don't you?'

'Of course. I'll let you get to bed now. We'll be in touch as soon as we have any more news.'

CHAPTER THIRTY-SEVEN

11.58 p.m. – Saturday

Rachel answered her phone on the first ring.

'How did he react to the news that we've got Jessica Toland in custody again?'

'He was pretty disinterested to be honest, Guv. He seemed to be preoccupied with what had happened to his wife and their cat. He only started paying more attention when I mentioned that we had a firm ID on Jessica being the driver of the BMW. He asked if anyone else was in the car, and I told him we couldn't see the back seats from the angle of the camera, like you said I should.'

'Did he sound relieved?'

'I'm not sure. It was difficult to tell over the phone, but if he and Jessica are in this together and he knows she's in police custody he'll presumably leave the house to go to his daughter, rather than her being left on her own wherever they've been hiding her. And if he does, PC Walsh will let us know.'

'Let me know, you mean. I want you to turn your phone off and go home and get some sleep. You must be exhausted.'

'No more than you, Guv. We're all putting in extra hours on this one. Nobody likes to think of that young kid alone and frightened.'

Rachel closed her eyes. At least she and Ruth had each other, apart from the times he'd taken her sister away to sexually abuse her. Nobody had ever been able to explain why he had abused one sister and not the other, particularly as they were identical twins.

It had left Rachel with irrational feelings of being undesirable to men that still persisted.

'Trust me, it's appreciated. Now go home and I'll see you in the morning.'

'Okay. Night, Guv.'

Rachel disconnected the call and relaxed back on her sofa with her feet up on the glass coffee table next to the remnants of the baked beans on toast she'd had for supper. She had left several of her officers dealing with the deluge of calls from the general public following the television appeal on the early evening news. She had to get out of the incident room with the phones constantly ringing. She needed to think, and for that she had to have peace and quiet without constant interruptions from junior officers thinking they had a lead. Somebody must have seen something, however insignificant it might seem, that could shed light on how Cassie Bailey simply vanished into thin air.

All those years ago, it had been the neighbour across the street, Iris McCartney, who had unwittingly provided the clue as to what had happened to the Hart sisters. She'd always been a bit of a curtain-twitcher, sticking her nose into other people's business, but if it hadn't been for her the girls might never have been found. It was something as simple as a box of sugary cereal protruding from the top of his shopping bags, when the whole neighbourhood knew he was a health freak, that had given the game away. Iris had asked him if his ten-year-old son, who had been at boarding school from the age of five, was coming to live with him and he'd shouted at her to mind her own business. She thought it was an excessive reaction and reported the encounter to the police, and they thought it suspicious enough to request a search warrant for his house.

Thank God for nosy neighbours, Rachel thought. Unfortunately the Baileys didn't have neighbours across the road from them, and neither of the adjacent neighbours could remember seeing or hearing anything untoward, apart from the speeding car. Just before she fell asleep fully clothed on the sofa, Rachel reminded herself that she needed to ask Hazel Bailey about the pumpkin whiskers again. Something was nagging her about them: *were they already in place when the red car sped off?*

CHAPTER THIRTY-EIGHT

Day Three – 6.30 a.m. – Sunday

Charlie had periodically nodded off in the chair he had pulled up beside the bed to be close to his sleeping wife, his head slowly dropping to his chest before the discomfort of the position would jolt him awake again. Naomi looked so peaceful, almost child-like, barely moving in her drugged state. Around 4 a.m., with his muscles screaming to lie down, he had been tempted to slip off his shoes and climb into the bed beside her, fully clothed. He longed to wrap his arms around her, to protect her from all the terrible things that were going on, but he knew it was too soon. There was no point in rushing the delicate process of trying to regain her trust. A long road lay ahead, and he would have to be patient if he wanted to be allowed back into her life. Their relationship would never be quite the same as it had been, but maybe they had both learnt something from the events of the past few months, and with time it could become even stronger.

At half past six, Naomi opened her eyes and looked puzzled to see Charlie sitting at her bedside.

'What are you doing here?' she asked, her speech a little slurred.

'I'm looking after you. You had a nasty shock.'

'Cassie? Did they find Cassie?'

'Not yet,' he replied gently. He watched as her face creased in anguish, clearly remembering the events of the previous evening.

'Pumpkin. My Pumpkin's gone. I should never have sent him to look for Cassie. He must have got his collar caught on a branch, or something. I can't believe he's gone.'

'I'm so sorry, Naomi. He was the best cat ever.'

'I don't want another one, Charlie. Don't think you can replace him by getting me a new kitten. I never want to experience this feeling again.'

Charlie reached for Naomi's hand to stroke it, praying that there was nothing worse to come for his already fragile wife. 'I won't do anything you don't want me to,' he said.

'I don't know what I want. My life is crumbling around me and I don't seem to be able to do anything to stop it. It feels like I'm being punished for something, but I don't know what I've done wrong,' she said, her voice flat and dispirited. 'I've tried to be a good person, Charlie, but maybe I didn't try hard enough.'

'Sometimes bad things happen to good people. The world can be a very cruel place for no apparent reason. You try and get back to sleep.'

'If I close my eyes, you will still be here when I wake up, won't you?'

She sounds so vulnerable, Charlie thought. 'Don't you worry, I'm not going anywhere,' he said, gently squeezing her hand.

Naomi did drift back to sleep for a couple of hours, but Charlie forced himself to stay awake, not wanting to let his wife out of his sight for even a moment. When she finally stirred again two hours later, he had the difficult task of trying to persuade her to eat some breakfast so that she could take the prescribed drugs.

'I'm not hungry.'

'Neither am I, but we both have to eat something, even if it's only biscuits with our hot chocolate. Do you remember our first night in this house? We'd bought a bottle of champagne to celebrate but ended up having hot chocolate instead. It's been our favourite ever since. Come on, what do you say?'

'I suppose so.'

'Good. Are you all right to get yourself to the bathroom while I go and warm the milk?'

'I feel a bit wobbly, but I'll be okay. What did the doctor give me last night? My head feels like it's full of cotton wool.'

'A sedative injection, and I'm afraid you're going to have to take some pills or Dr Moss said you'd have to go to the hospital where they can keep you under observation.'

'Not much of a choice, is it,' Naomi said, easing herself upright and swinging her legs down until her feet made contact with the soft carpet.

'Which is it to be?' Charlie said, supporting his wife at the elbow as she gingerly got to her feet.

'I'm not going to hospital, and that's final.'

'Fine. I'll bring your tablets up with your hot chocolate.'

Naomi pulled a face as she closed the bathroom door on him.

Charlie's eyelids were beginning to droop as he waited for the milk to boil. Lack of sleep and the worry of the past two days were catching up with him. *I wonder if Mum could make some soup for lunch and come and sit with Naomi, to give me a couple of hours' rest?* He tried his mother's mobile number, but it went straight to voicemail. For a moment he was puzzled. *Where could she be this early on a Sunday morning? If she was taking Alfie for a walk, she would have taken her phone with her.* Then he remembered her saying the previous evening that, despite not being particularly religious, she was going to go to church to pray for Cassie's safe return. He hoped her prayers would be answered. *But that doesn't help me out this morning,* he thought, only just catching the pan of hot milk before it boiled over on the hob. *Maybe Kate could spare a couple of hours?*

'Sorry to bother you, Kate,' he said, balancing the phone between his shoulder and his ear and reaching into the fridge for the squirty cream. 'Would you be able to pop round and sit with Naomi for a bit? The doctor said she shouldn't be left unattended, and I'm knackered after sitting up with her all night.'

'Doctor? What's happened?'

Charlie realised that Kate didn't know about Pumpkin. 'Mum was round for supper last night and after we walked her home, we went over to the field to look for Pumpkin. He didn't come when we called and now we know why. We found the remains of his collar in the ashes of the bonfire.'

'Oh no! That's awful. Of course I'll come round. Naomi loved that cat. She must be in pieces.'

'That's putting it mildly. The doctor says she's on the verge of a breakdown. He's got her on sedatives and compulsory bed rest.'

'Poor love. Wouldn't she be better off in hospital?'

'She wouldn't go. She's still clinging to the hope that Cassie got herself lost and is going to walk back in here at any moment and, if she does, Naomi wants to be here.'

'It sounds like you're losing faith.'

'Oh, I don't know, Kate. I keep trying to stay positive, and then all of a sudden this feeling of doom overwhelms me,' Charlie said, pausing halfway through adding a spiral of cream to the top of the steaming liquid.

'It must be so hard for you. Dealing with your own feelings is bad enough, but you're taking Naomi's on board, too. She's lucky to have you.'

'I'm no saint, as we all know. Which reminds me: I got a call late last night from the police. They found Jessica, and they're bringing her back to Reading for questioning. It was her car, well, the one that she hired, parked on our road on Thursday night. The police are pretty sure now that she is somehow involved in Cassie's disappearance, they just can't work out a motive yet and whether or not she was working alone.'

'Maybe it was another attempt to come between you and Naomi. She was pretty successful last time, and she may have thought this would make your split permanent.'

'Well, she couldn't have got that more wrong. If anything, this has brought Naomi and me closer together,' he said, closing the fridge door after putting the cream away. 'We've talked about that night, and I think Naomi is starting to understand how low I was feeling when I went on my drinking binge. It doesn't excuse what I did, but at least she's starting to see things from my point of view.'

'Hang on a minute, Charlie. What is it, Ricky? Can't you see I'm on the phone?'

Charlie could only hear Kate's end of the conversation.

'What try-out for the Tigers...? Why isn't it on the calendar...? Can't Dad take you...? Right, well, you'd better go and get your stuff ready. Are you still there, Charlie?' she said, speaking into the phone again. 'It seems Ricky has a football trial that didn't make it onto our family planner, and Alan can't take him because he's with the other two at mini-gym. I'm sorry, I won't be able to come this morning, but I could pop in later if that's any good to you?'

'Not to worry, Kate, our kids should always come first. I'll try my mum again in a bit. Thanks for the offer of later, though, I might take you up on it,' he said, picking up the mug of hot chocolate along with Naomi's tablets. 'Oh, and I hope Ricky makes the team,' he added, but it was too late. Kate had already hung up.

CHAPTER THIRTY-NINE

10.03 a.m. – Sunday

Jessica sat facing DCI Hart, her arms folded across her chest, a belligerent expression on her face.

'Am I under arrest?' she demanded.

'Not yet. This is a voluntary interview under caution. We need to ask you some questions regarding your whereabouts on the evening of Thursday, 30 October.'

'I was at home.'

'Alone?'

'Yes, alone. I'm always alone since that dick of a husband of mine and I parted company.'

'Not always.'

'If you're referring to Charlie Bailey, that was a one-off, and I wouldn't have taken him back to mine if I'd known where the drunken idiot lived.'

'We have reason to believe that you were perfectly aware of his home address, but we'll come on to that later, although I do have a question concerning that night, or more precisely, the following day. How did you know Mr and Mrs Bailey's phone numbers?'

Jessica tapped her gel fingernails on the table and breathed in deeply as though she was being patient with a small child. 'Charlie handed me his phone when we were in the pub. He wanted to text his wife, but he was too pissed to hit the letters, so he asked me to do it for him. He gave me his access code and started to dictate a message, and then snatched his phone back saying he'd changed his mind. Satisfied?'

'That's not what he said.'

'You seriously expect him to remember anything accurately about that night? He was so drunk, he couldn't even remember if he'd shagged me.'

She has a point, Rachel thought, trying to hide any obvious feelings of distaste she had for the woman by pretending to check the notes in front of her on the desk. She had to have had access to his phone or she couldn't have known Naomi's number.

'All right, we'll leave that for now. Back to the night Cassie Bailey went missing.'

'I've told you everything I know about that kid's disappearance, which is precisely nothing. I didn't take her. Can't you get that through your thick heads? Hook me up to a lie detector if you don't believe me.'

'We may well do that, Mrs Toland, should the need arise, but first I wanted to give you the opportunity to explain a few of your recent actions to us, starting with hiring the BMW. You told us during the course of your previous interview that you were short of money, and yet you hire an upmarket vehicle and leave your own car in the garage of your home. Would you care to explain why you did that?'

'Not that it's any of your business, but the Fiat was playing up, refusing to start. I didn't want it to break down after I'd finished a late shift at the pub, so I hired a car to be on the safe side. There's no crime in that, is there?'

'No, but it would have been more cost-effective to hire a smaller, cheaper vehicle. After all, there was only you using it, wasn't there?' Rachel was looking Jessica directly in the eyes, hoping for a telltale reaction, but she was met with a steely stare. 'Or maybe you could have hopped on a bus to get to and from work like thousands of other people in this town do?'

'They don't finish at midnight, do they? The bus stops running before that and anyway, it's a long walk my end, especially in high heels.'

'Well, a bus to work and a minicab home would have been a lot cheaper, wouldn't it?'

'Look, I may not have much money, but I'll spend it how I choose. I was sick of driving around in that stupid bubble car that my husband bought me, which they'll be repossessing soon anyway. I just fancied treating myself to a decent car for a bit.'

'And that of course is your prerogative. Can I just ask you why you hired it for three weeks and yet there was still ten days of the rental period to run when you were picked up, about to board a ferry to Spain on Friday night? Sudden change of plans?'

'Actually, a family crisis, if you must know. My brother called me to say my mother, who's staying with him at the moment, is not well. If she bloody dies after you've prevented me from leaving the country, I'll sue your arses off.'

She's a cool customer, Rachel thought. 'I'm sorry to hear about your mother. I wasn't aware she was visiting your brother in Spain. My information is that she is a resident in a council-run old people's home in Wigan and that no member of her family has visited in the past five years.'

'How dare you go prying into my family's lives like that?' Jessica said, her voice rising in volume.

'Police enquiries,' Rachel replied. *Finally, I've touched a nerve and got a reaction. Now I need to find some more of those buttons to press.* 'We had to be sure that Cassie wasn't with your mother.'

'Why would she be?' Jessica demanded, struggling to control her irritation. 'I keep telling you, but you're not listening,' she hissed. 'I never laid a finger on the kid.'

'Then perhaps you'd like to explain why you were parked up the street from her house on the night she disappeared, and why you lied about being there in your previous interview,' Rachel said, watching Jessica's face carefully for any signs that she was feeling backed into a corner.

'You can't prove that.'

'Actually, we can. Although the CCTV camera on Beechwood Avenue was malfunctioning, we have footage from the one on Alderton Road, taken minutes after an eyewitness says a car matching the description of your BMW sped away and turned left into Alderton Road. We've enhanced the image it captured. Not only is the number plate a match with the vehicle you hired, it clearly shows that the person driving is you. I repeat, why were you parked a few doors away from Cassie Bailey's house on the night she went missing?'

'No comment.'

'It really would be better for you to answer our questions, particularly as a young girl's life may be in danger.'

'No comment.'

'It may have an impact on any future sentence if you tell us the truth now.'

For the first time since DCI Hart had sat down opposite her to begin the interview, Jessica lowered her gaze. *We've got her*, Rachel thought.

'I want to speak to my lawyer.'

'Absolutely. Interview suspended at 10.17 a.m.'

CHAPTER FORTY

12.23 p.m. – Sunday

Hazel had been worried to see the missed call from Charlie when she turned her phone on after the church service. She had rung him immediately and was relieved to hear that all he wanted was that she make some soup and bring it round for them all to share for their lunch. As she'd ladled out the steaming broth into three bowls, she'd been glad she had made potato and leek rather than pumpkin and sweet potato. *That poor dear cat*, she'd thought, *he'd never hurt a fly. What a terrible end to come to, and yet another shock for Naomi.*

Her daughter-in-law had stirred from her drug-induced slumber when she had heard Charlie telling his mum, in little more than a whisper, about the tragic events of the previous evening. Her face, already pale, had taken on a ghost-like quality. Hazel couldn't stop herself from throwing her arms around Naomi and holding her to her chest like a young child. Naomi made no attempt to push her away, leaning into her as though she was trying to take strength from her. Hazel couldn't help but notice that Naomi was little more than a bag of bones.

No objection had been raised when Hazel said she had made soup for lunch, and she made sure the accompanying pieces of bread were really small so that they could be easily dipped in the hot tasty broth.

Once Naomi had finished her soup and swallowed some more of the prescription drugs, she lay back on her pillows again and closed her eyes while Charlie and Hazel took the dishes down to the kitchen.

'Will you be all right to sit with her for a bit while I grab forty winks, Mum?' Charlie asked.

'Of course. I gave Alfie his lunch before I came out, so I can stay as long as you need me.'

'Thanks, Mum, you're a treasure.'

'I'm your mum. You know I'd do anything for you. Have you heard from the police at all, this morning?'

'No. I expect they're snowed under with all the information piling in from the general public after the appeal yesterday. I hope we did the right thing.'

'If it leads to one tiny clue that helps us get Cassie back it will have been the right thing. You had to try it, Charlie, it's been two days now.'

'I know, and still nothing concrete. Please God, let's hope the appeal may have triggered a memory in someone watching.'

'Oh. That reminds me. I don't know how important it is, but when DCI Hart first spoke to me on the phone, she asked me if I could remember whether or not the pumpkin had sparkler whiskers stuck in its face. I've visualised standing on the pavement looking at this house so many times since I heard the news about Cassie, and I'm ninety-nine per cent sure there were whiskers when I saw it at around 10 p.m. Do you think we should let the police know?'

'I'll ring them now,' Charlie said, dialling the number. 'If nothing else, it could narrow the time frame for Cassie's disappearance. Someone must have opened the front door to add the whiskers between me heading home at around 9 p.m. and you passing with Alfie at 10 p.m. I'll put it on speakerphone so you can tell her yourself, Mum.

'Hello, can I speak to DCI Hart, please?'

'Who's calling?'

'It's Charlie Bailey, Cassie Bailey's father.'

Hazel could picture the look of pity on the desk officer's face.

'I believe DCI Hart is currently in the interview room. Is there anything I can help you with?'

'Can you give her a message, please? My mother has remembered that the pumpkin cat did have whiskers when she saw it at 10 p.m.'

'Did have whiskers,' the desk officer repeated. 'I'll pass that information on as soon as she's free.'

'Thanks,' Charlie said, hanging up abruptly.

Hazel couldn't help wondering if her son had ended the call so quickly to avoid having to listen to any platitudes from the officer. *People were only trying to be kind, but it didn't really help. He must have heard them all in the past couple of days, but it hadn't brought them any closer to finding his daughter.*

'I didn't know you'd been coming here every night to try and catch a glimpse of Cassie,' Hazel said.

'And I didn't know that you'd changed your dog-walking route. It seems we've both been keeping secrets from each other.' Charlie opened up his arms and pulled his mum into a hug. 'I'm so sorry, Mum. I know this has been incredibly difficult for you. I'll make it up to you, I promise.'

Hazel rested her head against her son's chest in the embrace she had wanted to give him for the past five weeks. She brushed a tear surreptitiously from her eye as she pulled away from him. 'Well, you could start by oiling the garage door. Not that I'll be needing it for a while.'

'That's a deal. I'll go up to Cassie's room for my lie-down. I've got my phone with me in case they ring back.'

'Take as long as you need, I'll keep an eye on Naomi.'

It feels so good to be needed, Hazel thought, watching her son climb wearily up the stairs. *But how I wish it could be under different circumstances.*

CHAPTER FORTY-ONE

1.45 p.m. – Sunday

DCI Hart checked the time on the recording device. It had taken longer than she would have hoped to get Mrs Toland's lawyer down to the police station, but, in fairness, it was a Sunday and he was probably hoping for a weekend off to spend time with his family. *That's a massive assumption. What makes me think he has a wife and children? Because he's very attractive and it's still the norm, even in this day and age. Most people are not like me, unable to allow another person to get too close.*

When Tim Berwick, from the same law firm who had dealt with Jessica's recent divorce, had finally arrived shortly past 1 p.m., she had emphasised the need for urgency. Before taking him through to meet his client, she had pointed out that a child's life was potentially at risk. He had nodded saying, 'I realise that.' It obviously had an impact on him, as only thirty minutes later he permitted the interview to continue.

Jessica's demeanour was totally different from how it had been that morning and in the previous interview. She sat almost demurely, with her hands in her lap and her eyes trained down on them.

'Interview with Mrs Toland recommencing at 1.45 p.m. Can you please tell me your whereabouts on the evening of Thursday, 30 October?'

Jessica sighed deeply. 'I was in my car parked on Beechwood Avenue.'

'Just to confirm, that was a red BMW that you had hired from Manor Autos ten days previously.'

'Yes.'

'And what time did you arrive in Beechwood Avenue?'

'It was a little before nine,' Jessica said, remembering her panic when, as she was about to park, she had noticed Charlie walking down the path away from his front door. She had kept her eyes on the road ahead and driven past him, hoping he wouldn't notice her, and then parked up around the corner for a few minutes, hands gripping the steering wheel to prevent them from shaking, before driving around the block to try again. *I should have taken that as a bad omen. He wasn't supposed to be anywhere near the house at that time of night.*

'You're sure of that?'

'Certain.'

'Why were you on Beechwood Avenue?'

Jessica cleared her throat. *I'm only going to get one shot at this. I have to make them believe me that I never laid a finger on that child.*

'I was watching the Baileys' house.'

'For what purpose?'

'I was going to go and apologise to Naomi and tell her the truth about what happened, or rather didn't happen, the night Charlie got drunk.'

'I see. And you thought that 9 p.m. was an appropriate time to go and do this?'

'I didn't think it was the sort of thing her kid should hear and, as I don't have kids myself, I wasn't sure what time it would go to bed.'

'She.'

'What?'

'We're talking about a five-year-old girl, Mrs Toland.'

'Right, whatever.'

Jessica felt rather than saw the look her lawyer shot her. *Keep it civil*, he had warned her.

'So why didn't you go and knock on the door? We know you were still in the vicinity an hour later.'

'I was nervous, I guess. I'd had to pluck up the courage to go and see Naomi, and it wasn't turning out to be as easy as I thought it was going to be.'

'Why didn't you go ahead with your plan?'

'Because an old lady turned up with her dog and stood staring at the house. I hadn't realised how long I had been sitting there, and when I checked the time, I figured it was too late to go knocking on Naomi's door, so I just drove off thinking I could go back the next day.'

'What made you change your mind?'

'I've just explained to you,' she said, a note of irritation creeping into her voice, 'the old woman turned up.'

'That's not what I meant. Why did you change your mind about visiting Naomi the next day?'

'It didn't seem the right thing to do, what with her kid going missing.'

'So, is that why you rang Mr Bailey on Friday afternoon? You were going to tell him that you intended to inform his wife of the actual events?'

'Yes, that's right,' Jessica said, trying to keep the relief from her voice. She had wondered how she was going to explain that call if the police had traced it back to her phone, and now the DCI had done it for her. *Brilliant.*

'That all sounds very plausible, Mrs Toland, except for one thing. We hadn't released anything to the media about Cassie's disappearance at that point. You couldn't possibly have known about it unless, of course, you are the person responsible for it or, at the very least, you know who is.'

Jessica's fake nails dug into the flesh of her thighs. *Shit, the bitch has outsmarted me. Keep calm; don't let her see you're rattled.* She turned to her lawyer. 'You see? I told you, they are trying to pin this kidnap thing on me. I've offered to take a lie-detector test to prove I didn't go into the house and take the kid. Why won't they just hook me up and we can get this over with once and for all? This is the second time they have brought me in for questioning without any proof that I had anything to do with it.'

'Can I have a moment with my client, please?' Tim Berwick asked.

'If you think that will help us get to the truth. Every minute that passes is damaging the chance of finding Cassie alive. Interview suspended at 1.58 p.m.'

The moment the police officers had left the room, Tim Berwick turned to Jessica. 'You need to come clean with me and tell me everything you know about Cassie Bailey's disappearance.'

'Whose side are you on?'

'Lawyers don't take sides, Jessica, we're not in the school playground now. I'm here to represent your best interests, but I can only do that if I know you are telling me the truth. Did you enter the house and take the child?'

In his job as a defence lawyer, Tim sometimes had to deal with people who he didn't particularly like, and this was one of those occasions. But he was a professional and he had to accept that it came with the territory.

'No, and that is the truth. I swear on my mother's life.'

'But you know who did?' he persisted.

'Maybe.'

'Start talking. It will be a whole lot better for you if Cassie Bailey is found alive.'

'Before I do, I need to know if they can arrest me based on the evidence that I was in a car parked near the Baileys' house on the night the kid disappeared.'

'No. You gave a perfectly reasonable explanation for being there,' Tim said. Although he wasn't sure he actually believed the reason she had given, it was plausible. 'Everything they have presented so far is circumstantial, but I'm sure they will want to question you further on how you knew the child was missing. How did you know?'

'I'll tell you in a minute, but this is just between you and me, right? You can't tell them what we talk about unless I say you can, that's right, isn't it?'

'You have instructed me to be your legal representative and, as such, I am here to give my advice for the best outcome for you as my client. Everything we talk about is in strictest confidence at this stage, but I should warn you that if you tell me something and you then say something different to the police, I would no longer be able to represent you knowing that you were lying to them. Likewise, if I hear anything that I believe would be to your benefit to disclose to the police and you ignore my advice, I would be within my rights to walk away from the case.'

There was a part of him that hoped she would trip herself up by telling different versions of events to him and to the police. When he had taken the call earlier from his colleague, Nigel Adler, who had acted on Jessica Toland's behalf during her recent divorce, there had been no mention from him regarding how unlikeable she was. *I'll be having words with Nigel when I see him at the office tomorrow.*

'Okay. Here's what happened. I was supposed to take the kid that night, but I bottled it.'

'Go on.'

'I'd had a phone call earlier in the evening assuring me that Naomi would have taken sleeping pills, so I would be able to get into the house and take Cassie without being disturbed.'

'Wait – you were going to break into the house?'

'No, I had a key.'

'Who gave you the key?'

'I'm getting to it. I was just supposed to take her from her bed and drive her to a cottage in the middle of nowhere, then stay with her for a couple of days before flying out to my brother's place in Spain to start a new life.'

'So, why didn't you?'

'Exactly like I told them: this old woman turned up outside their house and just stood there, staring at it. It freaked me out. I asked myself what the hell I thought I was getting myself into. I may have done some unpleasant and unkind things in the past, but I've never broken the law. I changed my mind and made a run for it.'

'So, assuming you are telling me the truth now, who did take Cassie?' Tim was looking her straight in the eyes. In his experience, people sometimes momentarily lost eye contact when they were about to lie.

Jessica stared straight back at him. 'I don't know for sure, because we agreed not to contact each other again, but I have a pretty good idea. The trouble is I don't feel comfortable talking about it while I'm in the police station. How do I know they haven't got this room bugged and aren't listening in to our conversation right now?'

'The police aren't allowed to do things like that.'

'Well, you would say that, wouldn't you. You're all on the same side.'

'Like I said earlier, it's not about taking sides,' he replied, trying to keep the exasperation he was feeling out of his voice. 'It's my job to defend you, but if you know where this young child is being held, I'd strongly recommend you tell the police.'

'If I tell them about the cottage, assuming that's where she is, will they be able to arrest me as an accomplice? I didn't go through with the stupid plan, so I've done nothing wrong.'

Now we're getting somewhere. If I can encourage her to give the police the details of this cottage, maybe the little girl will be back with her parents before bedtime.

'Technically,' Tim said, 'but you knew of a plan to kidnap a child and you did nothing to prevent it. They might want to hold you for the permitted twenty-four hours, pending further investigation of the information you provide them with. Or, if that information leads to Cassie Bailey being found alive and well, you may get away with a caution if, as you claim, this is a first offence.'

'And if I don't tell them?'

'I don't think they have sufficient grounds to hold you, and certainly not enough to place you under arrest. But I would ask you to consider your actions very carefully. If you knowingly withhold evidence regarding the location where Cassie is being held and she is later found dead, you would be in very serious trouble.'

'You're talking prison?'

'Absolutely,' he said, thinking that maybe the threat of prison would persuade Jessica to do the right thing.

'Thank you for your advice, but at this stage my freedom is the most important thing to me. If you get me out of here, I promise I'll make a phone call to DCI Hart with the location of the cottage within an hour of my release. If you don't, I won't talk and that could mean something bad happening to Cassie.'

'You really are a piece of work.'

'Yes, but I'm a piece of work that's paying you to defend me against false accusations. I told you I didn't take the kid from her bed, and that's what I'm being accused of. Can you get me out of here today?'

Tim studied his client's face. *Could he trust her to phone the information through to the police within an hour as she had promised, or would she go on the run the moment she was released from police custody? It's a chance I'm going to have to take. If I don't get her released and she refuses to cooperate, it could mean the difference between life and death for Cassie Bailey.*

'I believe so,' he said, reluctantly.

'Then let's get them back in here and get on with it.'

CHAPTER FORTY-TWO

2.04 p.m. – Sunday

The mist of the November morning had lifted to reveal a beautiful, blue-skied autumn day by the time the car came to a halt on the gravel driveway of a small detached cottage. It had taken her less than an hour to get there and yet it was a world away from the sprawling suburbs of Reading, surrounded as it was by open fields dotted with occasional copses of trees. The single-track country lane that led to the cottage ended abruptly just beyond the opening to the driveway, becoming a footpath that saw very few walkers outside of the height of summer. She had first discovered it several years previously when she had harboured dreams of becoming a novelist as a means of escape from an existence she hated, but, as with most other things in her life, she hadn't had the drive to pursue it.

When the plan to kidnap Cassie had first started to form in her mind, the cottage seemed the obvious choice for a hideaway. After an initial call made using a pay-as-you-go phone ascertained that it was available, she had gone into the estate agents' office wearing a long dark wig to hide her blonde hair and paid two months' rent in cash. It was only ever going to be a short-term stopgap before moving on to her new life with her new family and her new identity.

'Come on, boy,' she said, reaching for the cat basket on the back seat of her car, 'Cassie will be pleased to have some company.'

The soles of her trainers crunched on the gravel as she strode towards the house and turned the key in the lock. Despite the bright sunshine outside, the hallway was quite dim as she pushed the front door open and set the cat carry basket down on the dark red quarry tiles.

'Cassie,' she called, 'where are you, darling? It's Auntie Kate. I've brought someone to see you.'

She heard nothing in response but the sound of a distant tractor. Closing the door behind her, and leaving the basket in the hall, Kate checked the lounge where the selection of toys and books she had bought for Cassie appeared to be untouched, before glancing in the kitchen and then making her way upstairs. The back bedroom, the one that Kate had painstakingly set up to resemble Cassie's bedroom at home, with the same unicorn bedcovers and bedside lamp, was empty and the bed looked as though it had not been slept in.

She gave a cursory glance to the front bedroom, which also appeared to be empty, before going back into the smaller room.

'Are you hiding, Cassie? Were you afraid because the nasty lady left you on your own? You can come out now. It's me, Auntie Kate,' she said, opening the door to the built-in wardrobe gently so as not to distress the little girl further.

What the hell? Where can she have got to? Maybe Jessica locked her in the downstairs bathroom so that she couldn't hurt herself while she was here on her own. She'd better have left her plenty of food and drink.

She ran down the stairs, through the kitchen to the scullery at the back that had been converted into a bathroom. The door was open and there was no sign of Cassie.

Kate rushed back through the house, panic starting to set in, checking every cupboard and possible hiding place. *How could this be? Jessica was supposed to bring Cassie here after taking her while Naomi was drugged up on the sleeping tablets.* Kate allowed herself a smile. She had totally fooled Naomi into believing they were herbal ones, when they were actually part of a stash she had saved following her bout of postnatal depression. *No wonder they knocked her out, particularly with the tiny amounts of food she eats these days.* Her smile disappeared as quickly as it had formed as her eyes frantically darted around for any trace of the little girl. *Why hadn't Jessica stuck to the plan?*

It had been agreed that Kate would go to the cottage on Monday morning after Alan had left for work and she had dropped the boys at school and Montessori. Jessica would hand Cassie over and head off to Spain to be with her brother. Alan was under the impression that Kate was going to be cat-sitting for a friend who was away on holiday for a few days. It was similar to the story she had told Charlie, apart from the bit about it being a friend of Alan's she was doing a favour for. *Why did I tell him that? Charlie could easily have let something slip to Alan. Maybe I was looking for sympathy. Whatever – it's irrelevant now I've been forced into a change of plan.*

Earlier that morning, after suggesting that Alan take their boys swimming again, Kate had hastily packed as many of her clothes and toiletries as she could squeeze into two large suitcases and locked the front door of the house she had shared with them all for the last time. The note she'd left had simply said that she didn't love Alan any more and that she thought the boys would have a better life staying with him.

In most people's eyes, Alan was the perfect husband. It was he who had suggested a bolthole of some kind, when she had expressed an interest in pursuing a career as a writer and said there was no way she could concentrate at home with her two infant boys. He'd also given the go-ahead for a full-time nanny if that's what his wife wanted. She had been on the point of renting the cottage for the winter months, at a much-reduced out-of-season price, when she had discovered she was pregnant again. The only thing that prevented her from having a termination was the hope that this time it would be a girl. The scans during the early part of her pregnancy were inconclusive, and by the time they could say with some certainty that it was another boy, it was too late for an abortion. From that moment, she had loathed her bump and when Lucas was born, she had initially refused to hold him. Everyone thought she was suffering from post-partum baby blues, but in truth she was dealing with the crushing disappointment of not having the one thing she craved: a daughter. She couldn't bear the thought of him tugging at her breasts like an animal, so Lucas was bottle-fed from birth.

A plaintive miaow from the cat basket in the hall interrupted Kate's thoughts. She undid the plastic hinges on the sides of the carry basket, took the top off and lifted Pumpkin out. He swayed a bit, clearly still under the influence of the quarter of a sleeping tablet Kate had given him to stop him attracting attention by miaowing after she had locked him in their garden shed in the early hours of Saturday morning while she had been babysitting Naomi.

'Go and find Cassie,' she said, urging the ginger tom in the direction of the stairs with the toe of her purple trainer. He took a few tentative steps forward before sinking onto the tiles and resting his head on his front paws, the mark where his collar had been clearly visible.

'Come on, you useless cat,' she said, scooping him up and placing him on the bottom stair. 'Prove to me that I did the right thing by putting just your collar on the bonfire.'

He staggered over the first couple of stairs, then seemed to gain momentum as he took the rest of them at a run. He went straight into the back bedroom and emerged a few moments later with Cassie's favourite teddy in his mouth, the one Naomi believed had been dropped on a trip to the garden centre with Kate. The six of them – Kate, Naomi and the four children – had searched for the bear for over an hour before a tearful Cassie had accepted a new one bought at the checkout. It had been easy for Kate to slip Cassie's favourite teddy into her roomy handbag when no one was looking. She knew she would need to surround the little girl with as many familiar things as possible to make her more accepting of the situation. That was where Pumpkin came into her plan. He was Cassie's best friend in the world, and would hopefully help the little girl to settle with her Auntie Kate in the house in North Wales that she had bought for cash with some of the £250,000 she had withdrawn from her and Alan's joint pension fund. Dropping Pumpkin's collar in the bonfire to make it seem as though he had perished in the flames had seemed like a good idea at the time, but now she was not so sure. Charlie had been there to take care of Naomi and that, on top of Cassie's disappearance, seemed to be reuniting the couple.

It seems Jessica is not the only one I've misjudged, Kate reflected, watching Pumpkin flexing his claws into the teddy's soft round tummy. Charlie had been proving more difficult to manipulate than she had imagined. She shrugged her shoulders in acceptance. *Having someone to share my new life with would merely have been the icing on the cake. What I really wanted was Cassie, so it'll have to be plan B, with just the two of us. But first I need to find her. Where can she be?* She sank down onto the sofa.

Kate didn't move for the best part of fifteen minutes, picking up each of the girly toys she had bought for Cassie and running her gloved hands gently over them. Then she turned her attention to the books: tales of fairies and unicorns and happy ever afters, the sort of stories that she longed to read aloud but knew her boys would poke fun at. She could feel the energy slowly seeping out of her. *All I ever wanted was a chance at a happy life… Naomi's happy life, but it's all gone wrong somehow. There was me thinking that Cassie was secreted away here safe and well when everyone else was panicking about her whereabouts. Now I know how they're feeling. Why didn't Jessica bring her here? She knew the address; she told me she had programmed it into the BMW's satnav. Even someone as stupid as her couldn't have messed that up, unless… she's not so stupid after all. Maybe she always planned to double-cross me and blackmail me for more money...*

I'm the stupid one, for agreeing to pay her the second half of the kidnapping fee before I had Cassie safely with me. Now I've no idea where she is. She wasn't with Jessica when they stopped her in Portsmouth or in London. If that bitch has hurt my little angel, I'll kill her with my bare hands, Kate thought, clenching her fists until her knuckles turned as white as the cotton gloves she was wearing. Then another thought occurred to her. *What if this isn't just about more money? Maybe Jessica wants to keep Cassie herself, and the kidnap money was to help her get started in a new life. She could be shopping me to the police right now, to throw them off the scent.*

'I need to get out of here,' she said aloud, jumping to her feet and scaring a dozing Pumpkin in the process, 'but first I have to get rid of any evidence that Cassie was meant to be brought here.'

Feverishly, she gathered up the toys and books and emptied the fridge of its contents, including the little girl's favourite foods, stuffing everything into the two 'bags for life' she had left in a kitchen drawer. She raced up the stairs and removed the unicorn duvet cover and pillowcase, revealing the plain white ones beneath, and piled the clothes she had lovingly selected for Cassie on the top. Then she unplugged the bedside lamp, replacing it with the original that she had stored in the wardrobe, and wrapped it and the clothes in the bedcovers. A quick check around the bedrooms to make sure she hadn't left anything that would tie her to ever being at the cottage, and Kate was down in the hall, shoving the covers in the cat basket and squeezing the lid back on it. She almost forgot to take Cassie's favourite bubble bath from the bathroom, but remembered just in time, throwing it in her handbag as the cat basket was now full. Pumpkin had been watching her frenetic activity from the safety of the doormat.

'Get out of the way!' she yelled at him, helping him with her foot. Surprised at the way he was being treated by the person who was usually so kind when she looked after him, Pumpkin scooted through to the lounge and cowered behind the sofa.

'Chrissakes! I haven't got time for all this,' she shouted in his direction, wrenching open the front door and running across the gravel to her car. She threw the laden cat basket and carrier bags onto the back seat and slammed the door shut with such force the Nissan Juke shook. Pumpkin had now ventured back into the hallway and was observing her warily. Kate knew she had to be calm to entice him out of the house.

'Come on, Pumpkin,' she said in a tone of voice he was more used to from her, 'it's time to go, mate.'

He sat down on the tiles, making no attempt to move.

She couldn't leave him in the cottage for the police to find when they inevitably discovered its location from Jessica; she had to get him out. That's when she remembered the cat treats that were lying in the litter tray in the footwell of her car. She reached in and retrieved the plastic container, shaped like a cat's head, and shook it as she approached the front door. Pumpkin obligingly moved towards her, rubbing against her legs as she eased the lid off the container and dropped a handful of treats on the doormat. He wolfed them down and looked up at her for more.

'Here you are, boy,' she said, dropping a couple more on the ground, allowing her to reach behind him and close and lock the front door. 'Want some more? Come on then,' she said, walking over to the edge of the drive and throwing the remaining treats over the garden wall into the field next door. Pumpkin was over the wall in a flash, vacuuming up treats as quickly as he could, unable to believe his luck.

Kate strode over to her car without a backward glance, muttering, 'Greedy ginger freak,' under her breath.

CHAPTER FORTY-THREE

2.52 p.m. – Sunday

When Rachel had halted the interview with Jessica Toland for a second time, she had been hopeful that Tim Berwick would be able to make his client see sense and divulge any information she may have concerning the kidnapping of Cassie Bailey. It was disappointing when the lawyer had summoned them back into the room; he demanded that they either charge Jessica or let her go, as the evidence against her was circumstantial and inconclusive and wouldn't stand up in court.

With a final throw of the dice, Rachel had once again questioned how Jessica knew about Cassie's disappearance. The woman had explained it by saying that she had seen a police officer standing on the Baileys' doorstep and had asked a neighbour what was going on. It would be entirely credible, if it had come from anyone but Jessica. They would need to speak to the neighbours to confirm or disprove it. There had been nothing further she could do if she wanted to avoid Jessica accusing them of harassment. She was compelled to let her go. Tim Berwick had looked apologetic as the two of them stood up to leave and, although she wasn't certain, she thought she had seen the lawyer mouth the word 'sorry' at her before following his client out of the room. *It must be bloody difficult defending the bad guys*, she had acknowledged.

*

To say Rachel was surprised when the call came through less than fifty minutes later was an understatement. She was sitting at her desk deciding on their next course of action when PC Drake knocked on her door.

'DI Wilson says you need to pick up on line one, Guv, Mrs Toland is on the phone. He says he's putting a trace on the call so to try and keep her talking.'

Rachel was intrigued. *Why would Jessica Toland be calling less than an hour after she had been released from police custody?*

'DCI Hart.'

'I have some information for you regarding the whereabouts of Cassie Bailey.'

'Go on.'

'She's being held captive in a cottage near Buckleberry.'

'And how can you be so sure of this when less than an hour ago you said you had nothing to do with her kidnap?'

'Because I was supposed to take her from her bed on Thursday night, drive her to the cottage and stay with her for a couple of nights.'

Despite all the lies Jessica had told her over the previous thirty-six hours, Rachel sensed that she may now be telling the truth. 'So why didn't you?'

'I bottled it. The old woman and her dog showed up as I was about to get out of the car and let myself into the house. It made me realise what a risk I was taking. You may not like me, but I've never broken the law and there was a chance the whole plan could go horribly wrong. It just wasn't worth it.'

Let herself into the Baileys' house? What was Jessica doing with a key? 'So, if you didn't take Cassie, who did?'

'I don't know for sure, cos she told me not to make contact with her, but I'm guessing Kate didn't entirely trust me to go through with her crazy plan, so she was also watching the house that night. She must have seen me drive off in a hurry and decided to go ahead with the abduction herself, knowing that she might never be able to persuade Naomi Bailey to take sleeping tablets again.'

'Kate? As in Kate Birchell? The Baileys' best friend?' Rachel could feel beads of perspiration pricking her forehead. *How could I have overlooked Kate when everyone else has been under suspicion at some point in the investigation?* 'Why would she take Cassie from them?'

'She's obsessed with the kid, which is weird because she has three of her own. I think maybe it's because she wanted a girl and hers are all boys, but to be honest, I didn't ask too many questions. I was only ever in it for the money.'

'She paid you to kidnap Cassie?'

'Well, I wasn't going to do it for nothing, was I? I don't even like the woman, but I needed some money to get out of this shithole and start a new life somewhere sunny and warm, and she knew it.'

'How would Kate Birchell know that you were short of money?'

'Everyone who reads the local paper knew. My ex-husband's bankruptcy was a big news story for them, and they made me out to be a right cow for divorcing him because of it. I had hate mail and everything. That's the main reason I want to get out of this dump. I've had enough of people talking about me behind my back.'

'So how did Kate get in touch with you?'

'She came to my house after the idiot reporter had put a picture of it in the paper with the name of my road, pretending to be all sympathetic, but I could see straight through her. I knew she was after something, I just didn't know what. She asked if I still had a thing for Charlie, and when I said yes, she told me his marriage was going through a rough patch. It was her who told me about the job at the Golden Lion. She said if I was patient, she thought there would be an opportunity to make a move on him. Thank God I didn't have to wait too long. Working in that pub was like working in a morgue. My chance came five weeks ago, but although I succeeded in splitting Naomi and Charlie up, he was clearly not interested in me and, to be honest, now I know what he's got in his pants, I'm not interested in him.'

'Forgive me, but I don't see how all this stuff with you and Charlie is relevant to Cassie's whereabouts.'

'It isn't. Kate tried to persuade me to take the kid by feeding me some bullshit saying if Cassie went missing while she was in Naomi's care, Charlie would leave his wife and come running to me. I wasn't having any of it. I agreed to take the kid, but only if she paid me.'

'But you're now claiming you didn't take her and that Kate did? I need the address of that cottage. We need to find Cassie before Kate does anything to harm her.'

'Why would she do that? I told you, Kate's infatuated with her. She's planning a new life away from here for herself and Cassie. A friend of my brother's did false papers for them both.'

'The friend's name?'

'I'd rather not say. I don't want to get my brother in trouble when he was only doing me a favour.'

Rachel tapped her pen on her pad. She doubted Jessica would be that considerate about another human being, even if they were a blood relative. 'So where was she planning on starting this new life?'

'She didn't tell me. She probably thought I would try to blackmail her or something to keep her secret.'

'A thought which never occurred to you, of course,' Rachel said, unable to keep the sarcasm from her voice.

'Look, I didn't have to ring you with this information, I could have just disappeared.'

'True.' Rachel realised that she needed to tread more carefully. Getting Cassie back to her mum was the most important issue, not scoring points against Jessica. 'We really appreciate you ringing in when you didn't have to. Why did you, if you don't mind me asking?'

'Call it a guilty conscience if you like. There's something a bit weird about Kate's obsession, and I didn't think it was fair that the

Baileys' kid should have to live with her when she's done nothing wrong. I don't like Naomi but she's probably a much better mother to Cassie than that psycho would be.'

'Well, you'd better let me have the address of the cottage before Kate goes on the run with her.'

'Larkhill Cottage, Pendlebury Lane, Dingley End.'

Rachel was scribbling down the address and was about to ask for the postcode, but the line had already gone dead. She tore the piece of paper off the pad and hurried out into the incident room.

'Listen up. That was Jessica Toland on the phone. She has given me an address where she says Cassie Bailey is being held. Errol, get the car, and we need two back-up teams to come with us to this address,' she said, handing him the piece of paper.

'Yes, Guv.'

'Graham, make sure the border authorities are on high alert. I don't want Jessica Toland slipping out of the country. She may not have kidnapped Cassie, but she could have prevented it from happening. I'm sure we'll be able to make a charge of "obstructing the course of justice" stick.'

'On it, Guv. The phone trace couldn't pinpoint her exactly, it only showed that she is still in the Reading area.'

'Strange. I'd have thought she would have wanted to get as far away from here as possible.'

'Maybe she was waiting to make her move until after she'd made the call so we wouldn't know where she was heading.'

'Good point. When you get off the phone from the border authorities, I want you to go to Kate Birchell's home. According to Mrs Toland, Kate is behind the whole kidnap plot. I doubt she'll be there, but if she is, bring her in for questioning. At last it feels like we're getting somewhere,' Rachel said, going back into her office for her bag and phone before heading for the stairwell and the waiting car.

CHAPTER FORTY-FOUR

3.42 p.m. – Sunday

Gravel sprayed around, showering down like a violent hailstorm as two police cars and an unmarked vehicle screeched to a halt in front of the rented cottage. Officers spilled out and surrounded it as DCI Hart stepped up to the front door and rapped the knocker. There was no response.

'This is the police, Kate,' she shouted. 'Open up!'

Nothing.

'Can you break this down, Errol?' she asked the burly detective sergeant at her side.

'Looks pretty solid, Guv, but we can give it a go, unless there's another entrance around the back that would be easier.'

'Check it out,' Rachel said, before calling out again. 'We know the whole story, Kate, you might as well come out now. There's nowhere to run. Jessica told us everything,' under her breath she added, 'eventually.'

For once, it had seemed as though Jessica was telling them the truth but now, standing on the doorstep of the seemingly empty cottage, Rachel was wondering if it had been another pack of lies to throw them off her scent. The front door opened. It was Errol.

'It was much easier round the back,' he said. 'The kitchen's got a semi-glazed door and the key was in the lock on the inside. It doesn't look like anyone's home though.'

Damn, it looks like we're too late. Why didn't that stupid woman tell us about this place during her interview rather than ringing the information in? We'd have been here an hour ago, and that hour could have made all the difference. If Kate was here, she must have gone on the run with Cassie, and if she suspects that we're on to her, the little girl could be in serious danger.

'Search upstairs,' Rachel ordered. 'Every cupboard, every nook and cranny, anywhere that a small child could hide or be hidden. I want this place going over with a fine toothcomb.'

'Yes, Guv.'

Rachel was regretting her decision to invite Charlie Bailey to meet them at the cottage. Despite telling him to manage his expectations, he would be devastated when he arrived to find his little girl was not there.

'Are the forensics team on their way?'

'They should be here by 4 p.m. Bob's not very happy that he's missing the Manchester derby on TV.'

'Can't he record it, or watch it on catch-up?'

'You're not a football fan, I take it?'

'No.'

'It's not quite the same as watching it live.'

'Tough. I think locating a missing child takes precedence over watching a bunch of overpaid prima donnas kicking a ball around, don't you?'

'Yes, Guv,' Errol replied.

Rachel took out her phone and selected Graham's number. He answered on the second ring. 'We're too bloody late,' she said. 'There's no one here, assuming that Jessica was telling us the truth and this was the kidnap hideaway location. I still don't trust her. She's changed her story so many times.'

'She seemed pretty convincing to me, Guv. Why would she bother ringing the station with false information? By making the call, she's implicated herself in the conspiracy to kidnap Cassie when she could have just kept quiet.'

'Hmm, I suppose. Are you at Kate's? I'm presuming she's not there?'

'No, I'm on my way back to the station, but you presume right, she's not there. Her husband, Alan, was there with the boys and he's in a right old state.'

'What do you mean?'

'Apparently she's left him. He showed me a note she'd written while he was out with the children this morning. She definitely isn't planning on going back there.'

'So, if she's not there and she's not here, where the hell is she? What we really need is the name and address of the guy who forged her new papers. If we knew Kate's new identity, she wouldn't be that hard to find. I wonder why Jessica wouldn't give us that information when she was keen enough to tell us everything else? I didn't buy the "protecting my brother" story. Is there anything from the traffic boys on Kate's car? I'm worried she might harm Cassie in some way if she thinks Jessica's spilled the beans.'

'Nothing yet. Why do you think she'd hurt Cassie? I thought the whole point of abducting her was because she's obsessed with her?'

'These people's brains are wired differently to ours. If she can't have the happy life she'd planned with Cassie, she won't want anyone else to.'

'I'll get on to them, Guv. I'll call you as soon as I have anything.'

Rachel ended the call as Errol came out of the house.

'They're definitely not here,' he said. 'It doesn't look like anyone's been here at all. Beds not slept in, no limescale marks on any of the taps, nothing.'

'Right, get everyone out. If there is any forensic evidence to be found, we don't want to destroy it. Are there any outbuildings?'

'Just a shed. Already checked, and there's nothing in it apart from garden tools.'

'Guv, I think you should come and look at this.'

Rachel quickly crossed the gravel driveway to where PC Drake was peering over the perimeter wall. 'What have you got?'

'Well, it may be nothing, but they look like cat treats to me. Who would dump a load of cat treats in the middle of nowhere?'

'Maybe hikers come up this way and leave treats for the wildlife. I should imagine other animals would eat them apart from cats. It may not be relevant, but take a picture anyway and make sure it's in your notes. Good spot, constable.'

Rachel made her way back over to the cottage, her shoes crunching in the gravel. As she stepped into the hallway, she realised a small piece of gravel had got caught in the ridges of the sole of her shoe. She leaned on the door frame to prise it out with a fingernail and that's when she noticed something orange-coloured poking out from beneath the mat. Picking it up, she realised it was a cat treat, and that it was the same distinctive shape as the variety that had been dumped over the wall. *Maybe this is related to the case after all*, she thought, tapping Graham's name on her phone again.

'What was the name of the Baileys' cat?'

'Pumpkin. Why do you ask?'

'I know remnants of Pumpkin's collar were found last night in the burnt-out bonfire, but did they actually find his body?' she asked, pressing herself against the wall of the narrow hallway to allow the officers who had been searching for Cassie in the upstairs rooms to get past on their way out of the cottage.

'Just the collar, I think. What are you getting at?'

'I'm wondering if the delightful Kate planted the collar in the bonfire to make it look as though the cat had died.'

'What makes you think that?'

'We've just found a load of cat treats dumped over the wall in the driveway, but more importantly, there was one under the doormat in the hall,' Rachel said, rolling the orange-coloured biscuit between her finger and thumb. 'It could have been from previous tenants and missed by the cleaners, but the rest of the place is pristine, so it's unlikely. Maybe Kate brought Pumpkin here as company for Cassie if the little girl was more distressed than she expected her to be.'

'It's a possibility, and it would suggest that Jessica Toland was telling the truth.'

'It would also prove that Kate has been here, or someone else who had access to the cat.'

'So, you're still not convinced that Kate is behind the kidnap plot?'

'Just keeping all options open. Jessica could be lying about Kate's involvement to deflect attention from Charlie. Perhaps those two did hit it off that night, and they're planning on running away together with Cassie.'

'You think?'

'I don't know, but he hasn't showed up here yet after I called him about the tip-off. It would be a pretty big signal to suggest that he's behind all this if he's a no-show. We've already had a very convincing acting performance from Jessica, and Kate could win an Oscar for her role as most supportive friend. Maybe they're all in it together, with their different reasons to punish Naomi.'

'If Charlie does show up, is it proof that he's not involved? He could still be play-acting, knowing that his daughter is safe elsewhere.'

'That's a good point. Or he's genuinely expecting her to be here, and he's been double-crossed by one of the other two? The border authorities are on high alert looking for Jessica, so our priority now is to find Kate. The timing of her decision to leave her husband and their boys surely can't be a coincidence.'

'That's what I thought.'

'And it seems strange that she would desert her best friend when she needs her most. Kate is a key piece of this jigsaw, and we need the rest of the pieces to start fitting together. At least one of those three knows where Cassie is – we just need to figure out which one.'

CHAPTER FORTY-FIVE

4.07 p.m. – Sunday

The light was starting to fade as Charlie sped along unfamiliar country lanes as fast as he dared, all trace of the tiredness that had overwhelmed him earlier erased by his anticipation at seeing his daughter. He knew he'd been exceeding the speed limit on the M4, but he didn't care. His satnav was showing an ETA of three minutes; three minutes until he could hug his little girl again after more than five excruciatingly long weeks. Every pounding beat of his heart brought him closer to Cassie.

Earlier, it had felt as though he had only been sleeping for a few minutes when his mobile phone started ringing. He had reached for it with his eyes half closed.

'Hello?'

'Mr Bailey? It's Rachel Hart here.'

He was instantly awake, gripping the phone as though his life depended on it. 'Have you found her?'

'Not yet, but we have reason to believe we know where Cassie is being held and we're on our way there now.'

'Is she… is she…?'

'Like I said, Charlie, we're not there yet, so I can't give you any further information but, if our source is accurate, we believe she's unharmed, although we don't know for sure.' There was a slight pause, and Charlie had sensed Rachel Hart's hesitation before she continued. 'I thought that maybe you would want to meet us at the location.'

'Yes,' he had answered immediately.

'Obviously it will be a crime scene and must be treated as such, but it might be easier for Cassie to have one of her parents there after her ordeal.'

'Yes, of course.'

'And on that point, I think it may be wise not to say anything to your wife for the moment, in case this turns out to be false information. There is always the possibility that Cassie won't be where we are expecting her to be, and it might all be too stressful for Naomi in her current condition.'

'Yes, I can see that. I won't say anything to Naomi or my mum.'

'I'll text you the address and we'll see you there in about an hour. And Charlie, please manage your expectations. This might turn out to be a false lead.'

'In three hundred yards, take a left turn,' said the dulcet tones of the female voice artist he had selected to narrate instructions on his satnav. He had made that particular choice because she sounded a lot like Naomi, and he had occasionally wondered if the actress was red-haired and blue-eyed like her, too. He could almost believe Naomi was sitting at his side offering guidance from a map instead of lying in her bed in a drug-induced sleep.

'Turn left,' the voice instructed.

As Charlie swung the Ford Focus onto the narrow lane, which was really little more than a dirt track, the anticipation of seeing his little girl again after their enforced separation was almost overwhelming.

'You have reached your destination,' the voice informed him as he pulled up on the crowded driveway behind a small van. Before he had even turned off the engine, he could see DCI Hart striding towards him. He couldn't read her expression as he climbed out of the car, but he knew the news wasn't good when she started her sentence with an apology.

'I'm sorry, Charlie. She's not here.'

'What do you mean?'

'The forensics team have just arrived and they will do extensive tests, but to the untrained eye it doesn't look as if anyone has been staying at this cottage recently.'

The adrenaline that had fuelled Charlie's mad dash from home seemed to be draining out of him. He could feel his shoulders slump and there was a rushing sound in his ears. When Rachel spoke again it was like listening to her from the end of a tunnel.

'Are you all right? I did warn you that this was a possibility.'

'Of course I'm not bloody all right! She's supposed to be here, Cassie was supposed to be here and now she's not. Where is she?' he demanded, his voice increasing in volume. 'Why are you lot so bloody useless?'

'I can understand your anger and frustration, but please believe me when I say we really are doing our very best to try and find Cassie.'

'Well, your best isn't bloody good enough,' Charlie railed, getting back into his car, slamming the door closed and collapsing forward over the steering wheel.

Rachel tapped on the window, but Charlie didn't respond. She waited a few moments and tried again before heading back towards the cottage.

Charlie knew he was being unreasonable. It wasn't the DCI's fault that Cassie wasn't at the cottage. There were so many questions he wanted to ask: who had the misinformation come from, being the main one, but right at that moment he didn't trust himself to be civil. He took several deep breaths, trying to compose himself. The only saving grace was that he hadn't told Naomi where he was heading. *If I feel this devastated, I can only imagine what it would have done to her.* At that moment his phone buzzed with a text message. *She must have discovered that I'm not asleep in Cassie's room,* he thought, reaching into his jacket pocket for his phone. *How am I supposed to explain that I sneaked out of the house without telling her and Mum – what reason am I going to give?* But the message wasn't from Naomi. It was from a number he didn't recognise, and it started with the words *If you want to see Cassie again…*

Hands trembling, Charlie keyed in his passcode and opened up the message:

If you want to see Cassie again you'll do exactly as I say. She is alive and unharmed and will stay that way if you deposit £10,000 into my bank account, details to follow. Text 'yes' back to this number and I will call you to let you hear Cassie's voice. It goes without saying that if you show this to the police you will never lay eyes on Cassie again.

Typing three letters and pressing the arrow to reply to the message was about the limit of what Charlie could manage. He glanced over towards the cottage to make sure there was no sign of DCI Hart and then focused his attention on his phone, willing it to ring. Even staring at it as he was, it still made him jump when it did. He pressed the green arrow before the end of the first ring.

'Hello?'

'Daddy?'

'Cassie, are you all right?'

'I'm sorry about the pumpkin. I should have waited for Mummy. Can I come home now, please?'

Before Charlie could say anything else, the call was ended. Moments later, another text came through with a bank sort code, account number and the name Jake Camero. The message simply said to text the word 'done' when the transfer had been made.

Who the hell is Jake Camero? Why has he got my daughter? He glanced over towards the cottage again. The DCI was on the phone and heading in his direction. Without a second thought, Charlie turned on the engine, rammed the Focus into reverse and backed out of the drive at speed, sending gravel shooting everywhere. He had no way of knowing if Jake Camero was the person who had tipped the police off that Cassie was being held at the cottage. Perhaps he was watching to make sure Charlie didn't communicate with them. *I can't take that chance*, Charlie thought, watching the outline of Rachel Hart get smaller and smaller in his rear-view mirror as he drove away at speed.

*

'That's odd,' Rachel said into the phone.

'What's that, Guv?'

'Charlie Bailey has just driven off even though I'm pretty sure he saw me walking towards his car. He's either still upset that I dragged him out here on a wild goose chase, or he didn't want to speak to me.'

'You did what you thought was best. If he hadn't showed up, we would have known he's involved.'

'But if he's not, I've just put him through emotional hell. Perhaps I should have waited to call him until we knew for certain that Cassie was here.'

'Well, if he's not involved, now is probably not the right moment to tell him about the little girl in the Chiswick playground wearing Cassie's coat and wellies.'

'We don't know for sure that they're Cassie's until the forensics team have examined them.'

'It would be a pretty big coincidence for the child to have exactly the same coat and boots that Cassie was wearing when she went missing.'

'True, but let's not get carried away. Did the mother say where she found them?'

'She didn't find them. She insists they were given to her by someone in her block of flats.'

'Did she give a description of this generous benefactor? Please let it match with Jessica, and then we can formally charge her with child abduction when we find her.'

'Sorry, Guv. Not this time. It wasn't Jessica, in fact it wasn't even a woman. The description reads, and I quote, "he's good-looking in a foreign sort of way".'

Rachel shivered. All the while she had believed that Jessica, Kate or Charlie were in some way responsible for kidnapping Cassie, she had clung to the belief that the little girl was relatively safe. With this new development the case had taken a sinister turn. If Cassie had been picked up on the street by a random stranger and not taken to the nearest police station, he must have had other plans for her. She could feel the bitter taste of bile rising in her mouth as she tried to blot out a deeply buried memory. If Graham was talking to her, she couldn't hear him. All she could hear was a little girl's voice pleading, 'Please don't hurt me, please don't hurt me.' But he had hurt her; he had hurt them both. Rachel was glad that she was standing on the road alone; it wouldn't do for officers under her command to see her crying. She brushed the tears away with the back of her hand and cleared her throat before speaking.

'We need to get an e-fit impression done of this mystery man in Chiswick, and cross-reference it with the known child sex offenders' register as a matter of urgency.'

'On it, Guv.'

*

Ten miles away, Charlie pulled into a motorway service area and logged into his online bank account. He transferred £10,000 from his and Naomi's savings account, money they had been hoping to put towards a deposit for a bigger house when their little family expanded, into their current account. He carefully tapped in the details for Jake Camero's account, and when the page came up for him to check before confirming his instruction, he made sure that all the details were correct. His finger hovered over the confirm button, then he closed his eyes and hit it. The message that the funds would be in the payee's account within two hours flashed up. *Two hours. By 6.45 p.m. the kidnappers will have received the money and then they'll tell me where to find Cassie.* He texted *done* as he had been told to do, then went into the café to buy himself a coffee and wait for what he knew was going to be the longest two hours of his life.

CHAPTER FORTY-SIX

5.05 p.m. – Sunday

Kate pulled away from the kerb having dumped the cat carry basket in an almost-empty skip outside an office building whose frontage was covered in scaffolding. She was confident that it would be buried in rubble once the builders started work on Monday morning. Even so, she hadn't taken any chances, and she'd emptied the basket of its contents in case anyone passing took a shine to it. This was the fifth stop Kate had made.

The toys, books and clothes she had lovingly selected for Cassie, along with the unicorn bedding and lamp, had been placed in a collection bin outside a supermarket. No doubt they would soon be winging their way to a far-flung war zone or a natural disaster area, the charity organisers too grateful for donations to ask any questions. She had driven slowly past a row of restaurants and spotted an alley, at the bottom of which was a selection of waste bins near the kitchen entrances. She had dropped a few food items in each bin, soon to be covered with leftovers from the evening dinner service.

The cat food she had simply scattered in a park, depositing the wrapper in a bin. On driving away, she checked her rear-view mirror as a dozen or more stray cats appeared from nowhere to enjoy their unexpected feast. And she had watched the litter tray float down a river after she dropped it off a bridge, twisting and twirling in the current and gradually filling with water before finally sinking beneath the surface.

All the pieces of potential evidence that Kate had removed from the cottage were now scattered far and wide, and she was fairly sure that no one would ever trace them back to her. All she had to do now was get rid of the fake passport and papers she had bought from Jessica's brother's contact, and she would be in a pretty strong position to deny anything Jessica may have told the police about her. *It should be easy enough to mingle with a crowd around a bonfire and throw the stuff into the fire unnoticed. It's not as though I haven't done it before.*

Although it was already dark, thanks to the clocks going back the previous weekend, it was only a little after five, so she knew it was probably too early for community displays to start. They had lit the bonfire at the Beechwood Avenue display at six, with the fireworks starting at half past. *For once I actually enjoyed it, but maybe that was because of the added element of danger, having to get close enough to drop Pumpkin's collar into the flames. Was that really only last night? It feels like a lifetime ago.*

At that point, Kate had thought everything was going more or less to plan, apart from Jessica attracting the attention of the police because she hadn't followed instructions and gone into work on Friday evening. She'd assumed Jessica had gone ahead with the kidnap, and that Cassie was safely hidden at the cottage. Although she'd been a little concerned when Naomi let slip during their phone conversation the previous day that they had already questioned Jessica about Cassie's disappearance and were once again looking for her, Kate hadn't seen any cause for alarm. If Jessica had implicated her in any way, the police would have already called her in for questioning. There had been no opportunity to leave her family and go to the cottage to check on Cassie the previous evening and, as it turned out, the little girl wasn't there anyway. Pumpkin was locked away in her garden shed, drugged but otherwise none the worse for wear, and she was nudging Naomi ever closer towards a nervous breakdown with her little trick of throwing the cat's collar on the bonfire. It had all seemed to be going her way until Charlie's call that morning. She had needed to think on her feet and fabricate the conversation with her eldest son to give herself a reason not to go around to Beechwood Avenue to babysit Naomi. Then it was just a case of getting rid of Alan and the boys for a couple of hours so that she could make her getaway a day early. *Strange, I expected to feel some emotion knowing I would never see my boys again, but all I felt was relief and excitement that I would soon be starting my new life with Cassie.*

Kate had guessed she would have only a few hours before Jessica spilled the beans and she had been proven right when, only five miles from the cottage, she had passed two police cars and a third vehicle with their blue lights flashing, speeding in the direction from which she had come. *It's a good job I wasn't in the Audi. One of the police officers would surely have recognised it, and thank God I hadn't chucked the dark wig, although I probably should at some point.*

A big orange sign pinned to a lamp post loomed into view.

FIREWORK DISPLAY 6 p.m. Sunday, 2 November. Gates open at 5.30 p.m.

She joined the line of vehicles queuing to go into the car park and followed the directions of the parking attendant. Tucking the envelope containing all the fake documents into the pocket of her Barbour jacket, and grabbing her purse rather than taking her handbag, she joined the throng of people heading towards the bonfire. Parents holding the hands of excited children, and couples holding each other's hands, made her feel all the more alone.

I've closed the door on my old life and now I have no new life to move on to, she thought, trudging along, head down and hands in her pockets. *I could still go to the house in Wales, and it would back up the story that I've been planning on leaving Alan for some time, but there's no point if I don't have Cassie to share it with.*

Kate bought herself a mulled wine and moved towards the blazing bonfire. The crackling sound of the wood, punctuated by hissing and spitting, increased in volume the closer she got, and as pieces tumbled through the structure and thudded to the ground, showers of orange sparks rose up into the inky darkness. She stood transfixed, watching the flames lick at each new piece of wood before it caught alight and was duly consumed by the inferno. *What was I thinking, enlisting help from that lying bitch? I must have been out of my mind. I thought I was so damn clever, making her believe that Charlie was interested in her, but maybe it's me that has been taken for a ride. Someone took Cassie on Thursday night, and it wasn't me. If it was Jessica and she has hidden her somewhere else, maybe with the intention of blackmailing me to get her back, why haven't I heard from her? My poor Cassie, what has she done with you?*

The first firework took her by surprise, bursting overhead in hundreds of pink and green stars, as the thumping music heralded the start of the spectacle that everyone else was there to see. Faces turned skywards gave Kate the perfect opportunity to dispose of the papers in the belly of the bonfire. She watched the corners of the envelope crinkle and brown before bursting into flames, her only chance of happiness going up in smoke. She dropped her plastic cup of mulled wine to the ground and crushed it underfoot before pushing her way back through the crowd of people transfixed by the pyrotechnics erupting overhead. *All I wanted was to be happy. I deserve that, don't I, after all the years I've played witness to Naomi and Charlie's perfect life?*

Kate climbed back into the car and reached for her handbag to put her purse back in its usual place. That's when she noticed she had two text messages on her phone from a number she didn't recognise. The first had been sent more than two hours ago:

If you want to see Cassie again, you'll do exactly as I say. She is alive and unharmed and will stay that way if you deposit £10,000 into my bank account, details to follow. Text 'yes' back to this number and I will call you to let you hear Cassie's voice. It goes without saying that if you show this to the police you will never lay eyes on Cassie again.

'What the hell?'
She opened up the second message:

Too late. You lose. Charlie paid up. Enjoy your sad and lonely life. Thanks for the thirty grand to get me started in my new one. For the record, you deserve everything you've got... nothing!

CHAPTER FORTY-SEVEN

'All right, Guv?' DI Wilson said when DCI Hart answered her phone. 'Did forensics find anything?'

'Nothing. They're just starting to pack up now. The whole place is as clean as a whistle. I kid you not, you could actually eat your dinner off the floor. At least you could have done, before our lot started tramping in and out. Any joy with the e-fit?'

'Actually yes, that's one of the reasons I'm ringing. He's not on the sex offenders' register, but one of the local boys in Chiswick recognised him as Jake Camero, an Argentinian he arrested a few months back. Apparently he's an artist with a little sideline in forgery.'

Rachel's grip on the phone tightened. 'Do you think he's our guy?'

'Almost certainly, although I'm not quite sure how he fits into all this yet. Forgery is one thing, but kidnapping a child is something else entirely and doesn't fit with his MO. He's currently on bail awaiting trial, so he must know that one step out of line will see him locked up until his trial date. The Chiswick team are on their way to his place now to question him, so we should have some answers pretty soon.'

'Well, that sounds promising. If he is our forger, he may be persuaded to cooperate and give us the details of Kate's new identity in return for the promise of a lesser sentence. Have we had any other leads from the appeal that I need to follow up?'

'Nothing else relevant. We've been inundated with calls of sightings, as you predicted, but they've all been checked out by the local forces and they're all completely innocent. One old guy had to be rushed to hospital in Leicester, though, after he was approached in the park with his granddaughter. Suspected heart attack, but I think he's going to pull through.'

'That's why I held off on the appeal in the first place, it just muddies the water. Speaking of which, nothing from the divers, I take it?'

'No, I would have let you know. The canal's quite shallow and it doesn't have much of a current so they're fairly sure Cassie's not in there, but they're going to continue at first light. I do have one other piece of interesting info, though.'

'Go on.'

'The security team at the big Sainsbury's in the town centre always let us know if cars are parked in their car park after the store closes. There are two vehicles in there tonight, one of them is an Audi and it's the same colour, make and model as Kate Birchell drives. I've asked for their CCTV footage, and I'm going to check the DVLA database when I get off the phone.'

'It's a shame you're not female, Graham.'

'Guv?'

'We're very good at multitasking,' she said, smiling for the first time in days.

'Very funny. Right, I'm just pulling it up now. Yep. It's definitely her car. Apparently it's been parked there since 11.51 this morning, according to the ticket displayed on the windscreen.'

'It sounds as though she's abandoned it,' Rachel said, annoyed for not suspecting that Kate would switch to a different vehicle to facilitate her getaway. 'We need their CCTV footage pronto, Graham. We've had traffic cameras looking for the Audi and she's probably miles away by now driving something else.'

'Maybe another hire car? Do you want me to try and contact the local firms?'

'They were pretty useless getting back to us with the information about who hired the red BMW, and I don't think you'll have much better luck with this, particularly on a Sunday evening. They're almost done here, so I'll head back to the station and we can go through the CCTV footage together when it comes in. I was just wondering whether to give Charlie Bailey a call. If he's not involved, it must have been devastating for him to get here only to find that Cassie wasn't.'

'Good idea, Guv. Hopefully he'll have calmed down by now, and at least you've got a couple of new leads to tell him about.'

'True. I'll call him on the journey back. It won't do any harm for him to know how hard we're working to try and find Cassie,' Rachel said. Charlie's stinging criticism that the police were 'bloody useless' was still fresh in her mind. 'And as you say, Graham, we have progress to report.'

CHAPTER FORTY-EIGHT

'Here you are, love,' Hazel said, setting the tray down on Naomi's duck-egg blue duvet cover. 'Do you need me to plump your pillows up a bit?'

'No, they're fine thanks, Hazel. This smells good. I'm surprised you found anything to cook. I usually do the weekly shop on Fridays.'

'That's what freezers are for, and potatoes last for ages as long as they're kept dry.'

'Aren't you having any?'

'It's a bit early for me. I thought I'd wait for Charlie to wake up and then we can eat at our usual time. I'm a creature of habit, I'm afraid. He told me you needed to have your next tablets at around 6 p.m., so I did yours early.'

'Is he still sleeping?'

'Yes. Not a peep from him all afternoon. He must have needed it, bless him. I'll give him a shout in an hour or so if he still hasn't surfaced.'

Naomi put a forkful of mashed potato in her mouth.

'You really do make the best mash,' she said, savouring the creaminess on her tongue. 'I've tried to follow your instructions, adding butter and grainy mustard, but mine is never as good as yours, although Charlie tries to pretend it is.'

'He's a good boy.'

Naomi fell silent, concentrating on her food. *Hazel's right. Charlie is a good boy. A loving, attentive father, a caring son and the kindest, most considerate husband anyone could wish for, until I started obsessing about having another baby. Something that should have brought us even closer together has somehow driven a wedge between us. If only I'd realised what it was doing to our relationship, we wouldn't be in this situation now, desperate for news from the police and yet fearful of what the news may be.* She took some more mashed potato, but this time it was harder to swallow.

'Have the police been in touch?'

'No, sorry, love. No one's called on the house phone and Charlie's got his mobile in Cassie's room with him so it would have woken him up if they'd called on that. Try not to worry too much. I'm sure they're doing everything they can. That DCI Hart really seems on the ball.'

'I know they're doing as much as they can, but every minute that passes without Cassie is like the cruellest form of torture. And all I keep thinking is, will she get over whatever ordeal she has been put through? Is she ever going to be the same little girl again?'

'She's brave and resilient. Children have a remarkable way of coping with things that would floor us adults. Of course, it depends on what she has endured, but she'll have you and Charlie supporting her.'

'And you, Hazel. She'll need all of us. I'm so sorry I stopped you from visiting her. These past three days without seeing her smiling face has been hell on earth for me, and yet I thought it was okay to stop you and Charlie from seeing her for the past five weeks. You must think I'm heartless.'

'I don't think any such thing. Heartbroken, more like, and probably with good reason. It has been especially hard for you, with no one to turn to for advice since your mum died.'

'I had Kate.'

'Thank goodness you did, but it's still not the same as having your mum to talk to. I – I kind of hoped that I would take on that role for you, but I suppose the circumstances of this situation made it impossible.'

'It did, really. No mother takes kindly to hearing their child being criticised. How would you have reacted if I'd come to you and told you Charlie had been unfaithful? I think somehow you would have found a way to place some of the blame on me, and I couldn't face that because I knew it was justified, to a degree. I've been such a fool, Hazel,' Naomi said, tears trickling down her cheeks. 'I didn't realise how lucky I was to have what I had until I lost it.'

Hazel reached for the tray and put it on the floor, then drew Naomi into a hug, allowing her to sob quietly into her chest. 'You haven't lost it forever, sweetheart, it's just misplaced for the moment. When Cassie comes home, you'll have the chance to put everything right.'

'But what if she never comes home? What if we're destined to live the rest of our lives wondering if she's alive or dead? We'd be looking at every dark-haired child of a similar age to Cassie and wondering if it's her. I don't know if I could bear it.'

'Let's not think like that. Let's believe she's on her way home to us right now. And if she is, she'll need her mum strong and well. Do you want me to fetch Charlie?'

'No, I'm all right,' Naomi said, pulling away from Hazel and wiping her eyes with an already sodden tissue. 'It just overwhelms me, sometimes.'

'Well, I'm here for you whenever you need me, and for what it's worth, I think my son was wrong to cheat on you, whatever the circumstances. "Until death us do part" should mean exactly that in my opinion, through good times and bad.'

'Thanks, Hazel, that means a lot, but it wasn't entirely Charlie's fault, I know that now.'

'Now then, do you feel up to finishing your dinner? It might be a bit cold. I could pop it in the microwave if you like?'

'No, it's fine. Delicious as your cooking always is, I can't really taste much today. I'm only eating so that I can have my next lot of drugs. I think my little outburst would suggest the effects of the last lot are wearing off.'

'Here you go, then,' Hazel said, putting the tray back in front of her daughter-in-law. 'I'm just going to nip downstairs and get my phone. Sheila normally rings me around this time on a Sunday and she'll be anxious to know if there's any news.'

A couple of minutes later, Hazel was back upstairs. 'Well, that's odd. I could have sworn I left my phone next to my keys on the shelf near the front door. I didn't bring it in here, did I?'

'I can't see it. Did you check the lounge and the kitchen?'

'Yes, just now. I must have left it at home. Would you be all right for a few minutes if I popped home to get it? I could let Alfie out for a wee while I'm there.'

'Take your time. I'll be fine, and Charlie's in the next room if I need anything urgently.'

'Well, let's get your tablets down you and then you'll probably doze off again. I'll be back before you know it.'

Once Naomi had swallowed the pills, Hazel took the tray with the remains of her dinner down to the kitchen. She could hear PC Walsh stamping his feet to try and stay warm on the other side of the front door as she shrugged her coat on.

'I'm nipping home for a few minutes to fetch my phone,' she said to him, 'I'll make you a hot drink when I get back, if you're allowed.'

'That's very kind of you, but I probably won't be here. I was supposed to be relieved at 6 p.m., but no one's turned up yet. Would it be all right if I use the toilet?'

'Relieved. Toilet. Very amusing.'

PC Walsh looked confused.

No sense of humour, today's youngsters, Hazel thought, shaking her head. 'Of course. It's the first door on the left before you get to the kitchen.'

'Thanks.'

Hazel pulled the door closed behind her and set off up the road.

CHAPTER FORTY-NINE

6.35 p.m. – Sunday

An oily film had formed on the top of Charlie's half-drunk latte; he had abandoned it because his throat was too tight to drink. Every few minutes he checked his phone, willing there to be a message from the kidnappers with details of where he could find his daughter. Over and over, as the minutes ticked away, he asked himself if he had done the right thing by sending money to them without informing the police of what was going on. *If I'd told the police and the kidnappers had found out, I would never have seen Cassie again. But what's to say they'll stick to their word? And what's to say she's still alive?* His daughter's voice on the phone, asking to come home, had been heartbreaking. *I had no choice; I had to send the money, even though it's a gamble. I hope to God it pays off.* He ran his fingers through his hair for the hundredth time.

The sound of Charlie's phone ringing startled him; he hadn't been expecting it. It was DCI Hart. He pressed the red button to dismiss the call. The kidnappers had given him strict instructions not to have any contact with the police, and he wasn't prepared to risk his daughter's safety. A few minutes later, she called again. *For Christ's sake, leave me alone, I'd have picked up the first time if I wanted to talk to you.* Then he started to worry. *Whatever she wants must be pretty important for her to ring twice.* He had just reached the decision to answer his phone if she called again when the text message he had been waiting for came through:

You're lucky it's me that took your kid. If someone else had found her on her doorstep, locked out of the house, she'd have been sold to an Eastern European gang for child porn by now or be dead. You should tell your precious wife to take better care of her, seeing as you both say you love her so much. I got the money so you are welcome to her. She's in Pangbourne Cricket Pavilion. Adios lover-boy.

Jessica! Charlie thought. *That bitch was behind this all along. There's probably no such person as Jake Camero, just a fake account she set up to get the ransom money. I can't believe she's put us all through this hell for ten bloody grand! If she's done anything to harm Cassie, I'll bloody kill her.*

The legs of the chair he had sat in for almost two hours scraped across the floor, such was his hurry to get to his car and enter the details for the cricket pavilion into his satnav. His phone started to ring again as he was waiting for it to accurately pinpoint his location and give him a route. It was DCI Hart. He switched his phone off. At that moment, he suspected he knew far more about his daughter's whereabouts than she did. He wanted to be the one to find and comfort Cassie after her ordeal rather than scaring her further with police sirens and flashing blue lights.

'Come on, you pile of shit!' he shouted at the satnav as it took its time before finally offering him a choice of three routes. He hit 'fastest route' rather than 'shortest route' and screeched out of the motorway services car park at far more than the permitted twenty miles an hour. The screen was showing an arrival time of 7.05 p.m. as he moved straight into the outside lane of the M4 and pressed the accelerator pedal of his Ford Focus almost to the floor.

Less than thirty minutes later, as the clock on his dashboard clicked on to 7 p.m., Charlie's car screeched to a halt in the deserted car park of Pangbourne Cricket Club. In the light cast by the full beam of his headlamps, he could see the outline of a building on the far side of the cricket pitch. It was in total darkness. Without a thought for his own safety, he leapt out of the car and ran across the grass, leaving the headlights on to light his way. His heart was pounding in his chest as he took the six steps up onto the veranda of the wooden structure two at a time. Using the torch on his phone, he could see that a pane of glass in the door, next to the handle, had been smashed. For the first time he considered the thought that Jessica may still be inside, but he dismissed it almost immediately. She had nothing to gain by hanging around. He presumed her priority now was to escape with his money, but he couldn't care less about that; all he wanted was his daughter back. Charlie pressed down on the handle and the door swung open, catching slightly on the fragments of broken glass that he stepped over as he entered the room.

'Cassie,' he called into the darkness. 'Where are you, darling? Daddy's here.' He stood still to listen for a response, but there was nothing. He flashed the torchlight around the large area where chairs were neatly stacked against walls covered with empty noticeboards. The cricket season was long over. It was the perfect hiding place in the depths of winter.

My God, what if I hadn't paid up? No one would have come near this place until next spring. He shuddered.

'Cassie,' he called again, this time with more urgency in his voice. Again he was met with silence, except for the ticking of a clock above the serving hatch at the back of the room, from where the wives and friends of the amateur sportsmen would serve tea throughout the summer months. He covered the distance in a few steps and shone the light from his torch through the hatch to illuminate the sizeable kitchen. On the work surface running along the back wall, next to an ancient cooker that was hooked up to a Calor gas bottle, were two large shiny tea urns. He shone the beam of light across cream-painted cupboards and back again, straining his eyes for a glimpse of his daughter. There was a large wooden table in the middle of the room where Charlie imagined the match-day helpers would form a production line, buttering bread to be passed on to others who filled the sandwiches before passing them over to the serving table beneath the hatch. Nobody was there now, of course, and he was just starting to believe that he might be on another wild goose chase when a movement caught his eye in the furthest corner of the kitchen. He pushed open the door next to the service hatch, rushing towards where he had seen the movement and he was just in time to see a mouse disappearing into a tiny hole in the skirting board. The flicker of hope was immediately extinguished.

'Where are you, Cassie?' he said, desperation creeping into his voice. 'What has she done with you?' Leaning back against the work surface, he had a clear view of the bench-like table under the service hatch. The cups, saucers and side plates which would be stacked up on a match day were probably neatly stored away in the cupboards, but it looked as though someone had left a sack of some sort under the table. As he moved to examine it more closely, he realised it wasn't a sack, it was a blanket, and sticking out from the top of it were a few curls of dark hair, just like his own. His pulse was racing as he pulled the blanket back to reveal Cassie lying on her side with her back towards him, her hands and feet tied behind her with blue washing line. She wasn't moving.

CHAPTER FIFTY

7.03 p.m. – Sunday

DCI Hart arrived back at the police station shortly after 7 p.m. and went straight to the incident room to check how DI Wilson was getting on with the CCTV footage.

'Perfect timing, Guv, I've just finished going through the footage from Sainsbury's car park, and you were right about Kate having a second vehicle. She leaves the car park on foot directly after parking. About an hour and a half later, a different woman with long dark hair approaches the Audi and removes two suitcases from the boot, then comes back for a cat basket and a litter tray. I say "different woman", but it is actually Kate. She's wearing a different coat, one of those wax Barbour jackets, and the hair is probably a wig, but the shoes are the same, very distinctive purple trainers I've seen her wear at the Baileys' house. The vehicle she transferred everything into is a bronze-coloured Nissan Juke, registered under the name Alison Dwyer to a house in North Wales. We've got her, Guv. I'll call the local force, and they'll be a nice welcoming committee for her when she turns up with Cassie.'

'Good work, Graham. Anything more from the team in Chiswick?'

'Not much, but they do confirm Kate's new identity. Actually, they thought it was all a bit strange. There was no one home when they got to Jake Camero's address, so they had to force the door. They said the place was really tidy, with nothing in the bins apart from the remnants of a recent pizza dinner and yet there was a scrap of paper lying on the kitchen counter with Kate's old name and her new identity details on it. They think it looks like the paper was left there deliberately for them to find. There was nothing else remotely connected with forged papers anywhere in the flat.'

'Does it feel to you like we're being played? Why give one of your neighbours a distinctive coat and wellington boots belonging to a missing child unless you want them to be noticed? This Jake Camero must have known his neighbour would describe him to the police, and because he's on bail he knew we would be able to track him down to his address pretty quickly. He then deliberately leaves information about Kate's new identity lying around. He wanted us to go to that flat and he wants us to be searching for Kate. The question is, why?'

'So that we're not looking for him?'

'Precisely. Obviously we need to have the North Wales force meet Kate, and hopefully she'll have Cassie with her, but if she doesn't, it could be a red herring fed to us by Jessica, and Kate was never involved at all.'

'But what about the change of vehicle and the disguise? Would she do that if she was just running away to start a new life on her own?'

'It's possible, if she didn't want her husband to be able to find her. Remember she went to the trouble of getting a new identity. It could be that she wanted to erase all traces of her old life.'

'True.'

'We need to locate Jake Camero, and I have a feeling that when we do, Jessica Toland will be with him.'

'I'll alert the airports and the channel ports to be on the lookout for them, particularly any flights or crossings going to Spain.'

'Send photos. We're talking about a forger here. There is virtually no chance that either of them will be travelling under their real names, and they may both be disguised: different hair colour or style, wearing glasses, you know the sort of thing. And if he was out on bail, we must have his fingerprints. Make sure you circulate them internationally. It's highly likely that "Jake Camero" isn't even Argentinian.'

'Oh, and I almost forgot, Guv. There's a note on your desk from earlier. Hazel Bailey remembered that the pumpkin definitely had its whiskers when she saw it at 10 p.m. on Thursday night.'

'Which means it's looking ever more likely that Cassie was in the red BMW driven away by Jessica Toland. Our top priority now is to find those two before they leave the country.'

CHAPTER FIFTY-ONE

Charlie could feel the blood in his veins turning to ice. *Oh my God, I'm too late*, he thought, his hand brushing the cold skin of Cassie's cheek as he tentatively rolled her small frame towards him on the floor beneath the serving table. She blinked in the bright torchlight and his heart felt as though it was about to explode with relief and love.

'It's all right, it's all right,' he reassured her, while lifting her and placing her on the table. Gently, he started to peel away the brown parcel tape that had been stuck over her mouth to stop her crying out, pulling her delicate skin as taut as possible to minimise the pain.

'Daddy, you found me!' she cried the moment the tape was removed. 'I thought I might be lost forever.'

Charlie hugged her closely for a few seconds then started rummaging in the drawers, looking for scissors or a knife to cut the restraints from around her hands and feet. 'Keep still, sweetheart,' he said, brandishing a bread knife, 'I just need to get these things off you and then we can go home.'

Moments later, after several frantic sawing actions, the nylon line frayed and then broke, and he scooped Cassie up into his arms to hug her properly. He felt like he never wanted to let go of her.

'I've missed our hugs, Daddy.'

'Me too, princess,' he said, swallowing down the lump in his throat. 'Come on, let's get you out of here. When we're away from here, we can phone Mummy to let her know you're safe.'

Charlie ran across the field towards the headlights of his car carrying Cassie in his arms, anxious to put distance between them and the place where she had been abandoned. He presumed Jessica was long gone, having got the ransom she had asked for, but he wasn't taking any chances. He buckled Cassie into her car seat in the back and jumped into the driver's seat before pulling away at speed.

'Are we going to ring Mummy?'

Charlie noticed the anxiety in her voice. 'In a few minutes. Let's get away from here first. Shit,' he added under his breath, noticing the low fuel light was on and the dial was indicating only enough fuel to drive fifteen miles; not enough to get them home. *Why didn't I think of filling the tank while I was stuck at the services waiting for that damn text message?* 'We need some petrol so we can call Mummy when we stop for that.'

'And please may I get a drink? I'm a bit thirsty.'

'Of course. I should have brought a drink with me,' he said, watching his daughter through the rear-view mirror. Her eyes were already starting to close. *She'll be asleep in a couple of minutes*, he thought, smiling indulgently.

It had started when she was a young baby. On nights when she was fretful and wouldn't sleep, he would strap her into her baby seat and drive around the neighbourhood. Minutes later, she would be asleep, just as she was now. He could hardly believe Cassie was here in the car with him. *Heaven knows what she's been through, but I'll make it up to her; I'll make it up to both of my girls.* He pictured Naomi's face eagerly watching out for them from the lounge window once he had let her know they were on their way home, and then the three of them embracing with happy tears.

He pressed his foot down harder on the accelerator pedal as he joined the motorway.

A couple of minutes later, a blue sign indicated that motorway services were a mile up ahead. *Not long now until I can tell Naomi the good news and she can speak to Cassie*, Charlie thought, a smile splitting his handsome features.

CHAPTER FIFTY-TWO

7.09 p.m. – Sunday

Kate waited a few moments after PC Walsh went back outside before slipping silently into the hall and gently lowering the lever to engage the deadlock. She had only managed to overhear a little of Hazel's conversation with the young police constable from the other side of the hedge where she was hiding, but it sounded as though she wouldn't be gone for very long. *I need to move quickly*, she thought, going through to the kitchen and putting some milk in the pan to warm up.

When she had arrived at Beechwood Avenue fifteen minutes earlier, having decided that a life in Wales without Cassie was a life not worth living, she had no idea how she was going to get into the house to confront Naomi. There was so much she wanted to say to her and so little time. She had been wondering whether to risk approaching PC Walsh, who she'd seen several times over the previous three days, in the hope that he was unaware of her involvement in Cassie's disappearance, but when the front door opened and Hazel came out wearing her coat and the police officer left his post and went into the house, she knew it was the best opportunity she was going to get. Within seconds of Hazel leaving, Kate was putting her key in the lock. Once she was inside, she hid behind the sofa in the living room until she heard the toilet flush and the front door open and close.

She hummed quietly to herself as she pulled the packets of sleeping tablets out of her bag and began crushing them with the back of a spoon before mixing the resulting powder with cocoa and sugar in the bottom of two mugs. Worried that there might be a funny taste, she added an extra spoon of sugar to each and then poured in a little of the milk to mix everything to a paste before adding the rest and topping it with cream. A mug in each hand, she climbed the stairs and pushed Naomi's bedroom door open with her foot.

'Hey Noms, how are you doing?'

Her friend's reaction to her being there would tell her instantly whether or not she knew about her involvement with the kidnap plot.

Naomi's eyes flickered open. 'Kate? What are you doing here?' she said, sounding groggy.

There was no sign of panic. 'I'm just relieving Hazel for a bit,' she said, putting the mugs on the bedside table.

'She must have forgotten to mention it,' Naomi replied. 'She's only popped home for her mobile phone, though, so you didn't need to come.'

'Charlie said you weren't to be left on your own when we spoke this morning.'

'Well, I'm not really. He's sleeping in Cassie's room. I could have called out if I needed anything.'

'No point in disturbing him. He sounded shattered after he was up with you all night. I'll push the door to so he won't hear us talking.'

'I'm afraid I won't be much company. The sedatives the doctor has me on completely wipe me out. I'm such a lightweight with medication. Your herbal sleeping pills proved that.'

'Yes, I realise that now. If you hadn't been so deeply asleep, none of this business with Cassie would have happened. I feel dreadful about it.'

'It wasn't your fault. I know you would never do anything to harm her. I keep trying to stay positive, but every hour that passes with no news eats away at the hope I have of getting her back.'

For once, Kate felt the emptiness and desperation that Naomi had been experiencing for the past three days. 'It's hard to stay positive when we have no idea where she is, but we've got to try. Look, I'm sorry I couldn't come round earlier, things got a bit hectic at home, but I'm here now and I remembered what you said about tea the other day, so I've made you a hot chocolate instead. I hope I've done it how you like it?'

'I'm not sure I can manage it after Hazel's bangers and mash.'

'You didn't finish all that. I saw your plate in the kitchen. You've got to keep your strength up,' Kate said, handing one of the mugs to Naomi. 'I've made one for myself, to keep you company. I know it's normally yours and Charlie's and Cassie's little family treat, but I'm almost family, aren't I?'

'Thanks,' Naomi said, accepting the mug of frothy liquid while wriggling herself into a more upright position. 'In some ways, you're closer than family. I know you're always there for me, no matter what. I'm so lucky to have you in my life,' she added, taking a small sip, followed by several bigger ones.

'Verdict?'

'Um, good, although I was saying to Hazel that nothing seems to taste quite the same as usual at the moment, not even her famous mustard mash.'

'It's probably stress, Noms. Stress can do funny things to people,' she said, taking a sip of her own drink and trying not to grimace at the unexpectedly bitter taste. *It's a good job Naomi's taste buds are slightly off*, she thought, forcing herself to take a bigger gulp.

'You're so lucky you don't suffer with it. You're always so calm and collected.'

'It might appear that way, but I've just learnt to hide my feelings better than most. I guess I'm a bit like a swan. I appear to be gliding smoothly across the water without a care in the world, while all the time my feet are paddling furiously beneath the surface to keep me afloat.'

'You never said.'

'There was no point. Come on, drink up while it's warm and then you can relax back again.'

Naomi obligingly took a couple of big gulps and then licked her top lip to remove the creamy moustache. 'I would have tried to help if I'd known.'

'Would you? I'm not so sure. You were always the more vulnerable of the two of us, the one who needed help and support, and I always gave it to you without question because you were the most important person in my life. That's probably what Charlie found so endearing about you. Do you remember how surprised we both were when he asked you out? It had always been the three of us, and then suddenly it was you two as a couple and me tagging along. I don't suppose you ever wondered what that was like for me? Not only was he taking my place as your best friend, I had to come to terms with the idea of you two being intimate. It wasn't easy, I can tell you.'

'I guess I never really thought about it from your point of view,' Naomi said, downing the remainder of her drink and reaching out to place the mug back on her bedside cabinet. She misjudged the distance and the mug overbalanced, falling onto the pale-coloured carpet. 'Oh no, did it make a mess?'

'Don't worry about it. It doesn't matter. Nothing matters any more.'

'Are you all right, Kate?'

'Of course. Why wouldn't I be?'

'You seem a little strange. Not like your usual self.'

'I'm just—'

Before she could finish her sentence, the phone began to ring.

CHAPTER FIFTY-THREE

'Are we there?' Cassie asked, waking up moments after the car pulled to a halt in the car park of the motorway service area. 'Can we ring Mummy now?'

'I'm just trying her now,' Charlie said, listening as their home phone rang out six times before going through to the answering machine. He hung up without leaving a voice message, disappointment rushing through him. Desperate as he was to let Naomi know that Cassie was safe, he wanted to hear her reaction to the news. 'She didn't answer,' he said, in response to the hopeful look on his daughter's face. 'She must be sleeping, but maybe the phone woke her up and she couldn't get downstairs in time. We'll try again in a few minutes when we've got our drinks.'

'Am I allowed fizzy orange? Mummy doesn't like me to have it too close to bedtime, but that might be a bit later tonight.'

'I don't think Mummy would mind, just this once,' he said, unbuckling her seat belt and lifting her down from the car.

'This is a bit like an adventure, Daddy.'

Charlie was amazed at how unaffected by her ordeal his daughter seemed to be, although he couldn't help noticing how tightly she was holding his hand. Having not seen him for over a month, he had wondered if Cassie would be a little shy with him, but he'd worried needlessly. It was as though they had never been apart.

Once he'd paid for their drinks, he led the way towards a table in the corner of the brightly lit café. The wooden chairs didn't look particularly comfortable and the Formica table could have done with a wipe, but he wasn't planning on stopping for long.

'Daddy,' Cassie said, after having a slurp of her drink, 'is Mummy still cross with me? Is that why she didn't come with you to fetch me?'

'Mummy's not cross with you, princess. She's not feeling very well, so the doctor said she had to stay in bed, just like when you had chickenpox.'

'That's what the lady said but I didn't know whether to believe her or not.'

Charlie gripped his coffee mug.

'When I got up to see what the noise was, Mummy told me to go back to bed. She had a cross voice. I thought maybe I could make her happy with me again if I put the whiskers in the pumpkin, so after she closed her bedroom door, I went downstairs to fetch the sparklers from my sandpit. But then I couldn't find the pumpkin. I know I'm not supposed to open the front door on my own, but I wanted to help so I climbed on a chair and got the key down. I'm sorry, Daddy, I won't do it again.'

Charlie wanted to hug his daughter and tell her it was all right, but he knew he should discourage her from doing it again. 'We all make mistakes, Cassie, that's how we learn things.'

'While I was putting the whiskers in the pumpkin to make the cat face, the door closed and that's when I noticed the lady behind me.'

Charlie felt a prickle on his skin. *So that's how Jessica managed to take her. She must have been watching the house, waiting for an opportunity, and Cassie inadvertently presented it to her on a plate. The bitch must have pulled the door closed while Cassie was concentrating on the pumpkin.*

'She asked me if I was all right. I wouldn't have talked to her if she didn't know my name because Mrs Johnson, my teacher, has told us all about not talking to strangers. The lady said that you and Mummy were her friends and that it was lucky she had been driving by because it was too cold for me to be outside all night. I believed her because she knew your name is Charlie and Mummy is Naomi, and she was right about the cold too because I was a bit shivering, even in my pink coat.'

Charlie was struggling to control his fury. He was seething inside. *How dare that evil cow pretend that she is our friend?*

'She knocked on the door, but Mummy didn't come so she said I could go to her house with her and she would bring me home in the morning. She was really nice to me, Daddy, and I was very cold and tired. Did I do the wrong thing?'

'You weren't to know that she was only pretending to be nice.'

'She put me to bed at her house and when I woke up, we had some toast and she said she was going to take me home. But I fell asleep in the car and when I woke up, we weren't at our house. That's when I started to feel a little bit frightened.'

Charlie could hear the tremor in his daughter's voice. She was putting on a brave face, but clearly they would need to be mindful of nightmares in the coming months.

'If you weren't at our house, where were you?' he questioned, gently.

'She said we were at her boyfriend's flat. I didn't like it much because it was high up when I looked out of the window and it had a funny smell.'

'Funny smell?'

'Yes. It was a bit like when we do painting and sticking at school.'

'Did the lady say why she had taken you there?'

'Yes. That's when she told me that Mummy wasn't very well and that I might have to live with Auntie Kate for a while if she didn't get better. I like Auntie Kate, but I'd much rather be with you and Mummy.'

Charlie was confused. *What did Kate have to do with anything? She disliked Jessica almost as much as Naomi did. Was that just another one of Jessica's lies to make Cassie think they were all friends?*

'She said she was going to check on Mummy, and that I had to stay with the man while she did.'

Charlie's heart was pounding now. *So Jessica wasn't in this alone. Jake Camero did exist, and that evil cow had left his five-year-old daughter alone with him. What sort of person would do that? If he's laid a finger on her, I'll find him and wring his neck.*

Trying to sound nonchalant, he said, 'So, what did you do while the lady wasn't there?'

'I watched Peppa Pig. The man had lots of DVDs and every time one finished, he put a new one on and then went back to the smelly room. I like Peppa Pig, but I don't think I want to watch it again for a while.'

'Did he give you any food?'

'I had biscuits, and then when it got dark outside, he went out and got pizza.'

'Was the woman there?'

'No. She didn't come back until the next day, just before the fireworks started. We watched them from the window and then she said we had to leave. I don't like the new coat and boots she got me. I like my pink ones better. I cried a bit when she made me wear them and she told me to shut up or she would smack me.'

Charlie's nails were digging into the flesh of his palms.

'I think that's when I knew she wasn't very nice. I fell asleep in the car, and when I woke up the tape was on my mouth and my hands and feet were tied up. There was something over me so I couldn't see where I was. I was very scared then, Daddy.'

'I'm sure you were. I would have been too, and I'm a grown-up.'

'I didn't know I was still in the car until it started to move again. Then we stopped and the door opened, and the lady pulled the tape off my mouth. That's when she let me talk to you on the phone.'

'I was so pleased to hear your voice.'

'I was happy to hear your voice too, Daddy.'

'Do you want to tell me any more? It can wait until later if you've had enough. You'll have to tell your story to the police, anyway. They've been looking for you while you were lost. Will you be okay with that?'

Cassie sighed. 'I suppose so. I'll have to tell Mummy about it too, and Granny Hazel and my friends at school. I'm going to get very fed up telling this story, I think,' she said, shaking her head from side to side with a resigned expression on her face.

But at least she's alive to tell the story. It could have all been so much worse, Charlie thought, a chill running through his body.

'Can we try Mummy again now? I want to tell her I'm sorry.'

He reached across the table and squeezed his daughter's hand while pressing 'home' in his contact list again. Instead of ringing out, it went straight to the answering machine. Despite knowing that Naomi's mobile phone was switched off, Charlie tried it anyway but wasn't surprised when it went to voicemail, as did his Mum's mobile which he also attempted to call.

'There's still no answer, princess. Let's get the petrol and get you home. Then you can tell Mummy how sorry you are, and then she'll give you a great big hug to show you how much she loves you.'

CHAPTER FIFTY-FOUR

7.23 p.m. – Sunday

When the house phone started to ring, Kate rushed from the bedroom down to the hall, anxious for it not to wake Charlie. It stopped just before she reached it, but she lifted the phone off its cradle and pressed the green button anyway so that it would ring out as engaged if anyone else tried to call. She waited at the foot of the stairs for a few moments, but there were no signs of life from Cassie's room. She climbed back up the stairs as quietly as she could and closed the bedroom door behind her again.

'Who was it?' Naomi asked.

'I didn't get there in time,' Kate replied. 'Don't worry about it. If it's important they'll ring back.'

Naomi was having trouble keeping her eyes open and her head was leaning to one side as though it was too heavy for her neck. If she hadn't already been lying back on her pillows, she looked like she would have collapsed onto them.

'I feel a bit weird,' she said.

'How do you mean, weird?'

'Dizzy and a bit sick, and my tongue feels sort of numb.'

'It must be your medication. It'll pass, and then you'll drop off to sleep again,' Kate said, reaching out to stroke Naomi's forehead. 'You can still hear me though, right?'

Naomi nodded.

'Good, cos I want to tell you something. It *is* my fault that Cassie is missing. I arranged for her to be taken from her bed on Thursday night.'

Naomi struggled to open her eyes and made a move as though to sit up, but Kate was applying sufficient pressure on her frail body to keep her prone.

'W-what are you talking about?' Naomi managed, her words a little slurred.

'Don't try to talk, just listen. We don't have much time.'

Kate watched the fear creep into her friend's eyes as though she was struggling to process the new information in a brain already dulled by tranquillisers.

'Charlie,' Naomi tried to call out.

'Shhh, I said don't talk. We don't need Charlie. We've never needed Charlie, except to give us Cassie. If you call out again, I'll have to gag you, and I don't want to do that to my best friend.'

Beneath her hand, Kate could feel Naomi's pulse slowly beating against her temples and her skin felt clammy to the touch.

'Where is Cassie?' she said slowly, every word a struggle. 'Where is my baby?'

'That's a good question. Right now, she should have been on her way to Wales with me to start our new life together, but she wasn't at the cottage when I got there. I don't know where that bitch has taken her. I should never have trusted her. She was always trouble at school.'

'Who?' Naomi murmured, her voice barely more than a whisper.

'Jessica. I paid her to steal Cassie for me.'

'*Nooo*,' Naomi wailed.

'Shhh, I told you to keep it down. I don't want Charlie barging in on us like a knight in shining armour to rescue his damsel in distress. He had his chance. He messed up. Now it's our turn.'

'I don't understand, Kate… Why take Cassie from me?' Naomi mumbled, with difficulty.

'I've had enough. For years, I've stood by and watched you and Charlie playing happy families. You had everything I didn't. You had the unconditional love of someone that you loved in the same way.'

'But you had Alan—'

'Alan! Do me a favour,' Kate said, the volume of her voice rising slightly. 'Surely you must have realised that I never loved Alan. I only married him because you'd married Charlie.'

Naomi's bottom lip started to quiver. 'I – I didn't know that you had feelings for Charlie.'

'Not Charlie. Those drugs really are making you slow on the uptake. You, Naomi, I have feelings for you. I always have had.'

'You like women? But you're married.'

'Not all women. I'm not gay, I've just always had a thing for you. When you and Charlie starting rowing because you couldn't get pregnant again, despite already having the most beautiful child in the world, I could see a tiny glimmer of hope. I had to have a plan in place for the moment one of your rows spiralled out of control. I couldn't believe my luck when Charlie rang me that night and I was able to push him straight into Jessica's waiting arms. You know, I actually knelt at my bedside and prayed that he would go off with her and leave you devastated, and then I would step in to comfort you. It would have been better for all of us: you, me and Cassie. But no, he kept ringing me and whingeing about his terrible mistake and how much he still loved you. And you – you kept refusing my help, wanting to do everything for yourself. If you would have just let me look after you the way I wanted to, then it could have been Cassie asleep now in the next room instead of Charlie.'

Naomi was barely awake, but she summoned up all her strength for one last attempt to attract Charlie's attention. 'Charlie,' she screamed, 'help me.'

Kate's hand moved swiftly from Naomi's forehead to her mouth. 'I warned you,' she hissed. 'Now I'm going to have to gag you.' She pulled a scarf out of her handbag and tied it quite tightly around the back of Naomi's head, forcing her mouth open. In doing so, she knocked her bag over, allowing the bottle of unicorn bubble bath she had bought for Cassie to roll across the room.

Naomi made a muffled sound, tears streaming from her eyes.

'You see how thoughtful I was?' Kate said, following Naomi's gaze. 'I even bought her some special bubble bath. Special bubble bath for a special little girl. I bought her pretty clothes, too, and toys and books. She would have had a happy life with me, but that stupid cow ruined it with her greed. And now there's no going back. I've left Alan and the boys. I always knew I would eventually, but this whole episode with you and Charlie pushed me into making the decision sooner rather than later. When I found out that Alan had had the snip without telling me, and that I was never going to get pregnant with my own little girl, I couldn't bear him touching me. All those nights I gritted my teeth while he was thrusting and grinding, hoping that would be the night he would give me what I wanted, were in vain. Are you still listening, Naomi?'

Naomi's head had lolled to one side, her eyes closed.

Kate shook her gently. 'Don't go yet. I'm not ready. The tablets are working more quickly on you. It must be because you're so thin, or they're reacting with whatever the doctor gave you to calm you down after you found Pumpkin's collar. I'm sorry I had to do that, really I am, but I thought Cassie might need him if she didn't have you. Don't leave me, Noms, please. We're supposed to go together – we always did everything together before Charlie came along and ruined everything.'

Naomi's eyelids flickered. She forced her eyes open, silently pleading for Kate to help her.

'I'm sorry, Noms, so very sorry. I wish it hadn't come to this. All I wanted was for you and me to be together and bring up Cassie as our daughter. When it was finally clear to me that the only person you really wanted was Charlie, even after what he did to you, I had to have Cassie. I couldn't go on with my sham of a life. You do understand, don't you? It hurt me to punish you by taking Cassie, but for once I put myself first after a lifetime of always looking out for you. When I got to the cottage and she wasn't there I was seriously thinking of ending my life right then and there, but I clung to the hope that Jessica was just being a greedy bitch and wanted more money from me. When the police passed me on the road to the cottage, I knew she'd grassed me up and that they would come looking for me. I got rid of all the pretty things I'd bought for our little darling and watched the papers that were the passport to our new future go up in flames. It was only when I saw the missed text messages from Jessica that I realised any future life without both you and Cassie was pointless. That's why I had to come here, I didn't want to die without you knowing how much I love you. You can still hear me, can't you, Noms?'

Naomi's eyes were closed again. There was no movement from her apart from the shallow rise and fall of her chest. Kate gently reached round the back of her head and untied the scarf. She touched her friend's lips, the lips she had always longed to kiss, with the tips of her fingers, leaning her body forward to rest her head on Naomi's chest.

'It won't be long now,' she whispered. 'I'm coming, and then we'll always be together.'

CHAPTER FIFTY-FIVE

7.36 p.m. – Sunday

Charlie could see through the plate-glass window that there was only one cashier taking payments for fuel, and the queue was quite long. He unbuckled Cassie's seat belt and took her into the shop with him. Even with all the doors locked he wasn't prepared to leave her alone in the car. Without drawing Cassie's attention to it, he tried their home number again. It was still engaged. He began to wonder if Naomi or his mum had got to the phone the first time he called, pressed answer then put it back on the cradle without ending the call. *That must be it. I can't imagine either of them on a call for so long, unless Mum's ringing Auntie Sheila.* Their conversations sometimes lasted an hour or more. He looked at the six missed calls from DCI Hart and decided to try and find out what she wanted.

'Mr Bailey. At last. Where have you been? I've been trying to reach you all evening. You didn't return my calls. There have been huge developments in your daughter's case.'

'Can I just stop you there, DCI Hart. Whatever it is can wait. I've got Cassie,' he said, looking down at his daughter and smiling.

'What?'

'She's with me.'

There was a pause.

'What do you mean, she's with you?'

'While I was at the cottage this afternoon, I was contacted by the kidnappers. They wanted money in return for telling me where Cassie was.'

'And you gave it to them? Just like that? Without informing us?'

'They said I'd never see her again if I told the police. I couldn't risk it. The most important thing is that Cassie is safe.'

'Of course, it's what we've all been working to achieve, and it's fantastic news, but didn't you think to inform us the moment she'd been found? It's Sunday evening, and I've got almost fifty personnel working on this case in some form or another, many of whom have barely slept in days.'

'Look, I'm sorry,' Charlie said, realising that he should probably have called Rachel the moment he and Cassie were safely away from the cricket pavilion. 'I only found her half an hour ago, and my priority was to get her back home as soon as possible. Surely you can understand that?'

'I can understand your feelings, but there are procedures. You should have let us handle things.'

'I can't believe this. I've got her back. Surely that's more important than your stupid procedures?' he said, his raised voice attracting the attention of other customers in the queue.

'Where exactly are you, Mr Bailey? I can have officers meet you and escort you the rest of the way home.'

'That's precisely what I don't want,' he hissed into the phone, lowering his voice in an attempt to prevent his daughter from hearing, 'Cassie's been through enough already. The last thing she needs is flashing blue lights, wailing sirens and uniformed police officers. She's my daughter, and I'll do it my way.'

Rachel couldn't argue with that. She'd had nightmares for months after the police had finally found her and her twin sister in the cellar of their next-door neighbour's house.

'She's Naomi's daughter too, Charlie. You are intending to bring Cassie home to your wife, aren't you?'

'Of course. What is wrong with you? I've tried to ring Naomi, but our home phone keeps going straight to answer machine. When I get off the phone from you, I'll try her again. I'd appreciate it if you keep this between us until I've spoken to her. I know you're only doing your job, but don't spoil this reunion for us. We should be back around half past eight,' he said, hanging up before DCI Hart could respond.

'Daddy, you've got an angry face,' Cassie said quietly. 'Did I do something wrong?'

'No, not you, princess,' he replied, squeezing her hand.

They were at the front of the queue when he realised that not only had DCI Hart not told him the reason for her multiple calls, he hadn't told her that Jessica and her boyfriend, Jake Camero, were the kidnappers. *It will just have to wait*, he thought, swiping his payment card and opting not to bother with a receipt. *We'll be home in thirty minutes. I can tell her then.*

CHAPTER FIFTY-SIX

7.38 p.m. – Sunday

Rachel Hart was shaking as she laid her phone down on her desk, staring into the space in front of her, oblivious to the frenzied activity of the incident room. She knew she had been totally irrational firing questions and veiled accusations at Charlie Bailey, but she hadn't been able to stop herself. *Maybe I shouldn't have taken this case on. The Baileys might have been better served if I'd left this to my DI. Perhaps it's all just too close to home.*

There was no doubting that it was an enormous relief now Cassie had been found safe and well, but from a police point of view their job was far from over. They had to catch whoever was responsible, and for that to happen they would need to interview the little girl. As Rachel knew only too well, what they said and how they said it could have a massive impact on the rest of her life. The question, 'Why did he hurt your sister and not you?' had haunted Rachel since she was six years old. The blame, the accusation, the guilt. Memories of being huddled in a corner in the back of an ambulance while the paramedics worked frantically to save Ruth's life were the basis of recurrent nightmares from which she always woke drenched in sweat and struggling to breathe. Ruth was the one he had physically abused, but no one could see the mental damage he had done to Rachel. *We'll have to tread very gently with Cassie*, she acknowledged, suddenly becoming aware of DI Wilson staring at her through the window of her office. She signalled for him to join her.

'Shut the door, Graham,' she said.

'Guv.'

'I've just had Charlie Bailey on the phone. He says he's found Cassie.'

'You're kidding.'

'I'm absolutely not. I just got off the phone with him a few minutes ago. While I was hanging around waiting for the forensics team to come up with some evidence at the cottage and you were wading knee-deep through hours of CCTV footage, he says he was waiting for a text message from the kidnappers with the details of where to find Cassie after he paid them a ransom.'

'He had contact with the kidnappers and didn't tell us? Doesn't he know how much danger that put Cassie in?'

'Apparently not. He said they only contacted him via text message for the first time this afternoon, shortly after he arrived at the cottage and found out that Cassie wasn't there.'

'Do you think the kidnappers were watching the place?'

'It's highly likely, and we all know who rang the information about the cottage through to us knowing we would go straight there.'

'Jessica Toland.'

'Precisely. She couldn't have known for sure that we would ask Charlie Bailey to meet us there, but it was a fair assumption. And she has Charlie Bailey's phone number.'

'And if she was watching the cottage, she would know if he spoke to you after receiving the text message.'

'He says he was warned not to speak to us. You know the sort of thing, "if you involve the police, you'll never see your child again". I suppose we'll find out more when we see the message, assuming there was a message, and that he has paid a ransom to get his daughter back.'

'What are you getting at, Guv?'

'Until we've had a debrief with Mr Bailey with the exact details of how the alleged kidnappers contacted him, I'm keeping an open mind. We've already discussed the possibility that Kate had nothing to do with Cassie going missing. Maybe she confided in her friend Charlie that she was planning on leaving her husband and starting a new life because she was unhappy. He might have used the information she gave him in confidence to invent a kidnap plot with the sole purpose of regaining access to his daughter.'

'It seems a bit extreme. And why would he ring you to say he was bringing Cassie home? Wouldn't he just disappear with her?'

'And have a life on the run, always looking over his shoulder? This way, he is the hero in Naomi's eyes, finding their daughter and bringing her home. You remember at the press conference yesterday, when we overheard the journos arguing about who they thought had abducted Cassie? Maybe the one who suspected Charlie Bailey was right after all. If I find out he has been behind this whole thing, I'll throw the bloody book at him for wasting police time.'

There was a knock at the door.

'Come in.'

'Guv, there's been a confirmed sighting of Cassie Bailey at a motorway services on the M4. An eagle-eyed member of the public spotted her, even though she wasn't in the pink coat, and sent us this photo. You'll never believe who she's with.'

'Her father?'

'How did you know…?' Errol started to say.

'Typical. An actual sighting now we don't need one,' Graham said. 'But it looks like he was telling you the truth and is headed back home. You'll need to get the blue light out if you're going to get there before him.'

'You heard him, Errol. Bring the car round.'

'Yes, Guv. Oh, and this was handed in for you at the front desk a few minutes ago.'

Rachel took the envelope from him and ripped it open. 'Well, that's interesting.'

'What, Guv?'

'It's from Jessica Toland's lawyer. Apparently she's fired him! There's a nice thank you for getting her released earlier when she was obviously as guilty as hell. He wants me to ring him. I wonder what that's all about,' Rachel said, grabbing her phone from her desk and dropping it into her bag.

'You could call him on the way to the Baileys' house, Guv. Keep me updated.'

'Tim Berwick.'

'Mr Berwick, it's DCI Hart here. I got your note.'

'Oh right, thanks for calling so promptly.'

'I assumed you might have some information for me?'

'Not really. I just wanted to apologise for the despicable way my client, or rather former client, behaved earlier. I did try to make her see that honesty was the best course of action, but she wasn't having any of it. All she was interested in was whether you had enough evidence to hold her on, and I had to be honest and tell her you didn't.'

'Don't worry, you were only doing your job, although how you can defend people like her when they are so clearly lying is beyond me.'

'Fortunately, people like Mrs Toland are few and far between. It's just unfortunate that I wasn't fully apprised of the woman before I took the case on. She did me a favour in firing me. It saved me the trouble of finding another lawyer to represent her.'

'I don't suppose you have any idea where she was heading when you left her earlier?'

'This may be slightly unethical, as she was still my client at the time, but I did overhear her on the phone arranging to be picked up from Pangbourne railway station.'

'That's actually very helpful. It could even help us tie her in with the kidnap plot, Mr Berwick.'

'Tim, please call me Tim. And if I can be of any further help, please call me. You've got my number now.'

Rachel could feel herself blushing. *Am I imagining it, or is he flirting with me?* 'Well, thank you for your help, er, Tim, I'll bear that in mind,' she said, hurriedly ending the call. She instantly tapped in DI Wilson's number.

'Guv?'

'Sorry, Graham, you were probably about to leave for the night, but I need you to check some more CCTV footage. Pangbourne train station from 2.30 p.m. onwards this afternoon. You're looking for Jessica Toland. Someone will be picking her up from the train.'

'Pangbourne? That's only a few miles from the motorway services where Charlie and Cassie Bailey were spotted.'

'Exactly. This could be where we finally find out who has been telling us the truth and who has been feeding us a pack of lies.'

CHAPTER FIFTY-SEVEN

'You're still here, then?' Hazel said to PC Walsh, who was back on the doorstep of 15 Beechwood Avenue, stamping his feet in an effort to stay warm.

'Yes. DCI Hart phoned a short while ago to say she and DS Green are on their way, so there was no point in replacing me. Just means a couple of hours of overtime. I don't mind. I could use the money.'

'Oh, I wonder if they've got some news?' she said, feeling the same mix of hope and fear she had experienced every time there had been contact from the police since Cassie's disappearance.

'She didn't say much, just that she'd be here before 8.30 p.m. to meet up with Mr Bailey.'

'Right, well, I'd better get our dinner on then, or he'll be right in the middle of it when she gets here. Can I get you a cup of tea or coffee while I'm in the kitchen?' Hazel asked, sliding her key into the lock.

'Ooh, tea would be most welcome. Milk and two sugars, please.'

'That's odd. My key won't turn in the lock.'

'Here, let me try,' PC Walsh said. 'No, it doesn't want to budge. It feels as though there's a deadlock on.'

'Really? I've never known either of them use the deadlock,' Hazel said. 'They usually just secure the door with the mortice lock overnight, and why would Charlie do that unless he thought I wasn't coming back this evening?'

'Charlie? He's not in the house. He went out just after three. I thought he might come back with you as the Guvnor is expecting to meet him here.'

'You must be mistaken. He's been sleeping in Cassie's room all afternoon.'

'No mistake. He definitely left around three o' clock. I'm surprised you didn't hear the front door. I remember distinctly, cos it was just before DI Wilson called to tell me they'd had a tip-off about Kate Birchell being behind the kidnap plot.'

Hazel reached out for PC Walsh's arm to steady herself. 'What are you talking about? There must be crossed wires somewhere. She's been Naomi's best friend since infant school. Why would she want to kidnap Cassie?'

'I'm only telling you what DI Wilson told me. He said Kate had left her family and was on the run with Cassie, and that I was to be extra vigilant and not let anyone into the house without checking with him first, present company excepted, of course.'

Hazel was beginning to get a panicky feeling in her chest. 'Well, if you're sure it's a deadlock and Charlie didn't put it on, it must have been Naomi, but I can't see how it could have been. She'd just had her latest lot of pills when I left her, and they're so strong they've been knocking her out. I don't think she could have made it downstairs, and anyway, why would she want to lock me out? Are you absolutely certain no one could have got in while I've been gone? You haven't left this spot?'

'Except for when I went to the toilet and you closed the door with me inside. I suppose someone could have sneaked in then, but only if they had a key.'

Hazel felt a shiver run down her spine. 'Kate's got a key.'

'But why would she come here? If she has kidnapped Cassie, surely this is the last place she would come to?'

'There's something not right, we need to get inside. Can you break the door down?'

PC Walsh looked at it with a dubious expression. 'I don't think so on my own, but I can radio for back-up.'

'You do that, and hurry. I'm going next door to see if they've got something we could force the door open with.'

'Urgent back-up requested at Fifteen Beechwood Avenue,' PC Walsh said into his radio.

There was a short pause and then a voice said, 'Go ahead, PC Walsh. What is it you need?'

'We need to gain entry to the property. We believe someone inside may intend to harm Naomi Bailey. Please send back-up, and be quick.'

As PC Walsh clicked his radio off, Hazel reappeared with Barry from next door who was wielding a tyre iron.

'Sir, you can't do that,' he said, putting his hand on Barry's arm as he went to swing the heavy implement into the air. 'It's breaking and entering. You could be prosecuted.'

'Don't be ridiculous. Mrs Bailey says it's a matter of life and death. Don't stand there like a lemon. Help me, man.'

There was a momentary pause before PC Walsh took the tyre iron from Barry's grasp and applied it to the area of the door around the lock.

'I'll pull on this, you push with your shoulder,' he ordered, taking control of the situation. 'Thank God it's an old-fashioned wooden door. We'd never get in if it was UPVC with an aluminium frame.'

There was a splintering sound and the door swung open.

PC Walsh was the first to the top of the stairs. He pushed the bedroom door open and was met with the sight of Kate slumped forward across Naomi's lifeless-looking body. At the sound of the door opening, Kate turned slowly to face him.

'You're too late,' she said, her words slow and laboured. 'If I couldn't have her, I didn't want anyone else to.'

'Oh my God,' Hazel said, appearing in the doorway. 'What have you done?'

PC Walsh was back on his radio. 'Forget the back-up, I need an ambulance at Fifteen Beechwood Avenue... now.'

CHAPTER FIFTY-EIGHT

The Day After – 10.45 a.m. – Monday

'Are you sure you're okay?' Charlie said, looking down at his daughter's pale face and squeezing her hand.

'Yes, Daddy, I'm sure. I'll be nice and quiet, just like you told me, and I promise I won't cry,' she said, squeezing his hand back.

Their shoes made a squeaking sound on the vinyl flooring as they made their way along the corridor towards the lifts. They got out on the second floor and followed the signs to the Chapel of Rest, as directed by the hospital receptionist. Charlie glanced in the direction of the stained-glass doors of the chapel as they passed, continuing on their way towards the private recovery room where Naomi had been taken late the previous night after having her stomach pumped. The hospital staff had told him that if she had arrived in their care fifteen minutes later it would have been too late to save her. The toxic combination of the prescribed sedatives and the sleeping pills that Kate had fed her had begun to shut down her internal organs. Charlie shuddered at the memory of arriving outside his house for what should have been a happy reunion, to be faced with an ashen-faced DCI Hart.

'You need to come with us, Charlie,' she had said.

For one minute, he had thought she was arresting him for wasting police time, but then he spotted the front door hanging on its hinges.

'What's going on? Where's Naomi?'

'They've taken her to the hospital but it's touch and go, I'm afraid. We need to get you and Cassie there as quickly as possible.'

Those fifteen minutes clutching his daughter and praying in the back of the police vehicle as it rushed across town with its blue light flashing, had been among the worst in his life. They'd screeched to a halt outside Accident and Emergency, then been rushed through harshly lit corridors, only to be forced to wait for what felt like hours in the relatives' room before they were finally allowed a few minutes with an almost-comatose Naomi. Charlie wasn't even sure if she knew they were there, but he had refused to leave until hospital staff allowed them to see her and assured him she was going to pull through.

*

'Mummy!' Cassie cried as they entered Naomi's room.

Naomi was lying on a bed hooked up to various drips and monitors. She opened her eyes and moved her fingers to beckon Cassie closer. 'Is it really you? Come here, let me look at you,' she said, her voice trembling.

Cassie ran over to the bed with Charlie close behind her. *My brave little girl might have promised not to cry, but I'm not so sure that I won't*, he thought, as he watched Naomi reach for their daughter's hand and hold it like she would never let it go.

'I like your jumper. It looks like Auntie Sheila's handiwork.'

'It is, Mummy, that's a very good guess. We spoke to her on the phone to tell her I was found and she said she is going to make me a unicorn birthday cake too.'

'That sounds yummy.'

'How are you doing?' Charlie said.

'I've been better,' Naomi replied, a faint smile on her lips.

'Can I hug you, Mummy?'

'Of course you can, sweetheart.'

'Just a little one,' Charlie said, lifting Cassie up onto the bed, 'and be careful not to touch any of the tubes.'

The little girl reached her arm across her mum, resting her head on her chest.

'Why do you have the tubes, Mummy?'

'They're to help me get better,' Naomi said, gently stroking her daughter's dark, unruly curls. 'I didn't know you were here last night, until the nurse told me this morning. I thought I'd dreamed of your voice saying "Mummy". I can't believe you're really here. This is real, isn't it? I'm not dreaming?'

'It's not a dream, Mummy. I'm very much really here, and Daddy's here too, just like it used to be.'

Charlie smiled, feasting his eyes on his two girls. 'That's enough of a cuddle for now, I think. There'll be plenty of time for that when we get Mummy home,' Charlie said, lifting Cassie onto his lap as he sat on the edge of the bed.

'We stopped at the pet shop on the way here, Mummy.'

Naomi looked at Charlie, raising her eyebrows in question.

'Do you want to see what we bought, Mummy?'

Naomi nodded, surprised that the hospital would allow animals in a sterile environment.

'Can I have the bag please, Daddy.'

Charlie handed it over.

'It's a new collar for Pumpkin.'

Naomi opened her mouth to speak, but Charlie interrupted her.

'He must have lost his somewhere, so Cassie asked if we could buy him a new one on our way here.'

'He'll have to be more careful with this one,' Cassie said.

'We all need to be more careful not to lose the things we love,' Charlie said, looking directly into his wife's eyes.

'I don't think he loved it, Daddy. It was green and sparkly and it made him look like a girl cat. I think he'll like this one much better,' Cassie said, producing a royal-blue velvet collar from the bag.

Naomi fingered the collar, 'Good choice. It will make him look even more handsome.'

There was a knock at the door and a nurse popped her head round it.

'Is it all right if we take Cassie to have the rest of her tests now? It shouldn't take long.'

'Are you okay to go on your own, sweetie?' Charlie asked.

'I won't be on my own, Daddy,' Cassie said, crossing the room and taking hold of the nurse's outstretched hand. 'I'll be with the nurse. And when I come back, I can tell you all about my adventure, Mummy.'

'Don't let her out of your sight,' Naomi said, an anxious note creeping into her voice.

'I won't, don't you worry. There are a couple more tests to do and we're only along the corridor. She'll be back before you've noticed she's gone,' the nurse replied as she and Cassie left the room.

'How are you really?' Charlie said, leaning forward and taking his wife's hand in his.

'Despite everything, I'm happy. It took almost losing you and Cassie to make me realise just how lucky I am to have you both. And Pumpkin, of course. I can't believe he's home. I vaguely remember Kate saying something about taking him to keep Cassie company. What happened?'

'I don't know how much Kate told you about the cottage where Cassie was supposed to have been held. One of the forensics team who had been sent to check it over spotted Pumpkin sitting on the wall as he was packing up to leave. He thought it was a bit odd that a cat should be alone in such an isolated place, and rang the station to see if it was anything to do with the case. I couldn't believe it when DI Wilson showed up first thing this morning and handed over a cardboard pet carrier. I'd been dreading having to tell Cassie that Pumpkin was dead after everything she's already been through.'

'He's certainly used up a couple more of his nine lives,' Naomi said, smiling. 'You know, I've been lying here this morning thinking how differently this would have ended if Hazel hadn't come back when she did.'

'It's hard to come to terms with the fact that Kate tried to kill you. What could have driven her to do that? And why did she want to take Cassie away from you? She was supposed to be your best friend.'

'She was my best friend, but I never realised she wanted more than that.'

'What do you mean?'

'She loved me, Charlie. In her head, she did what she did for love. She told me she had never loved Alan, and only married him because you and I got married. At first I thought she meant she had a crush on you, but it seems it was me she wanted to be with and to raise Cassie with – as our daughter.'

'I would never in a million years have suspected Kate of liking other women.'

'Not other women, just me. It probably started as an adolescent crush that grew and grew the more time we spent together. Lying here thinking about it, she always seemed to want what I had. She met and married Alan so quickly after we tied the knot and, if you remember, we were both trying for a baby at the same time, although she beat me to that one. I think the more dissatisfied she became in her life with Alan, the more she began to fantasise about having a happy life with me and Cassie, especially after she found out that Alan had had the snip so she would never be able to have a daughter of her own. I feel a bit sorry for her, if I'm honest. Have they said how she's doing?'

'She's out of danger. They've got her in a recovery room on the first floor, and there's a police guard on the door.'

'Why? Surely they don't think she'd try and hurt me again?'

'They're just being careful, I guess. After all, it was their police officer who let her slip past him into our house with almost disastrous consequences. They won't want any more mistakes.'

'What do you think will happen to her?' Naomi said.

'They'll probably do some kind of psychological appraisal, I would think. I guess it will also depend on whether you want to press charges.'

'I don't. She's been my best friend forever, and I honestly believe she would never have tried to hurt me if she hadn't been sick. Maybe they can give her the therapy she needs to be able to move on with her life, even though it won't be the life she thought she wanted with me. If they could make her see that what she felt for me wasn't love, more like an obsession, she might even find a bit of love in her heart for Alan. I'm sure he'd take her back, if they were able to explain to him that she's been suffering from mental illness. He absolutely adores her.'

'And that is why I love you. You're a wonderful, kind human being. You always try to see the good in everybody.'

'With the possible exception of Jessica. I've never been able to see any good in her.'

'Which, as it turns out, shows what a good judge of character you are. I don't know why any of us are surprised that she double-crossed Kate.'

'The only thing I'm surprised about is that Kate felt she could trust her in the first place. I couldn't believe it this morning when DCI Hart told me that they'd been in this together.'

'Well, she's not going to be bothering any of us any time soon. As we were about to leave home to come here, Rachel Hart rang to say that Jessica and her boyfriend, Antonio Chavez, also known as Jake Camero, were apprehended at Charles de Gaulle airport in Paris about to board a flight to Venezuela.'

'Venezuela? I thought she was intending to go and live with her brother in Spain?'

'That's what we were meant to think. She was hoping that while the British police were liaising with the Spanish police, she and her boyfriend could escape to his home country, which conveniently doesn't have an extradition treaty with the UK.'

'She really did have it all planned out.'

'Yes. Even giving Cassie's coat and wellies to a child who was similar-looking was no mistake. They wanted the police to search his flat after they had left so they would put all their resources into looking for Kate, giving them an extra few hours to escape. We should be grateful there are no direct flights from the UK to Venezuela. I couldn't bear the thought of her getting away with this after all the upset she's caused.'

'I should have had more faith in you, Charlie. I'm sorry.'

'What were you supposed to think after seeing that picture?'

'I know, but I'm still cross with myself for allowing her to manipulate me.'

'Let's not waste any more of our time talking about her. When did they say you can go home?'

'Go home? That makes it sound as though you won't be coming with me.'

'I didn't want to take anything for granted, Noms.'

'I don't think either of us will, ever again,' Naomi said, closing her eyes as Charlie leaned in to kiss her gently on the lips.

CHAPTER FIFTY-NINE

11.49 p.m. – Monday

Rachel entered the room as quietly as she could, twisting the knob until the door was completely closed to avoid the click it would otherwise have made, before releasing it gently. It was almost lunchtime, but the heavy blackout curtains were pulled closed and they were doing their job very effectively. She stood still for a few moments to allow her eyes to adjust, fearful of bumping into furniture and disturbing the sleeping figure whose outline she was just beginning to make out on the bed. The nurse said that she had refused her dinner the previous evening, despite their efforts to encourage her to eat, and she was in a deep sleep when they had knocked with her breakfast earlier that morning. They had decided it was best to leave her as Rachel had called to say she would be visiting; they wanted to avoid a violent outburst if possible.

Stirring from her sleep, Ruth said, 'Why didn't you come? I put my favourite dress on and my make-up, and I waited and waited but you didn't come.'

'I'm so sorry, Ruthie, I was tied up on a case,' Rachel said, moving towards the bed and perching on the edge of it. 'I rang reception to let them know. Didn't they tell you?'

'I thought they were lying. You always come on a Sunday. What was more important than me?'

'Nothing is more important to me than you are, but…' Rachel hesitated, not knowing how her sister would react to her reason for not visiting, 'a little girl had gone missing and we needed to find her.'

There was no response.

'Shall I open the curtains and let in some light, and maybe the window too, for some fresh air?'

Ruth still didn't speak.

Rachel walked over to the window and drew the heavy curtains, allowing the bright November morning to enter the room. She opened the window the couple of inches the safety catch would allow. It was the hospital's responsibility to minimise any opportunity for their residents to try and take their own life. She filled her lungs with fresh air and gazed out across the open fields. It took a large chunk from her monthly wages to keep her sister in the private residential hospital, but at least it meant she had pleasant surroundings, and most of the time she seemed quite happy.

'Did you find her?'

Rachel turned to face her sister, who was now sitting up in bed still wearing her favourite dress; smears of lipstick and smudged eyeliner distorted her pretty features.

'Yes, thankfully we did, late last night. She's with her mum and dad now.'

'Had she been raped or was she lucky, like you?'

Rachel could feel her throat tightening. No one, not even her sister, would ever understand the psychological damage the abduction had caused her, and the burden of guilt she would carry for the rest of her life because she had been left physically unharmed while Ruth had suffered repeated assaults. She forced a smile onto her face. 'She was lucky, like me.'

'Good. I'm glad. Can we get some lunch now? I'm really hungry.'

'Me too. Do you want to freshen up a bit first?'

'Of course. I can't go to the cafeteria looking like this. I look like a crazy person,' Ruth said, a hint of humour in her voice. 'I won't be long,' she said, closing the door to her en suite bathroom, just as Rachel's phone alerted her to a text message:

Hi Rachel, it's Tim (the lawyer). I hope I'm not being too forward, but I wonder if you fancy going for dinner sometime?

The sound of Ruth singing Pharrell Williams' 'Happy' at the top of her voice was coming from the bathroom. Rachel smiled and replied:

Sure. I'll check my diary and give you a call.

A LETTER FROM J.G. ROBERTS

I want to say a huge thank you for choosing to read *Little Girl Missing*. If you did enjoy it, and want to keep up to date with all my latest releases, just sign up at the following link. Your email address will never be shared and you can unsubscribe at any time.

www.bookouture.com/j-g-roberts

The original idea for this book came to me when I was on holiday, which is not unusual as that is when I have the most time to think. It started out as a short story about Pumpkin, the cat, going missing around Bonfire Night, and Cassie wandering off to find him and getting trapped inside an outbuilding. As a mum myself, the thought of my children going missing, for even a short time, filled me with horror and I quickly realised this should be the main storyline for my book, although, as you will have read, Pumpkin does make an appearance, or should that be a disappearance? When I sat down and started to write this book, the words just flowed and it soon became apparent that the story was too big and complex for a short story or even a novella – I just kept writing until the story was told.

It has been something of a departure for me to write a domestic thriller/detective novel, as my previous books have been more emotional/romance, but I have to say I have really enjoyed getting my teeth into the characterisation of the 'baddies' – just as well, really, as this is the first of the DCI Rachel Hart series and there are plenty more unpleasant characters to come in later books.

Jessica in particular was a joy to write, and it gave me real satisfaction whenever Rachel was able to catch her out in the one-to-one interviews – I love writing dialogue, and find myself speaking the words in my head in the characters' voices. I had mixed emotions writing Kate, though. On the one hand, what she did was despicable, but I found myself feeling really sorry for her too.

I hope you loved *Little Girl Missing*. If you did, I would be very grateful if you could write a review. I'd love to hear what you think, and it makes such a difference helping new readers to discover one of my books for the first time.

I love hearing from my readers – you can get in touch on my Facebook page, through Twitter, Goodreads or my website.

Thanks,
Julia Roberts

 JuliaRobertsTV

@JuliaRobertsTV

 www.juliarobertsauthor.com

ACKNOWLEDGEMENTS

Topping the list of people I would like to thank for bringing Cassie's story to print is my editor at Bookouture, Abigail Fenton. I submitted my manuscript to her in August 2018 and three weeks later received a lengthy email in response. It wasn't offering me a publishing deal, but she had taken the time to make suggestions for reworking the ending of a story she otherwise liked when she could have just said 'not for me, thanks'. It was also Abi who suggested that DCI Rachel Hart could become the central character in a series. Two months later, I was signing a three-book deal after she had pitched two further ideas to the Bookouture team – I'm so pleased they liked them. I should also give special mention to publicist Kim Nash, who has always been very encouraging about my writing, having read some of my previous independently published novels – thanks for the vote of confidence, Kim. I feel very lucky to be working with a team who are so dedicated to producing the best-quality work possible.

Once again, my family have each played their part. My daughter is usually the first to read and comment on a finished manuscript, but she recently started a new job, so the task fell to my son, an avid John Grisham and non-fiction reader. It's the first book of mine that he has read, and I was buoyed for days after his comment: 'it's actually very good'. My daughter has now finished it and I loved her WhatsApp comments while she was reading, trying to guess 'who dunnit'. I must also thank my long-suffering 'him indoors', who doesn't see me for hours on end when I'm writing, apart from to bring me cups of fruit tea. He also has to sit and listen to me reading him excerpts from my day's work, not to mention being a sounding board for ideas for the next in the series – he's a keeper!

Most of all, I want to thank you, my readers, for giving me your time – I hope you feel it was time well spent.